The
ENDS *of the*
WORLD

– A –
CONSPIRACY OF US
NOVEL

MAGGIE
HALL

G. P. PUTNAM'S SONS

G. P. Putnam's Sons
an imprint of Penguin Random House LLC
375 Hudson Street
New York, NY 10014

Copyright © 2017 by Margret Hall.

Library of Congress Cataloging-in-Publication Data
Names: Hall, Maggie, 1982–
Title: The ends of the world / Maggie Hall.
Description: New York, NY : G. P. Putnam's Sons, [2017] | Series: Conspiracy of us ; [3]
Summary: "In the final installment in the Conspiracy of Us trilogy, Avery West and her friends must
avert a deadly virus—and a murderous family set on ruling the world"—Provided by publisher.
Identifiers: LCCN 2016052363 | ISBN 9780399166525 (hardback)
Subjects: | CYAC: Adventure and adventurers—Fiction. | Secret societies—Fiction. | Love—Fiction. |
Voyages and travels—Fiction. | Virus diseases—Fiction.
Classification: LCC PZ7.H14616 En 2017 | DDC [Fic]—dc23
LC record available at https://lccn.loc.gov/2016052363

Printed in the United States of America.
ISBN 9780399166525
1 3 5 7 9 10 8 6 4 2

Design by Marikka Tamura.
Text set in Adobe Caslon Pro.

*To all the girls who are stronger at the end of the story
than they were at the beginning.*

PROLOGUE

The rumors spread, wide and fast as a plague.

Some of them were true: She has the eyes, they said. He has the blood of Alexander.

Some of them weren't: He's invincible. It's magic.

The One and the girl with the violet eyes, they whispered. *Their fate is the fate of the Circle.*

They didn't know the real secret of that fate. They didn't need to. They couldn't.

Rumors spread just as quickly outside the Circle of Twelve, but these were different. Terrorist attacks, the newest one a biological weapon in Paris. *Conspiracy,* they whispered. *Something's happening,* they said.

After the virus had been released in Paris, the world had gone quieter. But it was not the quiet of calm. It was the kind of quiet that held its breath, a bowstring drawn so tightly that it had to be let go soon, or it would snap.

And under it all was a race. For archaeology's greatest mystery, Alexander the Great's tomb, and in it, the cure to the virus that could demolish the Circle, that could start a war. Whoever was first to find it could dictate the Circle's future, and maybe the world's.

It wasn't this girl and this boy that would decide their fate. It was a long line of history, set in motion thousands of years ago, a line through some of the greatest conquerors the world has ever seen, and through their follies.

A fate written in the stars.

CHAPTER 1

At night, in the dark, were the only times I couldn't get it to go away. The screams, the smirk on Cole Saxon's face, the sound of my mother's first cough, when I didn't understand yet, and the second one, when I did. Her bloodied face. People falling all around me, choking on their own blood because of mine.

In waking hours—like now—my brain took those same memories and did something different with them.

The guy I was watching across the party was short, with dark hair, wearing a tuxedo. I could only see his back as he meandered from the bar to the edge of the property, gazing out over the twinkling lights of Jerusalem.

"Kuklachka," Stellan said in my ear.

I squinted. Now that he was closer, I could tell the guy's hair was curlier than I'd thought. Longer. He finally turned around, taking a sip of his champagne. It wasn't Cole Saxon. None of them ever were. I should be glad. If the Saxons actually showed up here, it would mean nothing good.

I turned to Stellan. "What?"

He rested a hand possessively on my lower back and leaned in close. "I asked if you wanted to go skinny-dipping in the fountain. Liven up this party a little." I stared up at him blankly. He sighed. "I asked if you'd happened to see the Rajesh family come in while I was talking to Elodie."

I should have smiled at the joke. That's what he was trying to do: loosen me up, make me look like a girl in a cocktail dress at a party should. But my brain no longer remembered how to create that feeling on its own. So I rearranged my features in a way that I hoped from the outside looked more pleasant and less robotic than it felt. "No. I don't think they're here yet. Maybe we should start with someone else."

He didn't even attempt a fake smile back.

A firework burst, loud enough to shake the ground. Nearby, next to the very fountain Stellan had been trying to joke about, Jack and Elodie both glanced up at the sky. Elodie leaned in to whisper to Jack, and she winced almost imperceptibly. She'd been shot and was still healing, which meant she was still at half capacity. She hated it. But she was here tonight, for us. Just like she was every day. For the past month, she and Jack had been with Stellan and me as friends. Tonight, they were here as our Keepers.

This party was a celebration, and we were the guests of honor. Tomorrow, we were to be initiated as the thirteenth family of the Circle of Twelve.

It had been almost a month since my mother had died, since Cole Saxon had released the virus in a crowded room at a Fashion Week show in Paris and my world—and the *whole* world—had been turned upside down. That night, we'd told the rest of the Circle exactly what the Saxons had done. We'd told them about how my half siblings, Lydia and Cole, with the blessing of our father, Alistair, had been murdering Circle members all over the globe, and blaming it on the Circle's longtime enemies, the Order, trying to scare the Circle into uniting behind them. We told them how the Saxons now had a biological weapon to make any attacks even easier.

What we didn't tell them was that the biological weapon was made of our blood.

Stellan and I were *the One and the girl with the violet eyes.* The couple foretold in the mandate, a prophecy of sorts that the Circle had believed in for thousands of years. But we'd recently discovered that the *union* we were to create, which the Circle believed would give them great power, actually meant that if Stellan's blood and mine got mixed and an unsuspecting Circle member ingested it, they would begin to bleed uncontrollably, and die within minutes.

Another round of fireworks lit up a bridge in the distance. Closer, the walls of the old quarter of Jerusalem were cast in various shades of purple. I could pick out one that looked just like my eyes. I wondered what kind of celebration the Melechs had made up to explain the display.

At first, all the on-the-nose, over-the-top Circle business had been dazzling: Living in the Louvre. A ball inside the Eiffel Tower. Fireworks over the city for a private party. Now I saw how it was a smoke screen. The fanfare served to remind them how important they were.

And now we were at the center of it all.

I'd spent the last month hoping it wouldn't come to this.

Announcing who we were to the Circle had been the only way to hold the Saxons accountable and keep them from hurting anyone else, but as the rage and fear had melted into grief and numbness, I wanted everything that came with it less and less. Being an official Circle family would bring power, yes, and there were certain things that appealed about that. But it would also bring politics and danger and worst of all, being a pretty little symbolic pawn in this world that had taken everything from me.

Despite our attempts, though, we hadn't been able to put off the initiation any longer. And it turned out it was a good thing we hadn't. We needed something from the Circle, and this initiation was the way we were going to get it.

From across the courtyard, I saw Laila Emir and her little brother staring at us. Stellan saw, too. He tucked a strand of hair behind my ear and grinned. I leaned into his palm with a coquettish laugh.

Beyond the Emirs, I glimpsed Daniel Melech in the crowd. He gave us a dirty look. The Melechs, though they'd organized this lavish party since the initiation site was here in Jerusalem, were the Saxons' most loyal allies. Their son Daniel was especially close with Lydia.

I wanted nothing more than to hold the knife I had strapped to my leg to Daniel's throat and force him to reveal where my sister was. Tell him about how I'd dreamed of putting a bullet in my brother's head every night for weeks, and that by helping them hide, anything they did was his fault, too.

I knew vaguely that I should be appalled at myself for thinking those things, but all I felt was empty. Ever since that night, it was like I was a robot with only one command programmed: *Stop them. Kill them.* I could lie and say it was only because I wanted to prevent them from hurting anyone else. Though I did want that, the truth was, the only real emotion that broke through the emptiness was the drive to ruin the Saxons like they'd ruined me.

A violet firework exploded, gold tendrils arcing from its center and cascading over the city like a weeping willow. An *oooooh* rose from the crowd.

I turned us a little more toward Daniel Melech and ran my fingers up and down Stellan's arm, glancing around at the crowd. Most of the Circle families we'd been waiting for were here now.

When we'd learned about the virus, we'd also learned something more: there was a remedy. Napoleon had left the remedy buried. *I fear it will only make matters worse,* he'd written.

He was right.

With the virus, the Saxons could manipulate their way into control of the Circle—or take it by force. The ideal, of course, would be to destroy the virus, but that was impossible—we *were* the virus. And any attempts by the team of scientists we'd hired to try to deactivate it in our blood had been unsuccessful. There was just one safeguard.

Lydia had called me every day for weeks after my mom had been killed. So had my father. When I finally answered, Lydia had promised that they'd never meant for my mother to be caught in the cross fire. All they'd wanted was to use what we'd found for the good of the family. The virus in Paris was entirely Cole's doing, and not sanctioned, she'd said. I knew it was true—Lydia and my father were too cautious to release something so deadly without a way to stop it.

So the Saxons were looking for this remedy. We had to find it before them. And since we couldn't destroy the virus, we had to destroy the cure instead.

There were more explosions in the sky, set to music only we at this party could hear. Tendrils of multicolored light twisted through the clouds, and I smiled blandly at something Stellan was saying.

We'd been following a virtual treasure map of Napoleon Bonaparte's since I'd come to the Circle. The final clue pointed to Alexandria, Egypt, as the location of Alexander the Great's tomb, where the cure was hidden. But even though we had the benefit of nearly unlimited Circle resources, we'd found nothing there. Nothing at various excavation sites. Nothing by ground-penetrating radar.

It was almost accidental how we came across the clue that finally pointed us in the right direction. I'd been reading Napoleon's diaries over again, combing through story after story that had nothing to do with our quest—battles and strategy and marriages and affairs. And I'd come across something that caught my eye—an entry that referred to returning an unnamed body to its rightful rest. The entry just before it had been torn out. Through some research, we'd discovered that Napoleon had been in Venice at that time.

Jack, with his seemingly endless memory for random facts, was the one who made the connection. There was a theory that linked Venice with Alexander's body. An archaeological rumor, started by a researcher who had never been able to prove it. Most of the community of historians scoffed at it. The theory said that in the ninth century AD, Alexander's bones had been mistaken for those of St. Mark, and had been taken to Venice, where they rested for centuries in San Marco Basilica. That Alexander's body had never been in his own tomb at all.

It was a ridiculous, desperate idea, but we were desperate people. We traveled to San Marco Basilica and, after some tests, found that "St. Mark's" bones weren't his at all—but they also weren't Alexander's. They dated from the early 1800s. "That's right when Napoleon wrote that diary entry," Elodie had said, finally excited about the idea. "He could have moved Alexander's body back to his real tomb and left some other body in Venice to cover it up."

But if Alexander's body wasn't there, it didn't help us. We would have been at the end of the road if Elodie hadn't remembered that the Catholic Church preserved relics of some of their most important saints at the Vatican.

Being Circle did come with some useful privileges, and one of those was that we were able to get into the Vatican and check. It turned out they did have a relic of "St. Mark's." A femur. We took it. We tested it.

Despite the evidence we'd seen, we were still shocked when the bone dated to somewhere around 350 BC. Alexander's time.

"There was a prophecy just after Alexander died that said whoever possessed his body would never be defeated. That was a major cause of the early Diadochi wars," Jack had remembered. "Is it possible that this bone could be the cure somehow?" But that hope was put on the back burner when our team of scientists discovered something else: a message, etched into a crevice in the bone.

From whence our queen made the twelve, our king's bone unlocks a map to the place of eternal rest.

Our king, we surmised, was Alexander, and the bone the one in our hands. *Our queen* appeared to refer to Olympias, Alexander's mother. She was the one who had created the virus as a way to bring her own line back to power. She'd done the modifications on the Diadochi—Alexander's twelve generals, who had split his kingdom between them to become the twelve families of the Circle—that both made them susceptible to the virus and gave them the violet eye gene. The ceremony when she'd done this had been the first and only initiation ritual the Circle had done.

Tomorrow, our initiation would be the second.

Ironic that I'd been pushing back against my "fate" with the Circle for so long, and now it was exactly where we needed to be. That didn't mean we weren't going to make a last-ditch effort to find whatever it was the bone *unlocked* before we had to go through with the ceremony itself.

Once we'd realized the clue had to do with the initiation ceremony, we'd gathered as much intel as we could. Jack and Stellan and Elodie knew a little about the original ceremony from the Circle history they'd been taught. Our friends Luc and Colette knew more as members of the Dauphin family, and Luc was able to snag some old texts from the Dauphins' library to fill in some gaps. There would probably be fire, we found. There would probably be chanting and invocations and some form of accepting us in. But we needed specifics. We assumed we were looking for an object. Something concrete that could be *unlocked*.

So tonight, we needed two things: to find out what this object that contained the next clue was, and to get hold of it before the initiation tomorrow, without the Circle knowing.

Stellan cleared his throat. I brought my attention back from scanning the crowd to find his hand extended to me. "Dance?" he said.

"Why?" I said through my forced smile.

"Because we appear to be on a dance floor, and it would look strange not to."

He was right. While I hadn't been paying attention, we'd ended up in the middle of a group of dancing couples.

I glanced behind him, saw Jack's eyes on us. With what I hoped wasn't too obvious a sigh, I put my hand in Stellan's.

"Have you seen Lucien?" he said, looping one arm around my waist. So that's why he'd had us wandering the party. Even though Stellan was technically the head of his own Circle family now, I wasn't sure he'd ever stop protecting Luc. "He was going to take Colette and see if they could find anything, but they've disappeared."

Stellan's usually light accent was a little thicker these days, his *th*s softening almost to *z*s. *Zey've disappeared.* It was because he'd been spending more time in Russia than he usually did. His little sister, Anya, was part of the thirteenth bloodline, too, which meant plenty of people might like to get their hands on her. He had her stashed somewhere safe, and went back every few days to move her to a new town in case anyone was looking for her.

"Luc's fine," I murmured, still watching the rest of the party. "This is a harmless way to let him feel like he's involved."

Stellan sighed and pulled me tighter against him. Some of the Circle didn't believe our relationship was real. That mattered because they still thought our "union" was what fulfilled the mandate, and to them, union meant marriage. There were whispers that we'd lied about having completed the marriage ceremony already—since we were so young, and I was an outsider, would I really have agreed to it like that? It was part of the plan tonight to show them just how very in love we were and put those doubts to rest, because they were completely right about the objections I'd have. Even if we had to be initiated, there was no way I'd go through with the marriage ritual, so we needed them to accept that it was already done.

We certainly looked the part of the perfect, pretty power couple: Stellan in a classic tuxedo, having perfected the look of *I'm too good for this place*, his blond hair mussed just enough to keep up the illusion. My dark hair contrasted with his, and my four-inch heels brought me just a little closer to his height, though he still towered over me. I was wearing some designer or another—Colette and Elodie had taken care of it. The dress was high-necked and black. It was beautiful, I supposed. A month ago, I would have had fun putting on something gorgeous and coming to some fancy party. Now my mom was dead and nothing else mattered.

"You doing okay?" he said. "I know being here is probably—"

"I'm fine." Maybe I was feeling a little tense, but nothing that was going to get in the way of what we were doing here.

Stellan twirled me. We'd rehearsed for tonight—for the politics and the Circle business and exactly what we needed to find out.

But the dancing didn't require practice. Stellan always knew just how to guide me in the direction he wanted to go, and I knew just how to respond to his touch. I wasn't even that good a dancer, but I fell easily back into his arms at the end of the turn.

He brought my hand up between us, and his fingers skimmed my knuckles. They were red and raw. Hitting something was the only way I'd found to blunt the sharp edges of the things that lived in my chest. It turned out that wrapping my hands with athletic tape didn't work very well.

I snatched my hand back.

"We could find you something softer than a heavy bag to hit when you don't have gloves."

"Or you could mind your own business," I said with a sweet smile, but I wasn't surprised that he knew what I was doing. At least it wasn't Jack who had caught me. He would have posted guards outside my room so I could no longer leave at night, just in case I got murdered on the way to the hotel gym.

"Having your hands look like you're part of a back alley fight club doesn't exactly go with formal wear," Stellan said. "Next time, tell me and I'll hold some couch cushions for you to hit."

When I said nothing, he pressed, "Or you could get a new hobby. Knitting? Crossword puzzles. I bet you're a crossword puzzle girl. Or"—his eyes flicked to my mouth and his lips curled up in a sly smile—"I could help you release stress another way."

In the past, that might have gotten a rise out of me. Now I was just annoyed that he thought he had license to hear my innermost thoughts because we'd made out once. We'd twirled too close to some cousins of the Wang family, so I giggled like I was playing along. "If you really want me to punch you, I'll punch you," I murmured. "Can you please drop it?"

"Actually, no. You've hardly said more than 'pass the salt' for weeks, and now I have you here and you can't run off." He curled a hand tighter into my waist to prove the point. "I'd like to at least know that inside that pretty little head you're not planning to murder *me*."

"Not currently."

"While we're at it, don't do that," I said. "The little doll thing. I'm not. Not yours, despite this arrangement, and not the Circle's, either."

"Avery," he said pointedly.

Over the past weeks, I kept thinking I'd pushed him away enough that he'd stop trying to draw me out, but he was persistent. Jack knew how it felt to not want to talk. Elodie was distracted and busy lately. But Stellan had zero boundaries. I pulled him down like I wanted to whisper something sweet and romantic. "If you have a problem with how I'm playing the role of your wife, tell me. Otherwise, I don't care, I don't want to talk about it, and I don't need your help."

Out of the corner of my eye, I saw Miguel Reyes approaching. "Time to play thirteenth family," I murmured.

There was a master of ceremonies for tomorrow who had been gathering information from everyone's records and putting it together into this initiation ritual, but we couldn't talk to him. We couldn't ask anyone directly, in fact. It would look too suspicious. There were a couple of families we could count as allies, but most still looked at us with a mix of awe and skepticism that we—this small outsider girl with strands of pink in her hair and her "husband," who had been a Keeper for the Dauphin family for years—had suddenly become the Circle's saviors. The fact that we were suddenly pumping them for information wouldn't make them less wary.

Luc had told us that some of the families were more thorough about passing down history than his, and might know specifics about the initiation, so we had a plan.

Stellan kissed my cheek with an exaggerated wink, like we didn't have a care in the world besides wearing fancy clothes and dancing and flirting, but when we broke from the dance, he didn't let go of my hand, and with the others watching I couldn't make him.

We finished our chat with the Reyes family—we hadn't expected them to know anything about the ceremony, and they didn't seem to—and then Stellan placed my hand in the crook of his elbow and guided me off the dance floor toward where George and Marie Frederick, from the American Circle family, stood by an expansive spread of hummus and kebabs and salads.

I went over in my head what we'd discussed about the Fredericks. To make sure none of the families caught on to what we were doing here, we were using ourselves as bait, becoming whatever version of us we thought they'd most respond to.

"Hello, Mr. Frederick," I said. "Mrs. Frederick." We asked about the weather back in Washington, DC, where they lived, and Stellan made some small talk about how *at least Jerusalem is a dry heat.* When we had them smiling, I said casually, "I can't believe the ceremony is tomorrow. I haven't even had time to prepare. I mean, I've hardly been able to think about anything but—"

I cut off and cast my eyes to the floor.

"Oh, sweetie pie." Mrs. Frederick had a soft southern accent that sounded strange to my ears after so long away from the United States. She took my free hand in both of hers. "My darling girl. I am so sorry."

The Fredericks had some vague attachment to me because I was American, and they had also been in that room in Paris just after my mom died. With them, our strategy was to play the victim card.

It felt a little gross to exploit our tragedies—by this time, the whole Circle knew that not only had my mom been killed, but that Stellan's family had died when he was young—but part of being in the Circle was learning to use every advantage you had.

"Do you think—" I sniffled a little and lowered my voice. "Could

The Fredericks, we'd heard, were especially interested in Circle ritual, and through the generations had incorporated some aspects of various ceremonies into their own country's traditions.

They glanced at each other. "You know, honey, it's hard to say exactly what'll go on," Mrs. Frederick said. "I'd be willing to bet there'll be pledges, so you'll have to be ready to give yourself up to the Circle, you know, like we all have."

I stifled a shudder. "Anything else?"

"You kids don't have to worry yourselves about it. All you've got to do is show up. We'll all help you out," she said warmly, patting Stellan on the back. We pushed just a little more, but when we could tell we weren't getting anything more, we thanked her and left.

"That strategy may have backfired," Stellan muttered.

I nodded. They didn't want to upset the sad orphan children with too much technical talk. "Zara Koning and Sakura Mikado are over there," I said. "Give me a few minutes alone with them, then come over."

He nodded and headed toward the bar. I needed a few minutes away from him anyway. I hoped being alone would ease the tightness in my chest. I wasn't used to being that close to someone for hours at a time lately, and he'd been right while we were dancing—as numb as I usually felt now, being here around so many memories was opening a few cracks.

Zara Koning, from the South African Circle family, was about my age, and Sakura Mikado, from Japan, was a few years older. I didn't know either of them well, but I knew they were both too savvy for any of our tactics, so I planned to be blunt.

After we exchanged pleasantries, I dropped my cool exterior. "I need your help," I said. "Is there anything you can tell me about the ceremony? The rituals are a part of life for you, but for me, they're still a little weird. No offense. I'd just rather not be blindsided."

They looked at each other, and Zara's expression softened. "They're not making you do the marriage ceremony, right?"

Sakura muttered something under her breath about *disgusting patriarchal traditions*.

"We've already done it, so I don't think they're making us repeat it," I said. Not as long as our romantic display tonight worked. I wasn't sure what was the worst part of the marriage ceremony: the fact that we would then actually be married, or the part that said the marriage had to be immediately consummated in front of people to be valid. I pushed the conversation back on track. "For the initiation, is there some creepy ritual object you pass around, or . . ."

Zara frowned. "I know at some ceremonies there's a chalice you drink out of—that's not that odd, though. Catholics do it every week."

I laughed a little with her, but my heart quickened. A chalice. That could be the object we were looking for. "Would it be the same chalice that's been around since the very first initiation ritual?" I said. "That'd be fascinating."

"I have no idea—oh, there's your *husband*."

Stellan rested a hand on my lower back, and I did my best to gaze at him adoringly rather than tensing. Like I was simply catching him up on the conversation, I told him about the chalice idea. He made a joke to Zara about how he would be glad if they gave us wine to get through the ceremony, then said something in Japanese to Sakura, and she laughed and pointed. When it came to politics—and acting—I might be okay, but Stellan would always be better.

We said our good-byes, and he told me Sakura had pointed him

with him anyway.

I glanced around for him, and found Jack's eyes on us again. Jack and Elodie were both shadowing us closely—just in case—and were also part of our show. Since we'd rather have gossip about our scandalous little family on everyone's minds than the fact that we were being especially nosy tonight, we were showing off Jack and Elodie. It was insolent and a little disrespectful of us, flaunting that we'd stolen the Saxons' Keeper and the Dauphins' house manager. And that now, against tradition, we were making them both our Keepers. It was exactly the kind of posturing a Circle family would do, so we did it.

I spotted Mr. Rajesh looking out over the city. His son, Dev, had been one of the Saxons' first victims. The Rajesh family was kind in a way I didn't expect from the Circle. Right after my mom died, Mrs. Rajesh had sent a giant care package of food. With Mr. Rajesh, we played close to our normal selves, with a side of sweet and dumb. "There's some kind of chalice, I heard, that you do the ceremony with?" I asked after we'd greeted him.

"No, not a chalice," he said. "I've heard that for this ceremony, they use a small box, almost a jewelry box."

The master of ceremonies was the head of the Vasilyev family. He wasn't here tonight, nor would he have been allowed to talk to us about the initiation if he were, but Stellan noticed his son across the party. We hadn't expected him to be here. We whispered quickly about a strategy, and Stellan asked the questions in Russian. *If we can be honest with you*, he was going to say, *we want to make sure nothing goes wrong during the ceremony. Obviously your family is trustworthy, but we know not all of them are. Have you heard anything from your father about items used during the ceremony, and could we inspect them beforehand to make sure there's no wrongdoing afoot?*

The man nodded sagely. Apparently some of the Vasilyev family were the Circle's resident conspiracy theorists, so it wasn't hard to convince him we were fellow skeptics. He glanced over his shoulder before he whispered something to Stellan.

When we left, Stellan pulled me onto the dance floor again. "We're going to have to get into the Melechs' private collection," he murmured in my ear. "He says there is a box, and it was stored here since the first initiation ceremony was held in Jerusalem. He thinks it's probably still here until tomorrow."

That was both the best news we could ask for, and the worst. We might have a chance at finding it—but getting caught snooping around the Melechs would be very bad.

We danced past Jack and Elodie, and I could tell they were dying to know what we'd found out. "What if we ask the Melechs for a tour?" I said, my fingers brushing Stellan's chest flirtatiously. "Jack and Elodie can come, too, and be extra eyes."

"Smart," he said, and I let him tuck my arm through his again.

The Melechs almost didn't agree. I wanted to add a jab about how we were sure they'd want to cooperate with anything we wanted, to put to rest those nasty rumors that they condoned the Saxons' actions, but luckily Stellan cut me off. He was right. We were playing a particular persona with the Melechs, too. They would never like us, but they'd let their guard down more if we could make them believe we were silly, spoiled kids joining the Circle for the parties and the private jets.

So while we saw the view from their formal dining room and heard how many guest rooms they had, I giggled, and hung on Stellan's arm, and nuzzled his neck whenever I saw something that could

want to see more pretty things. Do you have any . . . art?"

David Melech, as we'd hoped, had gone from wary to bored with our dumb questions. He looked at his phone and told Daniel and his wife to show us the museum wing, then left. I squeezed Stellan's hand as Mrs. Melech gave us the fastest tour she could manage. We were about to leave, disappointed, when my eye caught on something. "What's that?"

"Oh, that's a replica of a sarcophagus. It's one of the Circle's oldest artifacts," she said, a note of pride creeping into her voice. I squinted at the thing. It was a small box, the size of a jewelry box. "It's used in rituals," she finished, and I squeezed Stellan's hand. "Can I show you the way back to the party?"

She led the way out the door. Stellan and I followed as slowly as we could, trying to communicate silently.

When Daniel looked back at us, I could see the suspicion in his eyes. His parents might have bought our act, but he thought we were up to something. He had all night.

I giggled again, pretending not to notice. Then I reached down very obviously and grabbed Stellan's backside.

Stellan turned a surprised widening of his eyes into a saucy eyebrow raise so quickly, I was impressed. Daniel, as I'd hoped, had been watching every move, and averted his eyes in disgust. Stellan caught on to my plan, and when the Melechs turned around to see what was taking us so long, we'd slowed, my hands on his chest, him pulling me close to whisper in my ear as I blushed.

"We'll find our own way back," Stellan said dismissively, hardly looking up at them, like all we'd really wanted from this tour was a place to make out.

Mrs. Melech looked at Daniel, at her Keeper, and at Jack and Elodie. "I don't know if—"

Stellan leaned down and kissed me.

I stood on my tiptoes and forced my lips to follow his, in another kind of dance that he could lead and I could follow all too easily. We were lucky that was true, because we couldn't give away the fact that, far from this being a sign that Stellan and I just couldn't keep our hands off each other, this was the first time the Circle's new golden couple had kissed since our *actual* first kiss.

As numb as I'd been for so long, all my senses came suddenly, painfully alive. I heard Mrs. Melech clear her throat uncomfortably. I sensed every eye in the room on us. I noticed the spread of Stellan's hands on my waist and the stiffness of his collar under my wrists as my arms looped around his neck. I felt his lips parting mine. He tasted like—

The memories came in a rush. How his mouth had tasted like vodka and lime that night in Cannes, and the air was scented with the sea. His hands in my hair, mine undoing the buttons on his shirt, my head dizzy with drink and wanting. And then, different memories. A few days later. The smell of blood permeating that room in Paris, hot and coppery. My hands slick with it, crimson spatter all over my mother's clothes, her slim hand grasping at my wrist as I knelt beside her. Confusion. Screams. Death.

I pulled away with a gasp. The first thing I saw was Mrs. Melech's scowl, and I tried as fast as I could to put back on something nearing a smile. Tried to cover up how that kiss had, for some reason, just caused the most visceral flashback I'd had yet to the day my mom died.

Stellan's brows crooked down for a second at how rigid I'd gone, but I gave a tiny shake of my head. He looked back up, like he was

an order? By blood?"

He said it teasingly, but you could almost hear the atmosphere in the room shift.

"By blood" was an order the families gave to Keepers. It wasn't an ask. It wasn't just a cute use of the Circle's motto. It was a threat.

"You can't order us around until tomorrow," said Daniel, his faux-joke and fake smile colder than Stellan's had been. I knew that we, the thirteenth family, were technically the closest thing to leaders the Circle had—according to tradition, at least. What that would actually look like, after tomorrow, remained to be seen.

I found myself holding my breath, the fear that this wouldn't work and they'd toss us out before we got to see the box edging through the panic I'd felt a moment ago.

Finally, Mrs. Melech reluctantly put her hands to her forehead in the Circle's gesture of respect. Daniel curled his lip, but followed suit.

Stellan's hand tightened on my waist in a real way, not for show. I understood. No matter how much we didn't want this, there was something heady about having the most powerful people in the world submit to us.

They wanted us—the mandate, the union, the potential power we held—enough to give up their dignity. Enough to allow us to do what we wanted, knowing it might benefit them in the future.

Every once in a while, in a moment like this—a moment that

felt like control when nothing else in my life did—a tiny part of me wondered whether being part of the Circle wouldn't be so bad.

But I'd thought finding my family would fill the hole in my sad little heart, too. And instead, they'd killed my mother and unleashed a plague.

The Melechs left the room, and Elodie made a pleading face as she and Jack followed. She hated being left out.

"Are you okay?" Stellan said. "What was that?"

"Nothing. I'm fine," I lied, hurrying across the room without waiting for him to catch up. Even if I did want to stay with the Circle, this was one reason I never could. It would always mean memories I couldn't handle. Until I could leave, though, I would ignore them, like I had been for weeks.

The box was in a glass case. There was no lock. "Should we just—" I whispered.

Stellan was already opening the door. We looked inside, on the lid, on the outside of the box. "It doesn't even look very old," he said. "There's no way this is from Alexander's time."

I sagged with disappointment. "It's a copy at best. They probably already have the real one at the ceremony, if we're even right about what we're looking for. Does that mean—"

Stellan set the box back down and dragged a hand over his face. "I think," he said, "it means that tomorrow, we get initiated as the thirteenth family of the Circle of Twelve."

Stellan and I stood in a courtyard outside the Old City, waiting to be called in to the initiation ceremony. The plan was to watch for the box, and if it looked like what we needed, do something to pause this ceremony before it actually went through.

Above, palm trees rustled against the cream stone. We'd been to Jerusalem once before, when the Saxons were considering marrying me off to Daniel Melech, but I hadn't seen much of it that day.

For some reason, I had expected the city to be stuck in time, all old stone and desert and prayer, but I was wrong. It was also modern and clean and bustling. As I looked out the window on our car ride here, people crowded around bus stops, and bikes and cars shared the streets. Blue-and-white Israeli flags waved against a cloudless sky, and a riot of multicolored flowers peeked over balconies.

Jack had told me a little about the city's history the last time we came here. Jerusalem was one of the oldest continuously inhabited cities in the world. There had been so much devastation here—wars, natural disasters, being conquered over and over. And yet it had survived it all, on this same spot, a city of great importance to three major religions and to so many cultures through history. A melting pot and a highly contested land, a bustling modern metropolis and an ancient stronghold all in one. None of us were fans of the Melech family, but their city was a different story. If things were different, I'd want to spend time here.

Now I brushed those thoughts aside. The last thing I needed was to get sentimental about another city, especially considering what else we'd seen on the way here.

Just around the corner from where we'd stopped the car, I'd seen a group of girls about my age, wearing military uniforms and eating Popsicles in front of a coffee shop. They all held machine guns strapped across their chests as casually as I'd hold a backpack. Nearby, another group of girls in headscarves and jeans leaned against a 50% OFF SALE sign, looking at their phones. Down the street, a group of little boys played soccer.

The worrisome part was that at least half of each group was wearing white surgical masks.

When Cole had slipped the virus into champagne glasses in Paris, a dozen people had died. The world outside the Circle had quickly embraced various theories: it was a deadly new flu, or something in the air. Some even got it right and called it a biological weapon. What they didn't know was that from this, at least, they were safe: the virus only affected Circle members.

The fact that this meant my mother was somehow related to the Circle and hadn't told me was something I hadn't been able to think about yet. What we did have to think about was that, despite the fact that there had just been the one incident, the alarm was spreading all over the globe. We could only hope that if we prevented the Saxons from releasing it further, it would die down eventually.

I realized I was clutching my phone hard enough that my fingers had gone white. I shook them out, then turned on the phone, looking at news sites. *Mystery Virus Airborne?* one said. *Deaths in Paris Under Investigation.*

I flipped to another tab: the online version of Napoleon's *Oraculum, The Book of Fate.*

we'd thought he might have used it to hide a clue, but as far as we could tell, the book had nothing to do with Alexander or Olympias's virus. I sometimes still looked at it anyway. In this online version, you chose one of the questions, selected one of the groups of stars below, read the answer. One of the questions caught my eye: *Shall I be successful in my present undertaking?*

I brushed a fingertip over one of the star groups at random, and it took me to an answer:

Choose not the path of fear, but that of love.

"Cryptic," Stellan said. I turned to find him looking over my shoulder. "If our political strategy consists of consulting an ancient Greek Magic 8 Ball, I think we need a new plan."

I clicked off the page and flipped him off.

"That's not very ladylike behavior for someone who's about to become a Circle queen."

"If I didn't know better, I'd think you were looking *forward* to this," I said. "I suppose you have gotten exactly what you wanted the whole time. Us together. The girl and the One. The only thing you're not getting is the public marriage consummation. Sorry."

"Yes, that's too bad," he said wistfully. "I do prefer all my romantic encounters to be forced by awkward, tragic circumstance and witnessed by hostile strangers." He plucked at the fabric over his chest. "Maybe I'm just here for the outfit."

Stellan and I looked ready for a cult initiation. Our thin white shifts hung loosely from our shoulders to our bare feet. No matter how much attitude Stellan gave it, his bare ankles made him look uncomfortable as he shifted from foot to foot. I could see the two tattoos on his back through the thin fabric, and also the outlines of his scars. They snaked over his bare shoulders and partway down his arms.

Stellan's "magic skin" was what had allowed him to survive the fire that left those scars. ("Stop calling it magic," Elodie would admonish every time we said the word. "It's highly advanced science we don't understand. Olympias was a genius.") The scars were how we had discovered what Stellan really was. The Circle's thirteenth bloodline—Alexander the Great's own line. The part of the mandate that said *The One walks through fire and isn't burned* was not metaphorical after all.

If the Circle knew the virus came from our blood, they might capture or kill us—either because they were afraid we could be a weapon, or because they wanted to use us as one. So since we couldn't tell them what the *union* really produced, Stellan's scars were how we'd proven our identity.

"The Great modification," the Circle had named it. It had long been rumored that Alexander was not a normal human, that something allowed him to never lose a battle, and to come back from injuries and illnesses that killed thousands of others.

I shuffled my feet on the rough pavement under my own shift. "The virgin sacrifice robes are a little cliché."

"It's cliché because every secret society in the world has taken their cues from the Circle for thousands of years, whether they realize it or not," he said, peering over my head. "To answer your question, no. As you already know, I don't want to become more of a Circle puppet than we already are. Maybe we get inside, see this box, and pull a fire alarm before we have to pledge ourselves to the world's worst people forever. But if not," he said, nudging me exaggeratedly with an elbow, "at least it'll be some comfort that if you can't put a bullet in the Saxons' heads, you can take the Circle

draw me out, trying to be friends. "No one's watching now," I said coolly. "We don't have to pretend to be a happy little couple. Save it for inside."

I wondered what was taking so long. We'd arrived half an hour ago and had been walked through the basics of the ceremony. They'd welcome us; we'd accept. We'd pledge our loyalty. We'd get the tattoos that signified our commitment to the Circle.

Jack and Elodie were pacing at the gate, making sure no unsuspecting tourists wandered in. Occasionally, I saw Jack glance back at us with something besides a Keeper's responsibility on his face.

Despite the fact that he'd nearly gotten us killed reporting on me to the Saxons for what he thought was my own good, and despite the fact that I hadn't forgotten how it felt to learn he'd been lying to me, I trusted that Jack was on our side now. He had promised his loyalty to us, and if nothing else, I knew he'd honor that. He didn't know how not to.

That didn't mean it wasn't awkward. Especially at times like now, or last night, when I could see him deliberately overlook Stellan's hand resting on my back, how I reached up to whisper in his ear. With everything else going on, that unresolved tension was the last thing I wanted to deal with, which was why I hadn't. The boy I'd cared so much about until he broke my trust and my heart. The one who was my "destiny," who I'd had this purely chemical, completely unwanted attraction to until we'd finally given in to it after too many drinks.

And then my mother had died. And then nothing mattered.

I turned when Elodie's boots clicked across the courtyard. She and Jack didn't have to wear the ceremonial robes, so she was in her usual black top and black pants. Her platinum-blond hair was as sleek as usual, but at her hairline, there was an odd patch of what could have been darker hair. I'd never seen Elodie with even a hint of grown-out roots. These really were different times. "They're ready for you. Give me your phones. They'll go in the car with everything else."

There were no weapons allowed inside Circle ceremonies. Stellan had given his up easily enough to make me remember he was just about as deadly without them. I wasn't. I could feel my little knife strapped to my thigh. I hadn't gone anywhere without it since my mom died, and I wasn't about to start now. Elodie was taking just one thing in: a slim bag strapped across her back with Alexander's bone inside, just in case.

When she'd stashed our things away, Elodie led us forward, and Stellan stiffly offered me his arm. I felt the rustling of the thin linen shift against my legs as I walked, the late afternoon breeze flapping its hem.

Elodie took her place on one side of us, Jack on the other. I felt Stellan draw me just a little closer, the ropes of muscles in his forearm tight and tense under my palm. When the four of us were alone, there might be uncomfortable moments. But here, even I had to admit it was us against the world.

With Stellan and me leading the way, we took the steps down into the darkened cave to candle flames flickering low, and a sea of people in black.

A low chant started at the center of the group, and it moved outward until it filled the chamber. We stopped to acknowledge each person, both bowing low and raising our hands to our foreheads as if in prayer. Each person responded with a modified version of the gesture, their raised hands opening before us into a sign of acceptance. Arjun Rajesh smiled. The Fredericks and the Mikados nod-

have both of us under his thumb: Stellan had been his Keeper, and the Dauphins had once tried to kidnap me and marry me off to Luc. But finally, he raised his hands, too. I felt Stellan tense just a little, and then I felt him stand straighter.

Despite everything, goose bumps rose on my arms, just like they had when the Melechs had obeyed our order last night. We were standing at the center of a group more powerful and dangerous and ancient than I could have imagined existed until recently, and they were accepting us as equals and more. *It's seductive being wanted,* Stellan had said once. He wasn't wrong. We both felt it. We both liked the feeling it gave of being in charge of our lives.

I could tell as both our heads swiveled, searching for the next clue, that we were both still hoping it wouldn't be our fate.

As we passed, the Circle members pulled up the necklines of their black robes into heavy hoods, forming a shadowy knot that enveloped us more and more thickly as we approached the center of the cavern.

Above the crowd, on one of the walls, a symbol was etched. *Our* symbol—the symbol of the new thirteenth family. There had never been a question what it would be. I touched the locket around my neck that bore the same symbol. The thirteen-loop knot. I'd had this locket nearly my whole life, since I found it in my mom's things when I was little. I wasn't sure where the symbol had come from, but I knew it had been instrumental in the quest that had led to where we were now. Our mentor, Fitz, had used it to signify clues he wanted us to pay attention to, and before him, so had Napoleon. And now, if we did finish this ceremony, we would all be tattooed with it.

"This ritual is one the Circle hasn't performed in thousands of years," said the man who must have been the master of ceremonies.

I looked around the cave. It was so dark, I couldn't see anything beyond the assembled Circle members. Did someone have the box, or could it be hidden in here?

". . . brings together the full Circle once again as we welcome back to the fold a line that has been lost for as long as we can remember," the man was saying. "The acceptance of the new thirteenth family is an important step in our growth as a Circle. I now present to you the candidates for the new thirteenth family of the Circle of Twelve. The Korolev family."

I felt Stellan look down at me. We were taking my symbol, so we were taking his name. It only seemed fair.

Behind the mass of Circle members, I could see Keepers standing against the far wall. Jack and Elodie, though, were near us. I met Elodie's eyes for a second, and she gave the smallest shake of her head. She hadn't seen anything, either.

"Repeat my words," the moderator said, translating into English after a long speech I couldn't understand. "I pledge fealty to my brothers, and may nothing come between us, to my death." We repeated the words. "I pledge to do no harm to my own, or risk losing my life. My blood, my family, my brothers, stronger as one than apart. The thirteen as one, a world ruled by blood."

"By blood," came a murmur from the group.

From all corners of the room, bells tolled, their light tinging reverberating off the walls. The chanting started up again, low, the bass to the bells' soprano, and then the crowd parted to reveal a fire that had just been lit. I was startled for a moment that they'd let smoke touch this ancient place, but this was the Circle. Of course

flared high, blinding me and releasing the pungent scent of herbs. I felt Stellan wince. Fire was one of the only things in the world he was afraid of.

The moderator called something in a language I didn't know, and a smaller group of people stepped forward, holding knives.

"A baptism by flame unites the lines," the moderator said. This was the last part of the ceremony before the tattoos. I felt a tug in my gut. Were we really going through with this?

"Rule by blood!" the moderator announced.

"By blood," the crowd murmured again.

Sergei Vasilyev came forward. He sliced a line across his forearm and let the blood drip into the fire as the flames tried to lick at his skin. Then the moderator handed him something.

It was a small box, its lid hinged open. "This same blood, combined as one, will make the Circle complete," he proclaimed. Combining blood. That sounded as familiar as the box itself.

Mr. Vasilyev let another drop of blood fall into the box, and handed it off to his right. The next Circle family head, and the next, all the way down the line, did the same. The fire crackled, growing as if fueled by the offerings.

I had my eyes planted firmly on the box. Stellan pressed closer, his hand over mine at his elbow. He'd seen, too, and by the look in their eyes, so had Jack and Elodie. It might be the same replica box we'd seen last night. It was the same size and shape. But it looked—different, somehow.

The chanting grew louder. Stellan and I were each handed a knife of our own. By unspoken agreement, we stepped away from each other. The chanting grew frenzied as I came to the edge of the fire. The heat was like a wall this close. I put the tip of the knife to the forearm farthest from Stellan, and drew the blade across my skin. I felt a bead of sweat drip down my chest. I held my arm over the fire, as far in as I could reach, and watched the dark droplets sizzle as they fell.

I stepped back. The box was placed in my hands.

I knew immediately that, though it looked just like the one we'd seen last night, it was not the same. This was far older, like the one at the Melechs' was a toy. I held my arm over it, and let my blood drip inside onto wood already stained red.

And then I saw it. Etched into the back wall of the box was our symbol.

If anyone had spotted it, they might have assumed it had been specially engraved for today. But this carving was not new. I looked up. Stellan's eyes were burning into me like he was trying to read my mind. I tilted the box so he could see, and then glanced back at Jack and Elodie and let my eyes widen a fraction.

The moderator cleared his throat and gestured Stellan forward. The chanting continued.

Stellan stepped to the fire, letting his blood drip. He rejoined me, and I reluctantly handed him the box. Once we finished this, the ceremony would be all but done.

I could see the same thoughts swirl behind Stellan's eyes. He took the box. His blood dripped inside. The bells chimed like a chorus of heartbeats. Row after row, the Circle members got to their knees.

That's when Elodie screamed.

I jumped so hard, I almost knocked the box out of Stellan's hands. The chanting cut off abruptly.

that it didn't make sense. This was her version of pulling a fire alarm, and it worked. Keepers were rushing to their families, hustling them toward the exit. People screamed, threw back the hoods on their robes.

"Get to the exit!" Elodie yelled. She grabbed the back of my robe, and Stellan's, and shoved us in the opposite direction. I saw what she was looking at. There were a couple of passageways off the back of the cavern. We were still holding the box. We'd take it and find another way out, pretending we'd gotten lost in the chaos.

I clung to Stellan's arm as we disappeared into the dark mouth of the tunnel, and we squinted into the box. The flames from the main cavern were the only light we had. I heard Elodie's voice, and Jack's, still ushering everyone out. "Look," I said. "The symbol is etched into some kind of metal strip that goes all the way around—"

And then there was a bang so loud, it sounded like the world above us had imploded.

CHAPTER 3

Before I could react, Stellan had pushed me to the ground against a wall, sheltering me with his body. In the darkness I felt dust rain from the ceiling, and a deepening rumble seemed to be coming from the rocks themselves.

"Jack!" I screamed, pushing to standing. "Elodie!"

"Luc's back there, too," Stellan said.

The ground under our feet started shaking, like an earthquake. I grabbed blindly for Stellan to keep from falling—then there was a grating rumble and a crash, and weak light came from a hole where the wall opposite us used to be. It must have led into the main network of tunnels that ran under the Old City. They were a major tourist attraction. A group of shocked sightseers, the cameras around their necks forgotten, screamed and shoved as they fled the blast. A couple of them looked through the hole and did a double take when they saw us. We probably looked like ghosts in our white ceremonial robes.

The rumbling grew louder behind us, in the direction of the Circle ceremony. I spun toward it. "We have to get them—"

I could tell Stellan didn't like it, but he said, "They had a way out. We have to save ourselves." He pulled me to the hole in the wall.

The stone scraped at my bare arms as I squeezed through, and then there was a massive crash, and bits of rock and dust slammed into us, throwing us to the floor. I sat up coughing, staring back in the direction of the ruined ceremonial chamber.

There would be no going back for Jack and Elodie and Luc.

We followed the crowd. Tears streamed down my face at the haze in the air. I couldn't stop coughing, and neither could Stellan.

We burst into the next chamber just in time to hear someone scream.

"Merde," Stellan said under his breath.

I ran into him, but I would have stopped still anyway. "No," I whispered, panic swelling in my throat. "Please tell me this isn't what it looks like."

Despite everything, until this very moment I'd assumed this didn't have to do with us. That it was a random terrorist attack—or even an accident. Cave-ins happened in old tunnels sometimes.

"This wasn't just a bomb," Stellan murmured.

At a glance, it might look like the girl had been injured by falling debris. Her face was bloodied, and she was limp. But there was another girl next to her, yelling. It was in English, so I could understand. *"Elena!"* she screamed. She turned to the rest of the tour group huddled around her. "She just started coughing blood, and then she collapsed!"

And if we needed more proof, on the other side of the cavern, a kid leaned over a man whose face was covered in red. Moments later, the son coughed, spraying blood across his father's already-stained white shirt.

They hadn't been hurt by the cave-in.

It flashed through my head again. My mom falling to her knees, coughing. The bloody tears seeping from her green eyes, faster and faster, staining the light carpet where she fell. It had happened so fast. It was real—it was too real—but now the images rolled through my head like a movie shot on old, scratched film. I wondered whether it really had happened at all. Whether this all could be just a recurring bad dream, and at some point, I'd figure out how to wake up. I dug one fingernail into my palm as hard as I could. I don't think that worked in dreams, anyway.

Stellan put an arm around me and pulled me close, and I let him. "How?" I whispered. The only illumination came from the dim can lights illuminating the passageway, and those were dampened by the swirling yellow dust. My bare feet were covered in dirt, and it streaked my white robes. "They couldn't have all eaten or drunk something."

"Aerosol," he said. "I wouldn't have imagined the Saxons would have enough blood left to do it. But maybe it takes even less in this form."

"Every Circle family was here," I said, horror mounting. "The Saxons must have been trying to take them all out at once."

Stellan rubbed his face, smearing a clean line through the dust yellowing his skin. "If it got out here, maybe it wasn't directed into the ceremony chamber. Maybe they were just trying to scare the Circle. Or maybe they did it wrong."

I coughed into Stellan's shoulder, and then had another thought. "Do you think *we* can get it?"

"I hope not. I think it's just whatever's in the air. We need to get out of here, anyway."

As we skirted past the dead and dying, I whispered, "Are these people Circle? Some of the people who died in Paris were second cousins or something, but . . ."

Stellan pulled me past the father and son now both on the ground, dead. "Maybe the Saxons mutated it. I don't know."

I didn't take a wide enough berth, and my bare foot slipped on blood. I tried not to think about how cold and terrible it probably looked that we weren't stopping to help. We were the only ones who

We joined a clamoring, crying group of people, and I took a huge breath of fresh air when we burst into the evening light. I could tell immediately we were nowhere near where we'd gone into the ceremony, and we had no phones to call Jack and Elodie.

"Do you think they would have stayed by where we went in?" I said. I refused to consider anything less than them making it out safely. "Ask somebody where that entrance is."

As he did, I remembered the little box under my arm. Out here in the light, the strip of metal around the top of it was far more obvious. It was the most likely candidate for this "map" we were looking for. Just in case someone took the box back from us once we found the Circle again, I pried at it. One end popped off easily, and I yanked until the other came free. The back of the metal strip was bright gold, and it had writing etched into it. In spite of everything, my heart jumped.

Glancing around, I tucked the strip of metal into the sports bra I had on under the ceremonial robe.

Stellan pulled me out of the crowd. We were in some kind of alley, with tall, straight walls rising on either side and a stone street down the middle, cars parked on one side of it. It was hot, with a bit of a dry wind that flapped our robes. "The main entrance to the tunnels is in the plaza at the Western Wall, but I don't think that's where we went in." He glanced down the alley, chewing his lip. "Elodie and Jack will be looking for us, too. Assuming—"

"They're okay," I said, suddenly feeling more nervous when I saw that he was nervous. "They *have* to be. Right?"

Stellan peered over my head, and then he stiffened. I wheeled around.

There was a machine gun pointed at my face.

The soldier on the other end of the gun barked something, and Stellan raised his hands over his head. I did the same. I saw a crowd of people behind him, one woman chattering excitedly, pointing at us. Two more soldiers joined the first.

Stellan argued with the soldier. He yelled something angry, gesturing with his gun.

"Turn around," Stellan said quietly. "Hands on the wall."

I guess I wasn't quick enough, because I felt the barrel of a gun jabbing me in the middle of my back until I stumbled forward into the stone. I spread my dusty hands, one still holding the box, on either side of my head like Stellan had. "Don't try anything," he murmured as another soldier kicked my feet farther apart. "They will kill us. They think we did this."

"What?" I said it too loud, and earned another jab from the gun and one of the soldiers yelling in my ear, so close I could smell the sourness on his breath. He ripped the little box out of my hand, and I cringed as close to Stellan as I could.

"They got a tip, and then multiple tourists pointed you out," he murmured. "They said they saw you setting a backpack down and running away. A short girl in a white robe, with dark hair pulled up on her head."

"What?" I whispered again. That made no sense—then, suddenly, it did.

I had a sister who looked just like me, and who would know exactly what I was wearing today. "Lydia," I whispered.

My head started to spin. Lydia had set us up. The Saxons had blamed the Order for their attacks for so long, and now they were shifting that blame to us. The Circle would think we'd brought them to the initiation to kill them. The whole world would think we were

Saxons were persona non grata. But like this? She'd know where the military would take us. She'd be waiting. The Melechs were almost certainly in on it. And if they happened to fail in capturing us, the Circle would still think we'd tried to kill them, and the Saxons would be exonerated. It was the perfect plan.

Our hands were cuffed behind our backs, and we were thrown into the partially open back of a truck.

I glanced at the soldiers. The two guarding us looked younger than me. They couldn't have known the truth of what was happening; they were just following orders. If we were going to escape, we had to do it before we were taken to anyone who was in on the Saxons' plan.

But we couldn't use Circle influence now. The best thing to do would be to look like tourists who had stumbled into a very unfortunate case of mistaken identity.

"Our friends are in there!" I tried. "They might be hurt—"

The gun in my face made me close my mouth.

The cut on my arm from the ceremony was still bleeding. It gave me an idea. I surreptitiously took some blood from it and wiped it under my nose. And then I nudged Stellan, hoped he understood the plan, and let my eyes roll back in my head.

CHAPTER 4

An hour later, we were in a sterile, sparse room somewhere inside a military hospital.

I was a little shocked at the compassion of these soldiers, actually. I had hoped my stunt would cause some confusion and we might be able to escape, but even though they thought I'd set off a bomb laced with a biological weapon in their city—in one of the most volatile regions in the world—they had let me get medical attention.

There were no Circle members at this hospital, and no one seemed to know who we were. This wasn't where we were meant to have ended up. We had to get out of here before the confusion cleared.

This room was nothing but three stone walls and a chain-link gate across the front, with a soldier on guard. I didn't let myself look down the hall. The last time I'd been in a hospital was in a basement, on my way to the morgue to officially identify my mom's body. I wondered whether the people who had died today would be brought here—

I shook myself. How were we going to get out of here? Assuming Jack and Elodie were okay, they had no way to find us.

They had to be okay.

I blinked that thought away, too. I hadn't gotten through the last month by letting things like that in.

Next to me, Stellan stared straight ahead. His white robe was ~~torn at the collar, his face streaked with dirt and sweat. I thought~~

toes were tapping out a nervous beat on the concrete floor.

"Are you okay?" I whispered.

He gave half a nod at the far wall.

I listened to the restless *tap tap tap* of his foot and remembered him telling me about waking up in a hospital with most of his family dead and burns across his whole body.

A shudder went through me. My gaze slid out of our cell, down the hallway, and I felt the tenuous control I'd had on my thoughts since the bomb went off slipping.

That last hospital I'd been in had had the same anemic hospital light, the same speckled tile and dingy walls, the same sterile, cold smell like metal instruments and cleaning solution. I wondered if Stellan's had, too. In mine, my mother's usually smiling eyes had been lifeless, her hair matted with blood. They'd told me I could touch her, but I didn't. I signed the forms to identify her. They asked me about funerals and autopsies, and I wanted to scream at them that they were vultures, that my mother had died just a few hours earlier. But those words—*my mother died*—couldn't have been true, so I couldn't say them. I don't know, I said instead. Jack had asked me a couple more times in the past weeks, whenever the morgue called. I don't know, I said, over and over. I'll think about it later. I don't *know*.

Stellan's foot was still tapping. Now, so was mine.

The next time I had to identify a body—how had it become my life that I could say a phrase like that?—the next time, it could be Jack's or Elodie's.

Tap tap tap tap went our feet. *Stop it,* I told myself. We had to make a plan. We had to—Images flashed like a jerky movie reel in my brain: Jack glancing back as he and Elodie pushed Circle members out of the ceremony chamber. The dead girl, and her friend screaming her name. *Elena!*

When I started to lose control in the middle of the night, I got up and punched things. That wasn't going to happen now. The only possible distraction in here was sitting right next to me, and he wasn't doing so great himself.

One of my legs was cuffed to my rolling chair, but the other was free. I very quietly rolled my chair close enough to reach out and touch Stellan's foot with mine.

He stiffened. "No one's watching. We don't have to *pretend* in here."

I heard the echo of myself outside the initiation. I didn't move my foot.

Stellan let his head fall forward, his hair hanging in his eyes. "I'm sorry. I don't like hospitals."

"I know. I'm sorry I had us brought here."

"Not like the alternative was better."

The soldier turned around. *"Sheket!"* he barked. It wasn't hard to grasp the meaning of that. I shut my mouth until he turned back around.

When he did, Stellan inched his own chair closer. With a glance at the soldier, he leaned in like he was going to whisper something to me. I inclined my ear to him, but he just sat there, his breath uneven. Our cheeks were almost touching. Stellan's skin was warm and he smelled like blood and dirt, but under it, enough like *him* that it cut through the sad, sterile hospital smell. Except for the fake canoodling at the party, this was the closest we'd been in a long time. The closest I'd been to anyone in a long time. I remembered what

I wanted to pull away. I wanted my walls to snap up. But just this tiny bit of allowing myself to feel things had shattered those carefully built mechanisms into dust. "All that time, they'd been saying we were a miracle. The Circle's salvation," I breathed. "But we're not salvation. We're destruction. The two of us are the end of the world."

I waited for him to tell me everything would be okay.

"I know," he whispered instead. "And now so does the Circle."

I felt his lashes blink against my cheek. Neither of us moved.

I don't know whether I was trying to comfort him or myself. But I leaned into him, letting my cheek touch his. He sighed then, so softly. And he nuzzled his head into me, like a kitten wanting to snuggle.

We sat like that, his face in the crook of my neck, listening to each other's breathing, and I felt the hummingbird flutter of my heartbeat slowly calm.

The guard's walkie-talkie crackled to life, and as he answered, Stellan pulled away, avoiding my eyes. "We have to find some way to get the cuffs off," he whispered, like that hadn't just happened.

I sat back, too, embarrassed at how much better I felt now. My head was suddenly clear enough to realize something. "I have a knife."

I glanced at the guard, who was still turned away, and scooted my chair even closer to Stellan, maneuvering my free leg behind him. "My thigh," I breathed, nudging my leg against his cuffed hands.

He understood immediately. Goose bumps rose on my legs as his cold hands worked my robe up until he could reach the knife. I kept an eye on the guard while his fingers fumbled with the strap. I felt when it came free. "Turn around," he whispered. "Give me your hands."

The guard had started fidgeting, looking at his watch. I rolled away from Stellan with a loud cough, so the guard turned around and saw us both sitting quietly. When he turned back again, satisfied that we were being good prisoners, I rolled over quickly and offered Stellan my cuffs.

There was a quiet scrabbling as he worked at the lock with the slim knife, and then a snick. The guard turned, and just in time, I swiveled and rested my head on Stellan's shoulder, playing the tired, dejected tourist.

The guard snapped something, and I sat up, pretending to be chagrined.

As I did, I felt my unlocked cuff slip. I twisted my wrist to keep it on, but it kept falling. At the last second, I shoved my other hand under it before it could smack the chair with a clang.

I held my breath, but the guard sneered and turned back around, none the wiser.

After a second, Stellan turned his back to me, and I loosened my hands and took the knife. Elodie had taught me to pick the locks on handcuffs, but I wasn't very good at it. My eyes flicked from the cuffs to the guard's back, and I worked the tip of the knife back and forth.

Finally—*finally*—I heard a click. Stellan immediately worked his hands free. In moments, he had his ankle cuff undone, then mine.

He leaned across to me again. "We have to get him in here," he whispered. "Pretend to be hurt again."

I nodded, and, my hands clasped behind me like I was still cuffed, I let my head droop forward. Stellan yelled something frantic. I heard the guard mutter into his walkie-talkie.

keys jangled in the lock of our cell. I barely sensed him leaning over me before there was a thud, and Stellan was lowering him to the ground.

CHAPTER 5

I disentangled myself from my chair, rubbing my elbow. "He called someone. We need to go."

Down the hall, the elevator dinged. I cursed. "There." I pointed to another elevator at the end of the hall. We ran to it, and I punched the button over and over.

Shouts came up from where we had just been. Our elevator doors dinged open. Empty, thank God.

We jumped inside just as a voice yelled something behind us. The doors slid shut. I started to press the Lobby button, but Stellan stopped me. "Too many people. We'll find a back stairwell from another floor."

He ran a finger over the listings of the floors, and pressed the button for 3. "The ICU," he said. "No one will be looking for us there."

We got off the elevator without anyone else getting on. The floor was quiet besides a nurses' station, staffed by one woman with her back to us. We walked quickly in the other direction and ducked inside the first empty room we saw. "We won't be able to get out of here wearing this," I whispered.

The rooms here were just glass boxes, some of which had dingy white curtains drawn across their fronts. Across the hall from the one we were in, something caught my eye. A pile of clothing sat perfectly folded on the chair by the window. It was the same uniform all the soldiers wore: a greenish khaki top and pants, with a wide brown belt. There were even boots. And farther across the room, I could see

"Stay here," I whispered.

I glanced down the hall, then inched across and into the room. On the patient's TV, a phone rang. I held my breath. She stirred, but didn't wake up. I grabbed the pile of clothes and the boots.

Down the hall, the click-clack of heels announced a group of doctors talking seriously and passing a clipboard back and forth. Across the hall, Stellan's eyes got wide, and he pulled his curtains shut. I yanked the one in front of me closed, too, trapping myself in the woman's room.

The doctors' steps went past at an efficient clip. I peeked out, then tiptoed back across the hall.

When our curtain was shut again, I closed my eyes, adrenaline buzzing through me. "I'll change; then I'll find you clothes," I whispered, and glanced at Stellan. "Turn around."

I wasted no time pulling the clothes on, then hurried back down the hall, slightly less nervous now that I was dressed like someone who was supposed to be here. I found a man sleeping a few rooms away, his uniform folded neatly on a cart in the back of the room.

I looked Stellan over after he'd changed, too. His uniform was too baggy on him, but it would work. "Tuck in the back of your shirt." I hesitated awkwardly but then said, "Come here." While he got himself tucked and refastened his belt, I grabbed some tissues from a rolling cart to get streaks of dirt off his face and rubbed at a smear of blood at his hairline, careful not to get his blood on me, just in case. "How do I look?"

The woman I'd taken my clothes from was definitely bigger than me, but the attached belt helped me cinch the pants tight. Stellan tipped my chin up and scrubbed at my face. "Your hair," he whispered.

I pulled the cap low over my eyes and tucked the pink ends of my hair inside.

We made it to the bottom of the fire exit stairs without seeing another person. The second we got outside, though, we weren't so lucky. I opened the door just as a trio of stern soldiers trooped by, their guns slung across their backs.

My first thought was that I wished I'd thought to grab the guns that went with these uniforms. That was stupid of me. My second was that although it would feel safer to stand here quietly until they were gone, it would be *smarter* to blend in with a group who might be headed toward an exit. I signaled to Stellan, and we waited until the group was a few feet away before following them.

It was working—no one gave us a second glance. The soldiers *were* headed for the exit and— I stopped still.

They were headed for a group of a couple dozen soldiers just outside the exit, all carrying riot shields and wearing full face masks. The officer who looked to be in charge saw us and the group ahead of us, and barked something impatiently. The soldiers in front of us sped up. They were about to head out into a city that had just had a major terrorist attack.

I glanced around frantically for an out. "We have to," Stellan said under his breath.

I swallowed and nodded. A mask and a shield were thrust into my hands, and the whole regiment turned and walked out the gate, Stellan and me right in the center.

We marched to a square a few blocks away that was bustling with people. It wasn't quite a protest, and it wasn't quite a mob, but a group of men were yelling at another group, and it was escalating even as we watched. It wasn't hard to figure out why: this city was full of age-old conflict. Conflict over religion, conflict over

an atrocity.

Turning the Circle against us wasn't the Saxons' only objective, I suddenly realized. The assassinations they'd been committing and blaming on the Order for so long had spread fear, oily and black. And now they'd set a match to it.

"How could they do this?" I murmured to Stellan. Around us, soldiers were pulling their masks over their faces and raising their shields. We did the same, and fell into formation. "The Saxons, but the Melechs, too. This is their own city."

"Because all the Circle cares about is the Circle, and especially their family," Stellan said, his voice echoing through his mask. "The Melechs live here and adopt parts of the culture to fit in, but you can't say they have loyalty to this place any more than you can say every British person is a sociopath like your brother and sister."

"So they don't care at all about their people?"

"They care about how much power their territories have, certainly. You can be sure Britain will benefit from the Saxons' actions, as will their allies. But a few lives lost to get what they want?" He shrugged. "It's nothing. Knowing exactly how to use the world as a tool to get yourself ahead is how the Circle has always worked. Sometimes the families like when there's conflict in their territories—it makes a place easier to manipulate."

From across the square, a flaming rag in the top of a bottle sailed toward us, smashing on the cobblestones just ahead of our group with a quick orange burst of flame.

The officer in charge shouted orders, and a few soldiers took off in the direction it had come from. I watched them subdue both sides of a fight that had broken out, attempting to keep the peace without hurting anyone. Stellan grabbed my arm and I followed him, jogging to the far corner of the square with a guy not too much older than us, who had a shock of curly hair and blue eyes so light, they were almost eerie against his olive complexion.

While we hurried along, Stellan talked to him in Hebrew and I prayed he wouldn't say anything to me.

Just then, though, Stellan pointed and said something, alarm in his voice. The guy answered and nodded toward a street behind us. Stellan and I started that way, and the guy jogged off in the opposite direction. The second his back disappeared around a corner, we ducked into a tiny alley and ditched our riot gear. I wished we could do more since this was so very much our fault, but what we really had to do was find the cure, and to do that, we had to get out of here.

"Do you have any idea where we're going?" I said.

Stellan nodded. Our rendezvous point was a hotel near the Old City. We'd started choosing one everywhere we went, just in case we got separated and couldn't return to where we'd been staying. "But I need to find a phone before we do anything else," he said, looking up and down the alley and directing us to the far end.

"Our phones are back in the car at the initiation site." We emerged on a major street and waited in a crowd of pedestrians for the light to change.

"I know," he said. "That's why I need to find one. Any phone. A pay phone. I need to call Anya's nanny and tell her all of this. Tell her to lie low."

Oh. That was probably half of why he'd been so on edge this whole time. "I don't know if pay phones even exist anymore. There will be a phone at the hotel. It'll be okay. I doubt they're even thinking about Anya right now."

He just nodded tightly and guided us down back streets, staying

have enough of the virus left."

Stellan nodded. "If I were betting, I'd say somewhere in the Emirs' territory, to make it look to the world like a Middle East conflict. That would spread fear faster than random attacks."

"We have to warn them, then."

Stellan looked grim. "It's unlikely anyone will believe us since they think we did it."

We rounded a corner and the hotel appeared. We both stopped, looking up at it. Neither of us had mentioned Jack and Elodie and Luc since the hospital—on purpose, I was certain. We couldn't afford to panic again. But as we'd made our way here, I'd been getting more and more nervous.

I folded my arms over the stiff khaki of my uniform shirt. "What if—" I said.

Stellan shook his head and started forward again. If they're not here, my mind rationalized, it doesn't have to mean the worst. The Circle could have taken them. Or maybe they were hurt—a broken wrist or something. Maybe—

The lobby door flew open, and Elodie rushed down the steps and crashed into our arms.

CHAPTER 6

Merde, you two. Where have you *been*? I thought—I thought you—"
She pulled away, still holding on to both of our shoulders. In the
light spilling out from the hotel lobby, I could tell her face was red
and blotchy.

She was okay. She was alive.

Then she pulled away and punched Stellan in the shoulder, hard.
"Where were you? It's been hours."

I was peering behind her. The longer the doorway stood empty,
the more times I glanced back at Elodie's puffy eyes, the more my
chest caved in on itself.

"Where's Jack?" I interrupted. I grabbed her. "Elodie. Where *is*
he?"

"He's okay. He's inside," she said, and my bones turned to jelly. I
sat down on the front steps of the hotel.

"Lucien?" Stellan said.

"He's fine. I saw him just after, and texted with him a few minutes
ago. He's going to call when he can."

Stellan sat down hard beside me, his head in his hands.

"Hello," Elodie said. "I asked where you've been. We ran around to the other entrance looking for you and heard that the police were looking for a dark-haired girl in a white robe. We figured that was bad, so we didn't go back to the Circle, but we've been searching all over this city. I'm assuming you didn't join the army while you were gone, so what happened?"

Jack threw open the hotel room door as we approached, and sagged with relief when he saw us. His black pants and shirt were so dusty, they were gray. So was his hair. "Took your time getting back here, didn't you?" He wrapped me in his arms so hard, my feet came off the ground. I buried my face in his dirty shoulder.

"Are you okay?" I muttered against him.

He set me down and nodded, then looked over my shoulder at Stellan. They stared at each other for a second, then pulled each other into what I could tell was a bruisingly tight hug.

Stellan pulled away and smacked Jack on the side of the head, raising a cloud of dust from his hair. "There's such a thing as a shower."

Jack patted Stellan's chest. "Sure thing, Officer."

Stellan went immediately to call his sister. I sat down and shook my hair out from under my hat. The hotel we'd chosen as a rendezvous was a cheap, seedy one that no one would expect us to stay in, and I could see its lit sign buzzing and flickering out the window while Jack and Elodie told me what had happened after the explosion. All the Circle had made it out without getting sick.

"Did you hear that other people were infected, though?" I asked as Stellan came back into the room. "People died who weren't Circle."

Jack and Elodie looked at each other. "We did hear, and we had a thought," Jack said. "It doesn't look good."

"The virus infects people with Circle blood," Elodie cut in. "Until now, we've been thinking of it in terms of close relatives of the twelve families. Biologically, though, that's not necessarily true. Circle blood has spread a lot farther than that in the past two thousand years."

I didn't understand for a second, but then coldness slipped over me. "Olympias meant the virus to kill the *Circle*—"

"But she was expecting to kill them in the first or second generation," Stellan said, catching on at the same time. "Who knows how many people have *some* amount of Circle blood now? If a distant ancestor is all it takes . . ."

"That must have been what happened with my mom," I said. I'd assumed she'd lied about being Circle. Maybe instead, she had enough of the blood to be killed by the virus, but not enough to know about it.

Jack nodded grimly. "Which means this could devastate far more than just the Circle."

I didn't want it to, but it made sense. I couldn't believe we hadn't thought about it before, actually. I put my head in my hands. "Are *you* guys feeling okay? I know you said the virus didn't seem to hit in the ceremony chamber, but—"

Jack and Elodie both nodded. "Fine."

Fine. They were fine. I closed my eyes for a few seconds. My hair fell lank around my face. It smelled like smoke, and like the herb they'd thrown into the fire at the ceremony. I bottled back up the flood of emotions that had tried to overtake me in the last few hours, and sat up straight again. "Okay. So I guess this is even more important now." I pulled the piece of metal out of my shirt. "The box was taken away when we got arrested, but I got this out first."

Elodie snatched it and examined it under a bedside lamp. "This is ancient. It actually could be from Alexander's time. I can't believe you got it out of there."

"Does it say something about his blood? Or the cure?" I asked.

"And what does Alexander's bone have to do with unlocking it?" Jack chimed in.

hadn't. "Did you get ahold of Anya?" I said.

"The nanny didn't answer," he said gruffly. "I knew she wouldn't. That's the protocol if I'm not calling from my number. I'll call again in a few minutes."

Elodie was poking carefully at an edge of the metal. "Have any of you heard of curse tablets?"

We shook our heads.

"They were common in Alexander's day. Thinly hammered sheets of iron with words stamped into them, usually asking the gods to curse someone who had wronged the person."

"You think that's what this is?"

"It looks like it, sort of. But they're meant to be bigger, squarer. This is more of a strip."

"Doesn't matter if the words are there." Jack pulled out his phone and brought up an app to translate ancient Greek.

Elodie frowned. "They're not, though. These are the letters, but some of them are backward, and they're not lined up with each other in a way that makes sense."

"Maybe it's some kind of code," Jack said.

"The last clue did say the bones unlock something," Elodie mused. "But it's not like the bone has to do with a *code*. Unless maybe the clue itself did?"

The three of them leaned over the metal under the lamp, and I sat back, thinking. They knew much more than I did about all of this, but there was something tickling at the edges of my brain.

"Did they even use substitution ciphers at that time?" Jack asked while Elodie wrote down all the letters.

"No," I said. They all turned to me. I jumped up. "No, Alexander used a very specific kind of cipher. It was one of the first recorded codes. We did a project in school. I can't believe I forgot. Where's that bone?"

Elodie was clearly skeptical about the *school project* part, but she produced the bone and unwrapped a scarf from around it.

I picked up the edge of the metal piece. It felt like thick tinfoil. "Is it strong enough to be folded?" I said.

Elodie shrugged. "If you have to."

I handed the bone to Stellan, and held the metal piece up to it. Then I wrapped it around in a spiral, covering the outside of the bone like a maypole. "This was the cipher," I said. "You wrapped the thing around a cylinder of a certain size, wrote the message on it, and unwrapped it. The person reading it had to have the right size cylinder to wrap it again and read it, or else it just looked like gibberish."

I finished wrapping and held it up. "Does that look any better?"

Stellan inspected it. "The letters are in the right direction now."

Jack grabbed the phone and entered them again, going around and around the cylinder of bone.

He finally hit Translate and let out a low breath before he met my eyes. "Who knew American schools would have more answers than three people who have been part of the Circle for years?"

He turned the phone to us.

They said a woman should never have power again, it read. *Now a woman holds it all.*

Elodie grabbed the phone out of Jack's hands. "The Diadochi

said that exact thing about Olympias. She was causing trouble for them. She must have written this."

"Why do you know so much about Olympias?" Stellan said.

She rolled her eyes at him, ignoring the question. "That doesn't tell us anything concrete, though."

I will hold all the secrets with me, where I await my son for our eternal rest, in the city named for him. My followers shall watch over us, at the thirteenth at the center of the twelve.

We stared at each other. That was exactly what Napoleon had said. Alexandria. The thirteenth at the center.

"So we have to go back to Alexandria," I said. "I wonder if Olympias's followers had some kind of headquarters? How would we find that out?"

Stellan looked up at the ceiling. "We already searched so much of Alexandria—"

Elodie's phone rang, interrupting us. It was Luc. She put it on speaker.

It was worse than we'd thought. Not only did the Circle believe we'd set the bomb and tried to kill them, but the Melechs had "discovered" that the virus was our blood—obviously the Saxons had told them to spread the word. "So needless to say, they are not particularly happy with you," Luc finished. "The fact that you're the girl with the purple eyes and *Stellan the Great* is not going to get you out of this."

We told him about the Avery lookalike who had set the bomb. "That makes sense," Luc said. "Rocco says he thought the Saxons might have been in Jerusalem. They're so secretive now, only a couple of their crew ever goes with them, so he didn't know for sure."

We all turned to stare at the phone. "*Rocco* says?" Stellan asked.

Rocco—whom we used to call Scarface until we recruited him to our side and learned his real name—was our very own double agent in the Saxon home. He'd broken my mom out of captivity, and he claimed to not have killed our friend and mentor Fitz like we thought he did—I guess Cole Saxon actually did that himself—but we still didn't fully trust him.

"I called earlier and couldn't get ahold of you," Luc said defensively. "I was worried. I wanted to see if he'd heard from you."

"How do you even have his number?" Stellan asked.

"You all have been gone for a month. *Somebody* had to keep an eye on what was going on in London."

"You've been talking to Rocco for a *month?*" Jack said.

"All right, I don't care," Elodie cut him off. "Anything else, Lucien?"

"Actually, yes," Luc's tinny voice said from the phone. "They are also saying you are conspiring with the Order."

Jack's eyebrows shot up to his hairline.

"They're saying that you have been in league with them for a long time and that you were becoming a full-fledged Circle family to infiltrate more deeply," Luc said. "Loads of people believe them. I have to admit, if I didn't know you, I'd think it was a convincing argument."

"What argument?"

"They say that they have proof that Avery's mother kept her away from the Circle for a reason. They're saying she was a member of the Order, too."

I stared at the phone. "My mom? The *Order?* That's ridiculous for so many reasons. If anyone here knew my mom . . ." I shook my head. "And anyway, all those assassinations being blamed on the Order were the Saxons. The Order probably doesn't even exist."

"They exist," Jack said.

"So maybe they used to cause trouble for the Circle, but it seems like now they're just a bogeyman."

"Not to the Circle," Jack said. "If they thought we did this because we're power-hungry, that's one thing. If they believe we did it for the

Stellan was nodding along. He briefed Luc on what we suspected about the possibility of more attacks and told him to warn other families as well as he could without implicating himself, and then we signed off.

"Will it look more suspicious if we run?" I said. We did have some families on our side—maybe enough of them that we could argue our case. "Isn't there anyone who would believe us that these Order accusations are ridiculous? The Rajeshes? Or we could get Luc to talk to his parents . . ."

"If the situation were different, maybe." Stellan crossed to the window and pulled back the curtain a sliver to peek out. "But so much as mentioning the Order makes everything different. I think we have to let the Circle think we're either dead or gone to ground until we're safely out of here. And . . ."

"What?"

He dropped the curtain. "We've been looking to destroy the cure because we thought they wouldn't release the virus without it. Obviously that's not true."

"They still did it in a very contained area. If they got the cure, it could be so much worse. Today doesn't change the fact that we need to find it before they do."

"I understand that. But what it does change is that we are in far more danger than we were hours ago. We have to be smart."

This time, Jack was the one nodding his agreement. He sat on the edge of the bed, facing me. "Avery, I hate to ask, but we need the whole story. Are you absolutely sure your mother wasn't . . ."

"Of *course* I'm sure." Even if the Order was real, the thought of my scatterbrained mom being part of some group of counter-Circle agents was laughable.

Elodie was perched on the desk chair, her posture rigid, gnawing a thumbnail. I realized she'd been quiet since we hung up with Luc.

"Don't tell me you believe it," I said to her. "You know everything they're saying is a lie."

Elodie drew in a breath. "I don't—"

"What is wrong with everyone?" I exploded. "My mom's dead. Do we really have to accuse her of things?"

"Avery, trust me, I'm not *accusing* her of anything. In fact—" She shook her head, but then stood up abruptly. "I guess I have to tell you. I'm sorry." She looked at each of us. "I didn't want any of you to find out this way. I didn't want you to find out ever, actually, but Jackie's right—you need the whole story."

The room was silent. "What are you talking about?" I said.

Elodie crossed her arms over her chest and looked at Stellan, who had pushed off the window where he'd been standing, then at Jack, who had gone rigid on the bed. "Promise me you'll stay calm and give me a chance to explain."

Stellan took a step forward. "Elodie . . ."

"Okay. Yes. It's true that Avery's mother was in the Order. And I know because I am, too."

CHAPTER 7

The neon hotel sign blinked and buzzed out the window. Inside the room, we all stood, frozen.

"The Order's nothing like what the Circle says," Elodie added quickly.

"Elodie." Jack stood, his hands clenched at his sides, like he wasn't sure whether to reach for a weapon. "You can't actually be saying you're part of a group that has sworn to destroy the Circle."

"That's not how it is. It's been a long time since we used violence against the Circle at all."

"The Order killed Oliver Saxon only a few years ago."

"That wasn't us." Elodie had her arms crossed, her shoulders nearly at her ears. I'd never seen her look this uncomfortable. "I think that was actually an accident. Think about it, you two: Keepers are taught from the very beginning of their training to be on the lookout for the Order, but have you ever seen a confirmed Order attack? Since Alexander's time, when we were known as the Order of *Olympias*, we've been charged with keeping the peace. That does mean reining in the Circle's power at times, but it's very rarely violent. In fact, every Circle member sees someone in the Order daily. We're in every Circle household. Just like I am. Just like Avery's mother was."

Stellan was silent and rigid, staring blankly at a spot on the wall above Elodie's head.

Jack wasn't. "You've been lying to us since we met you, then?"

"We're forced to hide our real identities." Elodie looked at me meaningfully. "And Avery's mom isn't the only person you know who's secretly in the Order." She glanced up at Jack and looked genuinely sad. "Emerson Fitzpatrick was, too."

"What?" Jack exploded. "Elodie, I don't know where you're getting this—"

"It's true."

Jack was still staring her down. "I can't believe that," he murmured. "Fitz was loyal. He was my friend—"

"All of that is still true as well," Elodie said.

"You know what I don't believe?" Stellan asked, interrupting the conversation. "That you've been keeping it from me our whole lives that you're part of the group that killed my family."

I'd forgotten about that. The fire that had killed Stellan's mom and burned him and his sister nearly to death was started by the Order.

But Elodie was already shaking her head. "The Order didn't kill your family." She sounded softer than usual, speaking right to Stellan. "The Circle did."

Stellan didn't move. Jack started to protest, but I silenced him with a hand.

Elodie went on, "I know because they killed *my* family, too. That's why I joined the Order in the first place."

Stellan just stared. Elodie went on, like the two of them were the only ones in the room. And then she switched to Russian. Stellan straightened, alarmed.

"I said," Elodie translated for us, "that I'm from Russia, too. I was never French." She turned back to Stellan. "My mother was Mongolian, my father Russian. I spent the first years of my life in a tiny village near the border, and when my brothers were born, my father moved us to a small town outside Chelyabinsk. That's where Stellan

mean it's why you joined the Order?" he said flatly. It was like Jack and I weren't even there.

"When I was a kid, there was a fire in my apartment building," Elodie said. "The building exploded. I woke up lying outside in the snow, surrounded by my whole family: My mom. My dad. My two little brothers. All dead. Maybe I was just in shock, but for some reason, I kept thinking of a few weeks earlier, when another building nearby had burned. Our neighborhood wasn't rich. Bad wiring, or someone building a fire inside on the coldest days . . . But two major fires so close together? And I knew my father had been rocking a lot of boats in the town." She twisted her fingers. "I left the bodies of my family in the snow and I ran. As far as anyone knew, I died that night, too. I was burned all over, but the worst of it was the back of my head."

She didn't look up, but she pulled her hands through her hair—and took off her short platinum-blond wig.

Part of Elodie's head was scarred and bald. The rest was covered in black hair, buzzed short. That was what I'd seen at her hairline. She slipped the wig back on, settling it into place over her real hair.

"When another apartment building a couple of neighborhoods away burned down, too," she said, brushing her bangs back into place, "I watched the aftermath. I wondered if I was wrong and it was all a coincidence, but then I found out that some kids had survived that fire, too. A baby, and a boy about my age."

Elodie's face was oddly calm. Stellan's breathing was labored. I realized I was holding my breath.

"I went to the hospital where you were," Elodie whispered. "I watched you every day. You and Anya. You'd been burned much worse than I had, but you'd lived. And one day, a man came to see you. He wasn't Russian, and he'd taken a particular interest in you. I could tell you didn't want to, but you went with him because you had no other choice. I don't know if it was because I knew somehow that you were connected to my family's deaths or because I'd gotten attached to you, but I followed you. That's how Fitz found me. He took pity on me, and brought me to France, too. Brought me into the Order." Elodie finally looked up, studying Stellan for a long moment. When he didn't respond, she turned to Jack and me. "I was planted in the Dauphin home to do various things, including watch out for Stellan, though I never really knew why until you all uncovered the thirteenth bloodline. Fitz never told me what he suspected. I don't think he told anyone."

I was still trying to wrap my head around any of it. Somehow, what came out of my mouth was, "Do you think the Dauphins killed your family?"

Elodie hadn't put the wig on quite straight, and a bit of scar tissue peeked out. She looked vulnerable, which didn't look right on her. "I don't think so. I suspected the Vasilyevs at first, but Fitz didn't think it was them. That's one reason I agreed to be in the Order—so I could keep investigating. I've never really stopped, even though I haven't found answers."

The shell-shocked silence hung heavy over the room. Finally Jack cleared his throat. "So now the Order wants to take down the Circle using the virus? Is that the conclusion to this story?"

I wasn't sure whether to admonish him for being so callous or to wait for the answer. Maybe both.

Elodie licked her lips, eyes darting between us. "The purpose of the Order is not to harm the Circle. Just to serve as a line of defense between them and the world."

story. Now he looked up. "Why didn't you tell us? Why didn't you tell *me*?" He said it so quietly, it was scary.

"I couldn't risk it," Elodie said. "I wanted to—"

Stellan stood up. Without a word, he stalked out of the room.

Jack turned to Elodie. "Stay here," he said. "Just—stay here."

He took my hand and pulled me into the hallway, shutting the door behind him.

"Do you believe . . ." Jack's face was slack. "Would Fitz really have . . ."

"I don't think Elodie's lying. And it doesn't sound like Fitz did anything evil. I just can't imagine him being part of something like what the Circle always thought the Order was. Him *or* my mom. Though—" Connections started forming in my head. "Do you think he was just studying me the whole time? Both me and Stellan?" I'd known that I'd been entangled with Jack—with *Charlie Emerson*, as Fitz had called him—through Fitz for years. But Stellan was part of that web, too. And Elodie. Fitz hadn't just been our mentor. He'd been our puppet master, pulling the strings that had brought us to where we were today. *Who* we were today.

But he'd also done so much to protect us. To take care of us. So much that it had gotten him killed.

This was not a path I could let my mind go down right now. My mom, Fitz— I fisted my hands in my hair. Elodie. Concentrate on Elodie.

"I should have known." Jack paced the worn floral carpet in front of the door, thumbing his gun at his hip. "I should have at least suspected. About Fitz. Especially about Elodie. I've let us be in danger. I'm sorry. We'll send her away. I'll make certain she hasn't bugged our phones, and—"

I caught his arm. "Wait, stop. Do you really think we're in danger? She's been with us the entire time and nothing bad has happened."

"We're Circle. She's Order. I know it's Elodie, and I know she's saying the Order aren't what we think, but I'm not sure that matters."

I glanced at the closed door and lowered my voice. "I understand if you don't trust her entirely right now, but—"

He took me by the shoulders and turned me to face him. I startled. Jack hadn't touched me for so long. It felt both familiar and strange to be inches from his chest like this, his serious gray eyes pleading with me. "Avery. I know you haven't been with the Circle as long as we have. There are things you don't understand. Please let me do what I need to to protect you. As your Keeper and—"

He cut off.

Being under Jack's gaze like this, with his hands on me—it was too much. All of today was too much. And as much as I didn't want to admit it, no matter what Jack had done, when I started feeling this vulnerable, there was a part of me that wished more than anything that I could go back to how things were, melt back into his arms and let him protect me and convince me everything was okay.

I ducked away from him. If I was going to get through this, I had to turn all that off. "I get it. But we need Elodie." He started to protest again, and I held up a hand to stop him. "Just like we still needed you, after . . ."

Jack's face shuttered and he stepped away from me.

"I'm sorry," I said. "I don't mean to—"

"I understand. What are my orders on how to proceed, then?"

I studied the worn carpet. I hated treating him like an employee, but maybe at this point, it was the only thing to do. "I really don't

to find it. We're going to continue to treat her like we always have. That's my decision."

I thought he might protest—either as Jack the Keeper or something else—but he just inclined his head.

Stellan's voice came up the stairs, obviously on the phone, sounding like he was leaving a message. He emerged from a stairwell to stand by the window at the end of the hall, and I heard the snick of a lighter. Jack and I waited while he lit one cigarette, and a couple minutes later, a second. Then he came back to where we waited in front of the room.

"We have fake passports, but this is Israel and there has just been a terrorist attack, and we're the prime suspects. We won't be able to get on a plane," he said gruffly.

I let my brain spin off of Elodie and on to what in the world we were going to do next. "Did you get ahold of Anya?" I said.

"No," he answered in a way that declared that the end of the conversation. He ran a hand over his face. His fingers were shaking a little, but even though he'd just had his whole world turned upside down, that was the only indication anything was wrong. I had to admire it. He probably had more control over himself—and as important, how other people saw him—than anyone I'd ever known.

"We'll have to get out overland," Jack said.

"Nowhere we could get to overland is an easy border with Israel, either," Stellan said. "This is a terrible place to sneak out of the country on a good day."

"I'm saying it will be easier than *flying*."

"Obviously." The two of them had no reason to be angry with each other, but the relief at seeing each other alive seemed to have evaporated under all this new stress.

The door opened, and we all turned. "The border with Egypt is sometimes less strict. We could go directly to Alexandria overland," Elodie said, standing in the doorway.

We all watched her silently for a second. "How could we get to the border—and across the border—without the Melechs knowing?" I said, signaling to everyone to let the rest go for now.

"We could hire a small plane. Or a helicopter," Jack said.

"We'd have to bribe the pilot to not say anything," Stellan said.

"Or threaten him," Elodie added.

As Circle, we'd gotten used to getting anything we wanted with a snap of our fingers. Suddenly, we were just regular people again.

That gave me an idea. "How about we take a bus?"

Elodie cocked her head to the side.

"A bus," I said. "Regular people transportation. We'd disappear in the crowd."

"Not a terrible idea," Jack said. "The border will still be difficult, though, since we won't be in their system." I must have looked confused, because he explained, "Israel is different from many countries. When you enter, you get an entry stamp and they check you in to their system, and they have to check you out, as it were, when you leave. We didn't have to show ID to get into the country, since we came in with the Circle, so the passports we use to get out won't be registered."

"We may be able to convince them that we had the entry stamps on separate pieces of paper and lost them," Elodie said.

"*If* someone can get us into their computer system," Stellan said. By *someone* he meant Elodie, but he wouldn't speak directly to her.

Elodie gave him a withering look anyway. "It'll have to be once

"What about Avery and Stellan?" Jack said. "Will anyone here recognize them? Not Circle, just regular people?"

Elodie pursed her lips. It's not like we were real celebrities, but when we'd had lunch with Colette in Paris a few days ago, there had been lots of people taking sneaky photos, and not all of her. I'd been all over the news for a while after Takumi Mikado died in my arms, then both Stellan and I had been all over the papers following the Paris attack. There was one photo in particular. It was a beautiful shot, I admit. My arms were covered in blood; there were smears on my face beneath my wide, haunted eyes. I was clinging to Stellan, and Colette held my other side. I'm sure the paparazzi had meant to get a picture of Colette, but it was me and Stellan the tabloids had picked up on. When it leaked that my mother had died in the attack, I'd become something even more fascinating, deified by tragedy.

The feelings I'd managed to force down started to build back up into a hard knot in my throat.

"Once we get to Egypt, it's less likely they'll be recognized," Elodie said. "Here—it's very possible." I could see the wheels turning in her head. "Disguises. Just until we get to the border. We'll be playing tourists anyway. I'll go get them."

"*I'll* go get them," Jack said, casting a suspicious glance at Elodie that she pretended not to notice.

Half an hour later, we looked like summer tourists in ridiculously loud outfits and sunglasses headed to the beach. The only problem was my hair. "Ironic that I originally did this as a disguise and now it's the most recognizable thing about me," I said, pulling at the pink.

"We don't have time to dye it again," Elodie said. She reached up to her own head, the thought plain on her face.

"You don't have to—" I said.

She pulled her wig off. "Just until we get to Egypt," she said, handing it to me.

I held it, trying not to stare at her head. We'd only seen it for a second before. Half of it was scarred badly. The other half was buzzed close to her head.

Elodie folded her arms across her chest. "What are you looking at? Let's go."

The bus was musty and tinged with the smell of someone's tuna sandwich. We were winding through terrain that had us on switchbacks, the bus shifting into lower gears, jolting over rough pavement.

I crossed my arms over my chest and tried to get my head in a position that wasn't killing my neck, and closed my eyes.

I hoped this worked.

Getting caught at the border would be as good as admitting guilt, as far as the Circle was concerned. Maybe we should have appealed to someone after all. Begged the Circle to believe us. Maybe I should have just confronted Lydia. I knew she was in Jerusalem.

In those too-short days between when I'd gotten my mother back and when I lost her forever, we'd argued. It was almost all we'd done.

We should leave, she'd said. Go somewhere safe.

Safe no longer existed, I'd countered. Not now that the Circle knew what I was. So we didn't run. We stayed. I was too confident in the goodness of human beings.

This time, we'd made the opposite choice. If I was wrong again, it could mean all our heads.

My eyes flew open.

Through the gap in the seats, I could see Stellan in the next row up, his head against the streaky window, snacking on a bag of chips from a bus station vending machine. Some weird flavor of Cheetos. All the words on the bag were in Hebrew. He'd used Jack's phone to call Anya's nanny twice more, and had finally reached her. I knew he'd told her to go to the safe house and stay there. I wondered if I was the only one who'd noticed his foot was still bouncing nervously anyway.

Jack was beside me, his arms crossed over his chest, eyes closed. I couldn't tell whether he was actually asleep. Across the aisle, Elodie was on her phone, working on the program to get us across the border.

If we got caught, Stellan and I would probably get a trial, as Circle family members. Jack and Elodie—

My chest got tighter. I closed my eyes again.

This time, I actually did drift off, because suddenly, I woke with a start. I couldn't breathe. I sucked in gasp after gasped breath. I was drowning. I was—

I was on a bus. It was dark and bumpy and dry. I could breathe *fine*. It didn't make the tightness in my chest subside. It didn't make the images in my head—the blood, the screams, the Circle with guns to our heads—go away. Jack opened one eye and looked at me, and I hugged my arms around myself and shivered. Outside, the bus's headlights illuminated a warning sign. I squinted. It had Hebrew, Arabic, and at the bottom, English: *Beware of camels near the road.*

The bus came to a sudden stop. Jack sat up straight and peered over the seats. Ahead of us, Stellan did, too. Two soldiers with guns and sniffing dogs got on. My whole body went cold.

Jack put a stiff arm around me. "They're not looking for us," he murmured into my ear. "They're checking for bombs, but we don't want them to see your face anyway. Pretend to be asleep."

I leaned my head on his chest, letting Elodie's blond wig hide my face, and he pulled his cap lower and leaned on my head.

The soldiers went past us to the back of the bus, then through to

the same relief. For just a second, I accidentally leaned into it.

"You okay?" he murmured. It was not a Keeper asking his charge whether she was safe.

I nodded.

"I don't mean just that little scare. You've been—"

I sat up. "I'm fine."

"Are you—"

"I said *fine*."

Across the aisle, Elodie peered after the soldiers. Stellan glanced back at us, and I saw his eyes flick to Jack's arm still resting around my shoulders.

The second the soldiers stepped off the bus, I scooted away from Jack, and he folded his hands in his lap.

The bus started back up and rattled on. My chest didn't feel any less tight.

"If you're not fine, it's understandable," Jack said quietly. "You're allowed to be sad. You don't have to pretend you feel nothing. I know you don't want to talk to me about it, but keep it in mind."

I wasn't *pretending*. I was doing it on purpose, and this was exactly why. In the past couple of days a few emotions had snuck in, and now they were all rushing back at once. That was probably why kissing Stellan at the party had triggered those flashbacks, too, and all of it together meant I was having a really hard time functioning as well as I should. Hence turning it off.

It wasn't cold at all in here—in fact, it was stuffy—but I couldn't stop shivering.

When Jack realized I wasn't going to answer, he began thumbing through his phone. He cursed under his breath.

"What?"

He handed me his phone.

Rome. The Vatican. At the head of the story was a photo of dozens of emergency vehicles assembled in the iconic columned square in front of St. Peter's Basilica, their blue lights garishly illuminating the church's façade. The same *mystery virus* had struck there just hours after it had hit in Jerusalem, killing half a dozen priests.

Stellan turned, and I handed him the phone. This was just what we'd talked about as we hurried through the streets in Jerusalem. His bet on exactly where the Saxons would hit next was wrong, but the sentiment was right.

"Religious extremism," he said. "So that's their strategy. Two of the world's most important religious cities hit. Get ready for a lot more chaos in the world."

I felt sick.

Elodie crossed the aisle and sat next to Stellan, who scowled at her. She snatched the phone.

"And *we've* just been at the Vatican retrieving the Alexander relic," Jack said. "It'll be easy to blame this on us within the Circle, as if they needed more evidence. How long do we think before the Circle go to desperate measures to stop it?"

"Because being out to kill us isn't desperate enough?" Stellan retorted.

Jack frowned. "That's not what—"

"Desperate measures like uniting behind a dictator," Elodie said. The two of them ignored her, scowling at each other.

"They had almost none of our blood left," I said, changing the subject. "They must have found a way to use just a *tiny* bit when they aerosolized it, which means they could do it again."

the world, no one knew who and what to be afraid of, so they were afraid of everything. It was a disease, brought in by foreigners, some were saying. The "biological weapon" theory was still popular. It really didn't help that the virus killed in such quick and spectacular fashion, or that grisly cell phone videos of it happening had showed up on social media after every attack. In some countries people were fleeing the big cities, causing hours of gridlock on the freeways. In others, there were lines outside hospitals—like they could really do anything.

"Is it really just about power?" I couldn't stop thinking it. "Lydia keeps saying it's about how much they love their family, but I don't think she really knows what *love* means."

Jack sat back in his seat. "I don't know. Love can cause people to do some pretty ugly things."

Elodie reached up to tuck her hair behind her ears until she realized the hair wasn't there. "Anyone who thinks love and hate have to be opposites is wrong." She darted a glance at Stellan, then at Jack.

"The border will be even harder to get through if people are this nervous," Stellan said, ignoring her.

Every time I took a breath, my lungs seemed to shrink. As the sun came up, I watched the landscape go by. It was dry. Stubby trees and sunbaked greenery, pastel in the morning light. The occasional stand of palm trees. It looked like the more desert-y parts of Southern

California. Soon, we'd gone through a resort town on the sea and the bus stopped for immigration procedures.

Elodie had finished the program that would upload when we were within range of the immigration computer. She'd handed out our fake passports—I was Brittany Barnes, from Michigan—and we'd rehearsed the story. In the concrete box that passed for the bathroom where we got off the bus, I had to give Elodie her wig back, to match our passport photos.

She adjusted it in the mirror. I could tell she didn't want me to see it, but the tension that had built up in her during the bus ride loosened the second she had it back on.

"Thank you for letting me use it," I said. She looked at me warily, like she wasn't sure whether the friendliness was real. Neither Jack nor Stellan had said a word directly to her the whole bus ride. I could see why they were upset with her, but from her side, it must have been terrible keeping this secret from every friend she had. And their reaction now must have been exactly what she was afraid of. It wasn't even my stress and it was making my chest tighter. "I understand why you didn't tell us. They do, too, even if they're not acting like it. I'm sorry."

She glanced at me in the cloudy mirror and sighed. "It's okay. I almost had you murdered once, so I guess we're even."

I turned off the single faucet and the pipes screeched in protest. "Do you mean Prada? That was *you*?"

"It was an accident. I only meant for them to get some information out of you. It was *very* suspicious having you show up like you did, you know. But they were new to the Order, and they got overzealous. And then Luc and Stellan killed them, and that was such a pretty dress that got ruined . . . *Not* my best plan."

I wiped my wet hands on my leggings. I had assumed that the attack that had left me bloody and terrified in a ball gown on my first day in Paris was Lydia and Cole, too, before they knew who I was. I remembered running down the stairs, being chased by a guy with a knife. I remembered dead bodies on a checkerboard floor, the

air should have made me feel better, but didn't. By the time we got to the front of the line, all of us tense and anxious, my chest had tightened so much, I could barely breathe.

We were waved to the desk, and handed over the four passports as a group. The official flipped through them, and then frowned. He asked about our entry stamps, and we launched into the dumb tourist act we'd rehearsed. *We had entry stamps on another piece of paper, but oops, were you supposed to keep them?* Elodie was saying to me.

I could barely reply with, *Oh no, did you throw them away with the brochure for the Dead Sea the hotel gave us?*

While we were arguing, Elodie was letting the program upload. I could see her glancing down at her phone. I met her eyes, and she shook her head slightly, her brow pinched.

The official's hand drifted to his gun. It might have been unconscious, but my chest got even tighter, like there was a balloon inside it, expanding and crushing my lungs. He took our passports and went into the booth. We could see the computer screen, and him typing things into it. A red screen came up. He looked back at us, typed something else. Another red screen.

"Okay?" Jack muttered beside me.

I nodded.

"What's wrong?"

Maybe there *was* something wrong. For hours I thought I was just nervous, but it was starting to feel like more than that. "I'm sure it's nothing. I just feel weird."

"Weird *how*?" Jack sounded alarmed. It didn't help. I must have looked really bad. He rested a warm hand on my back. "Do you need to sit down?"

I tried to swallow. It was hard. What if I *could* catch the virus? What if that was the reason my chest felt tight? Maybe it took longer to kill me because I was the source.

There was a soldier patrolling, and he stopped in front of me, frowning, his gun held across his chest. "What is wrong with you?"

"She had too much to drink last night," Elodie said, shooting me a look that said, *What* is *wrong with you?*

I gave the faintest smile.

Elodie let out a flirty laugh and pointed at our bus, distracting the soldier with some dumb question about tours. He gave me one last lingering glance, and then moved to talk to her. I could tell Jack was practically buzzing with alarm, mentally searching for what he could use for first aid. "Avery—" he whispered.

Stellan hadn't spoken to any of us since we'd gotten off the bus, but now he stepped up and slipped a casual arm around my shoulders.

"What are you doing? She needs—" Jack started to protest.

"I don't think you actually know what she needs." Stellan drew me out of the line, and I could see Jack deciding whether to follow and make a scene.

"Leave me alone," I murmured to Stellan, knowing I should be more annoyed than I was capable of right now. "I'm fine."

"You're not fine. You're shaking and sweating. That's not good at a border crossing where they're already on alert."

"Can I catch the virus?" I glanced at the back of the soldier with the gun, now walking away from Elodie, and at the official inside the booth, trying our passport numbers one more time. One more red screen. We weren't going to get through. We were going to get turned over to the Circle.

Stellan pulled me farther away and drew me close, his head to

breathing?" he murmured.

I nodded against his forehead.

"I think you're having a panic attack."

"This isn't in my head," I snapped. "I literally can't breathe." It felt like a fist was tightening around my sternum. It was getting a lot worse, and fast. I felt my vision starting to swim. I was going to die in the middle of the desert on the hot asphalt. "I'm sorry. I'm going to leave you to deal with all this alone. I'm sorry—"

Stellan took my face in his hands. "*Kuklachka*, listen to me."

I'd told him not to call me that. And unlike in the hospital, having his face so close to mine wasn't helping this time. I pictured it all again—kissing him. An explosion. Screams. Blood. I took gasped breath after gasping breath, but I didn't push him away. His hands were suddenly the only thing keeping me upright.

"It's not just in your head. It's real. But I do think it's a panic attack."

I shook my head.

"It's a terrible feeling, but it's not going to hurt you. You're probably not breathing *out* all the way, so then you can't breathe *in*."

I could only hear some of the words. *Breathe. Panic.* My entire world narrowed to my chest, and to the air I couldn't get into my lungs.

"Look at me." He shook me a little. "*Avery.* We need to get you looking calm before the border official comes back."

I blinked a few times and his face swam into focus.

Stellan held my face tighter. "Purse your lips like you're whistling," he ordered in a whisper. "Now blow out. Push out all the air you can. More." He pressed a hand into my stomach. There wasn't any more air. But I contracted my stomach as hard as I could, and pushed out another breath. "More. Good. Now pause."

I did, trying to trust him, even though it hurt. My chest hurt. My lungs hurt. A tear slipped down my face. "Now breathe in slowly, through your nose, into your stomach," he said. "Try to push my hand out."

I can't, I wanted to say, *that's the problem,* but I concentrated on his fingers through the thin fabric of my T-shirt, concentrated on my stomach expanding under them. It was at least ninety degrees out, and I was so cold.

"Good. Now out through the pursed lips again. Slowly. As much air out as you can. *More.* And in again. Push my hand."

It was the third breath before I realized that I was very definitely breathing. It still wasn't comfortable, but it wasn't getting worse. A few more breaths, and I could breathe almost normally again. I blinked up at Stellan, and his eyes searched mine, far more concerned than I had realized.

"How did you know?" I whispered.

He rested his chin on the top of my head with a heavy sigh. I leaned my forehead against his beachy tank. His heart was going a mile a minute. His fingers tightened on my stomach and he pulled back, his eyes on the horizon behind me.

"Are *you* okay?" I said.

He pulled away. "Get yourself together," he said roughly. "At least until we get across the border. Keep up those breaths and it shouldn't get worse."

The door to the guard shack banged open and I jumped. Inside, the red screen was still up on the computer. My chest started to tighten again and I breathed, *out out out* in. I shot a glance at Elodie, and she gave the barest shrug and frantically pushed buttons on her phone.

with machine guns behind him made it look less so.

"Only just yesterday," Elodie said in her fake, heavy British accent. Breathe into my stomach, then out. Elodie glanced at her phone again, and her face relaxed. "Try *one* more time?" she asked. "I'd feel so bad about holding up the bus when I'm sure we're in there. Please?" The rest of the line behind us shifted impatiently.

The official's eyes narrowed. "Step out of line," he said, but he left someone else to deal with the rest of the group while he took our passports back into the booth one more time. This time, mercifully, the screen popped up green.

We all let out a heavy breath at once.

Elodie turned to me as we were making our way back to the bus. "Are you all right?"

I glanced up at Stellan. "Yeah. Sorry. I'm—sorry. Let's get on the bus before they change their minds."

CHAPTER 9

I woke up just as the bus pulled into the station in Alexandria. The kink in my neck suggested I hadn't moved for too long. I was shocked I'd fallen asleep at all, but the panic attack at the border had left me more exhausted than I already was. Jack and Elodie were blinking awake across the aisle, and Stellan was hunched against the window next to me, his bloodshot eyes suggesting he hadn't slept at all. We were all still bleary when we climbed off the bus, and Stellan immediately took Jack's phone to call his sister again.

"Coffee," groaned Elodie. "What time is it?"

"About noon."

We wandered out of the bus station and into a grassy plaza filled with palm trees. Across the street was a semicircular bay, and a dock filled with bobbing blue and yellow boats. A lone fisherman in stained robes and a white turban came strolling up the dock, followed by half a dozen hungry-eyed and dirty-faced cats. As he reached the shore, the fisherman stopped and pulled an entire fish out of his bag, tossing it down on the rocks. The cats descended like little furry vultures.

Elodie flopped onto the grass. "Can we just get a hotel for the night?" she said dully.

"We don't know how much time we have until this catches up to us. Our pictures might be everywhere on the Internet already." Right before we'd tried to steal Napoleon's bracelet from the Cannes Film

the news already. Have you seen anything?"

Jack shook his head. "We're not implicated anywhere. I've been watching. That's almost worse. It means the Circle really thinks we did it and they don't want the rest of the world involved."

Elodie let out a hacking cough. And another, so hard that she sat up and buried her face in her hands. "Must have gotten something in my throat on that bus. I told you I'm allergic to public transportation."

I kept staring at her. That was a weird cough. Not that we actually had to worry about the virus, but . . . No. She was *fine.*

"Where's the clue?" I said. Elodie pulled it out of her bag. "*My followers will watch over us, at the thirteenth at the center of the twelve.* Where Olympias's followers could watch over her. That's what we're looking for. Elodie, you had someone researching whether there was an Order headquarters here in Olympias's time, right?"

She nodded. "I'll call and see what they've found."

I ran a hand over the scrubby grass as seagulls called overhead. "Can we stop somewhere and get us phones? And a toothbrush? And something besides this tiny knife? Can you even buy guns here?" I added, remembering once again that we no longer had Circle privileges.

"Black market," Stellan said shortly. I'd noticed how quiet and tense he'd been since Jerusalem, but it had only gotten worse since my panic attack at the border. He'd barely said a word to anyone the past few hours.

"We should get a taxi," I said just as I realized it was weird to have to say that. We'd spent time in Alexandria before. Usually in an area this touristy, there would be dozens of drivers trying to convince us that their air-conditioning was better than the next guy's. People really must be nervous if even taxi drivers were hiding.

Finally, I spotted one, a minivan waiting in the actual taxi queue at the bus station. "I'm going to look." When I approached, I was surprised to see a girl get out of the driver's seat. She wasn't too much older than me, wearing a full-length robe and a pretty, rose-patterned hijab.

"Hi," I said. "English?" She nodded and smiled, showing dimples and crooked teeth. "Could you take us a few different places around the city?" She nodded again and I motioned everyone over.

Elodie slammed the van door behind her after we'd clambered inside. She turned to the driver and said something in what I assumed must be Arabic, and the girl grinned.

Ten minutes later, we'd moved about four blocks. Judging by the number of cars on this freeway, I guess not *everyone* was staying inside. Lining the road were dingy-looking apartment buildings with swaths of chipped plaster that exposed the brick beneath. There were satellite dishes on every balcony, and a mess of electrical cords snaked between them. This part of the city was not nearly as pretty as the old city.

No one seemed to care about lane designations, and there were at least six cars across on this three-lane road. A little boy leaned out of the car next to us, waving frantically at the car full of foreigners. I waved back halfheartedly. I could have held hands with him if I'd put my arm out our window. I tried not to think about him contracting the virus.

I was understanding more and more why I had spent my whole life avoiding getting attached to anything, to any place, to anyone.

"How far is it to where we're going?" Jack said from the backseat

our driver answered in perfect English. "Or at any time of day," she added after a second.

I tried to shake the thoughts out, and when that didn't work, I repeated the slow, steady breaths into my stomach to keep from panicking.

We made stops at a huge shopping center for a couple of changes of clothes and new phones, and at a smaller, seedier market for weapons. I didn't know when I'd become a person who felt better carrying a weapon, but somehow I had.

I flipped on my new phone. I meant to look through the news, but I found myself searching *Napoleon Book of Fates*. I found the same website I'd seen before, and the list of questions again. My eye was immediately drawn to one: *Shall I be successful in my current endeavor?* I clicked on it, then on a set of stars.

The map to one's fate is seldom straightforward; that deemed adversity may be but a fork in the road toward what is longed for, it read. I wrinkled my nose. Seriously? The *map* to one's *fate*?

I clicked off it and pulled up a news site. I didn't like what I saw. "The *UK* just closed their borders," I said. There were curses around the car. "That's a huge overreaction. All that's going to do is make the whole Western world panic even more."

Jack held up another news article. "The United States has made a statement that no one needs to be alarmed and that the CDC is working on isolating the cause of the virus right away. The Fredericks are trying to calm this hysteria before it gets out of control."

"And the Saxons are doing all they can to fan the flames right back up," I said. "Closing borders sends even more of a message than a government statement. Do you think maybe people will be reasonable, though? The death toll from the virus is maybe a couple dozen right now. That's terrible, but it's not enough for worldwide panic, is it?"

"Unfortunately, the world pays more attention to frightened hyperbole than reason," Elodie murmured.

Our driver, Mariam, pulled over to the curb. We piled out, and Jack pulled a twenty-euro bill out of his wallet. I leaned back in the window. "We have to change money, but here's this for now. Can you wait for us?"

She nodded, then called after me as I started to walk away. "Miss?"

I turned back.

"Are you a spy?"

I cast a worried glance at Jack. We shouldn't have said so much in front of her. "We were just talking about the news," I said quickly. "You're not going to get in trouble, I promise."

She nodded again. "My sister loves the James Bond," she whispered solemnly.

Okay. We could worry about that later. For now, I thought we could trust Mariam. "We'll be back," I said, and followed the others inside.

Elodie had talked to her Order contacts. This museum was near the coordinates of what they believed to be a major Order headquarters in Olympias's time. We hoped it might have some history of the area that could help us.

"Look for references to twelves," Elodie said. "The 'thirteenth at the center of the twelve' could mean twelve columns on a building that was destroyed thousands of years ago, or statues, or anything."

But the museum was tiny, with nothing but a few display cases of stone shards and a couple old coins and bits of tarnished jewelry. No history of the area at all. I grabbed a brochure and we left.

symbol from my locket. Hours of searching, and we'd found *nothing*.

The next site was the new Library of Alexandria. It didn't have much to do with the ancient library, but it was on the same site, and the ancient one was important to the Order. Plus, we hadn't searched this area of the city closely last time we were here.

I could tell by a freshening breeze that we were back near the water. We trudged down a dirty sidewalk, and I dodged a shop owner desperately trying to get us to buy some of the fish laid out on ice in front of his shop, and another waving aromatic flatbreads at us. Jack hurried us past them like they might be Circle, lying in wait to catch us.

"Do we really think anyone could have made a tomb here?" Stellan's hands were shoved rigidly into his pockets. All this failure certainly hadn't made any of us *less* tense. "It's too close to the bay. The ground is too wet. This is going to be another dead end."

"Do you have a better idea?" Elodie asked. "Because I'd love to hear it."

"The library was dedicated to the Muses," I said wearily, but loudly enough to speak over whatever Stellan might throw back at her. "Which is not the same, but similar to the Fates—the Moirai— whom Napoleon based the clues he left on. Maybe there are statues of the Muses."

Here, at least, there were mock-ups of how the old library might have looked, and we did our best to count any statues we saw and to find what might have been at the center of the buildings.

I was standing in front of a rendering of what the inside might have looked like when Elodie coughed again. We all stilled. She stood back up like it was nothing.

She *couldn't* get the virus after this long, could she? What would it look like if she did? Would it be quick? Or slower, since it had taken this long? A tiny nosebleed that got worse?

Breathe, I told myself. *Out out out in.*

We spent another hour at the library, then found a bench in a wide plaza nearby. A vendor cart selling candy trundled up over the sparse grass, and Elodie bought one of everything.

I knew logically that we shouldn't start panicking yet, but it was getting late. Especially if Elodie was—no. *Don't.* But even if that wasn't a concern, every time I glanced at the news, things looked worse. And Jack wasn't the only one looking up and down the street nervously for Circle members. We knew all too well they had ways to track people, and it wouldn't take them terribly long to figure out there were only a few countries we might have made it to from Israel. We were all keeping hats and sunglasses on, but that would only work for so long.

Elodie was flipping from web page to web page on her phone, her knee bouncing nervously, munching on a handful of candied peanuts. Stellan was texting, to Anya's nanny, I was sure, a lollipop dangling from his mouth. A guy with a cart full of dinky plastic toys walked by, and he shook one of those annoying hand-clapper things at us. We all flinched.

Stellan put his phone away and rested an arm around my shoulders. "Tell me, my darling other half," he said, with a feigned nonchalance, "how long until we cut our losses and give up?"

I pulled away so his arm fell back to the bench. "Are you serious?"

Jack, pacing in front of us with one hand on his concealed gun, stopped. "We're the only ones who can find the cure before the Saxons do," he said, like he was explaining something to a child. "Which means we have the responsibility to stop them from doing worse

pop. "Duty. Of course, coming from you. How about some logic, though?"

This was just how they used to bicker when I'd first met them. The threads holding the four of us together were coming closer and closer to snapping.

Stellan leaned his forearms on his knees. "We've been searching for the cure all by ourselves partly because we didn't want the Circle to know about our blood making the virus. Now they know. What's stopping us from sending them a package of every clue we have, letting them take over, and washing our hands of it? Why are we still risking our lives?"

I heaved an irritated sigh. "You know exactly why. To—"

To stop the Saxons, I almost finished. That was the only reason I'd done anything lately. *Stop them. Ruin them.*

But I suddenly realized that, since the bomb in Jerusalem, I'd barely thought about ruining the Saxons at all. Instead, what had come to my mind just now was the tour group crying over their friend in the tunnels. The angry men throwing bottles at each other in the square because each side thought the other had attacked their city.

I remembered what Stellan had said: the Circle only cared about the Circle, and more specifically, about their own family. The world wasn't their concern.

"Because the whole world is in danger now," I said quietly. "From the virus or from the turmoil that's following it. Because as much as we didn't mean to, *we* started this, and *we* have to stop it."

Jack spread his hands as if to say *my point exactly.*

Stellan sat back heavily against the bench and gathered his hair up in the hand not holding the candy. It was long enough now he could have tied it back. He stared off into the middle distance, not acknowledging what I'd said, but not fighting it, either. I knew he agreed. I'd seen his face in the tunnels when we'd realized what had happened. I knew he wouldn't leave the Saxons with something that could kill Luc and Colette, or any number of other Circle members we cared about.

"At the least, can we agree that arguing about it is a waste of our time and our sanity?" Elodie gestured to me. "This one's having panic attacks. The two of you have your pouty faces on. Not that your pouty faces aren't adorable. But it's not helping."

Stellan leaned across me to Elodie. "I think we can all agree that *you're* not allowed to pretend everything's the same as it always was and that you can joke your way back into us trusting you. You can't."

Elodie's face fell. I sighed and pushed up from the bench, wandering a few feet away to lean on a lightpost. The crinkle in my back pocket reminded me that I'd taken a pamphlet from the first little museum. I pulled it out and perused it absently. I flipped it over to the back, where it talked about the museum courtyard, which we hadn't even realized was there. There was a close-up of flowers, and then a shot from above.

I froze.

The courtyard contained ruins from circa 300 BC, the brochure said. The ruins were just bits of stone, now made into a garden. I picked up my locket, and rubbed my thumb over the symbol there. The symbol had thirteen loops, with the thirteenth at the center.

So did the garden.

The ruins in the courtyard were in the exact shape of the locket around my neck.

CHAPTER 10

The museum was closed. A heavy iron gate had been pulled down over the entrance we'd used just a couple of hours earlier. We peered around the back and saw a drive gate, but it was locked, too, and guarded.

"We could bribe the guards," Elodie murmured.

"Wouldn't it be better if no one knew we were in there?" I whispered. "This museum is state run. It probably wouldn't get back to the Circle, but anywhere that has guards at a gate cares if random people traipse in and attempt an archaeological dig in their garden."

As we watched, a tall, brightly painted truck rumbled up to the entrance. The guards opened the gate, and he drove right through.

"Maybe we could sneak through when he drives out," I whispered, but realized as I was saying it that there would be no possible way for us to get through unseen.

Unless . . .

Jack thought of it at the same time. "A delivery truck," he said. "*Them* we'd be able to bribe."

We hurried to a major road a couple of blocks away and surveyed our options. Cars would be too obvious. A pickup truck piled high with melons wasn't ideal for camouflage. And then I saw it.

Like a lot of the places we'd been, this city was a mix of the modern and the far less modern.

A donkey stood placidly, chewing on a piece of straw. He was attached to a flat-bottomed cart carrying a pile of something covered in cloth tarps. The driver was bantering with a taxi driver and spit some kind of dark liquid out of the corner of his mouth into the gutter.

"The donkey cart," I said.

Elodie sighed. "Why do these plans always involve ruining my clothes?"

Jack spoke to the driver, and when he said I could, I peered under the drop cloth, relieved to find baskets instead of raw fish or garbage.

I looked back to see the driver grinning widely at the bills in his hand, and gesturing for us to do whatever we wanted.

Stellan held up the cloth, and we all wedged ourselves in among the baskets. When Stellan had draped the cloth over us and gotten in on the far side, I felt the driver climb onto the seat over our heads and click his tongue at the donkey.

We jolted violently when the back wheel came off the curb. Jack's arm wrapped tight around me, and I clung to the edge of the cart, wincing when I heard a spitting noise and something hit the cloth just over my head. A dark stain spread, and with it, the smell of what had to be some kind of chewing tobacco. *Gross.* Luckily we weren't far from the museum at all, and I could tell when we turned into the dirt alley. Now we just had to hope the guard wouldn't look under the cloth. But when we rolled to a stop, the voices were joking, and no one approached where we hid.

There was a screech of the gate opening, and it was only a couple minutes before we stopped and the driver swept the cloth off of us. He chattered nervously in Arabic, and Jack jumped up. "He says to hurry." We righted the baskets we'd knocked off, and huddled behind a truck parked against a far wall until the drive gate slid shut.

I peered around the truck's rear fender. We were in what looked like the museum's loading area. I could see the gardens ahead. They were far more impressive than the inside of the museum was—all those bits of stone inside were pieces of the rubble, I realized. These ruins could have been a whole building, with each of the loops in the symbol being a room. There were no guards inside the walls.

We crept out and made our way carefully across the ruins. Elodie leaned down and touched the stone reverently. Now we knew why she'd always been so interested in Olympias.

I wasn't sure we'd be able to tell when we'd gotten to the center, but moments later, it became obvious. Right in the middle of the courtyard, there was a fountain. It had three tiers, all intricately carved with scenes of people, leading to a woman at the top, presiding over them.

"Could that be Olympias?" I said.

"No one knows exactly what she looked like," Elodie answered.

I gazed up at her, and then squinted. "Is that—" I climbed onto the fountain's rim to look more closely, and sure enough, carved around the woman's neck was a necklace just like mine.

Jack climbed onto the fountain's edge with me. "There's a crack here. It's man-made, not natural." He touched where the woman connected to the fountain. "I wonder whether we have to remove the statue."

"Be careful," I said.

He pulled on the top, and nothing happened. Then he twisted.

There was a click, and a groan. And then a screech from the far side of the fountain. We all hurried to it to find a trapdoor opened to a set of rough-hewn steps into the ground.

"Merde," Elodie said in a hushed voice. The rest of our faces reflected the same sentiment.

in the middle of this huge city?" I whispered.

"If it's this close to the water, that might be why radar hasn't found it," Jack said.

"If it's this close to the water, whatever was under there might have been washed away," Stellan countered, but he peered inside. He and Jack and Elodie had put aside their argument in the square when I made the discovery about the gardens, but I could still feel the hair trigger.

Stellan started down the steps. Elodie stopped him. "We're still your Keepers. At least let the two of us go first. It could be dangerous."

Stellan's jaw twitched. I wasn't sure whether it was because he was still annoyed at anything Elodie said, or because he still wasn't used to being the protected rather than the protector. But he stepped back and gestured expansively toward the hole.

Jack and Elodie clicked on their flashlights and disappeared down the stairs.

"Anything?" I called after a minute.

"Not dead yet," Elodie replied, her voice reverberating out of the tunnel.

Stellan glanced at me and I nodded, then slung my bag around my back. We took the first step down into what might very well be the biggest archaeological discovery of all time.

We assembled at the bottom of the stairs. I skirted a mud pit, and looked around as Jack shined his flashlight on the walls. We were in a wide dirt tunnel, stretching as far as we could see in either direction.

Elodie jogged off far enough that I couldn't see her flashlight anymore, and came back reporting more of the same.

I scraped my feet along a patch of dry ground to dislodge some of the mud, and clicked on the flashlight app on my phone. "Should we split up?" I said. "Cover more ground?"

Elodie shined her flashlight on the walls. "Splitting up in the creepy underground tomb is how horror movies start." We set out together, the only sound the tramping of our feet on packed earth.

I wondered how long this tunnel had been here. Had Napoleon left it just as he'd found it, from Alexander's time? Was the dirt we were walking on first packed down by Order members two thousand years ago? I touched the cool, damp wall and rubbed the soil between my fingers..

Jack had walked ahead, running his light over the walls and ceiling of the tunnel. Stellan followed his lead. Elodie and I brought up the back, watching for anything they might have missed.

Elodie coughed again, and I couldn't help but swing my flashlight onto her. "There's two thousand years of mold down here," she said, squinting against my light. I lowered it. "Stop looking at me like that."

I fell into step beside her. "You're not feeling any different, though? I know we thought—"

"If I have some strain of the virus that takes nearly a day to manifest, there's nothing to be done other than finding the cure. So as I said outside, less worrying, more questing."

"I'm just trying— Never mind." I was trying to not feel like we were running out of time, in one way or another. *Breathe,* I reminded myself.

Elodie glanced down at me and sighed. "Listen. Everyone's tense."

"I know. You all have as much reason to panic as I do, and you're not and I need to get it together."

Elodie held up a finger. "No. I'm saying we've had years to learn to deal with all this. You're new at it, and you're doing fine."

"I—" It had almost sounded like respect in her voice. "Still."

Elodie sighed again, like the conversation pained her. "I heard what you said up there. None of this is your fault. Not the virus. Not what happened to your mother. I thought you should hear someone say it out loud, just in case that's what the panic attacks are about."

I winced and tried to hide it. "Besides that it's my blood, *I'm* the one who had the chance to kill Lydia and Cole, and I was stupid and let them go. And then *I* spent the next few days not concentrating hard enough on protecting my mom. She wanted to leave. If we'd left, she'd still be alive. But I didn't see what was coming. Probably because half my brain was too busy thinking about—" I glanced up at Stellan's back, and past him, barely visible in the dark, Jack's. I shivered with disgust at myself and lowered my voice more, even though they were far enough ahead they wouldn't be able to make out what we were saying. "So yeah. It's nice of you to say, but everything that happened is pretty directly my fault."

Elodie touched tree roots snaking across the wall next to us. "You want to know why your mom died? Because Cole Saxon killed her."

Our lights danced ahead of us. My hand felt sweaty around my phone. "Yeah, because I—"

"No." Her voice was firm. "Because you nothing. It was because.

He. Killed. Her. It was not your fault. You let the Saxons go because despite it all, you wanted to see the good in them. You spent some time brooding over which of those two you'd rather kiss because you're human and your brain was exhausted thinking about dying all the time when up until now the only thing you've had to worry about is school exams. I mean—" She gestured ahead at Stellan. He bent to inspect something then stood again, his lanky form in a white shirt and his blond hair bright spots in the dark. "Whose brain wouldn't prefer *that* to sorting out who your psycho family is planning to kill next?"

"Shh," I hissed.

She rolled her eyes. "Don't forget, I've been with both of them, too. I get it."

I sniffed. "You guys have the weirdest relationship."

"*Us* guys? Do you prefer the term *judgy* or *hypocrite*?"

Fair. "Why didn't it work out between you and either of them?" I said quietly.

"Because sometimes something is fun for a while and not true love forever. And sometimes things change. People change." I had just a moment to wonder which boy went with which comment when she went on, "Stop distracting me. I'm trying to be kind or sympathetic or whatever this unfamiliar sentiment is. You're making it even harder than it already is." Her snarky tone vanished. "I used to do this same thing, you know. I would go over and over the night my family died. If I'd stayed up late reading, maybe I would have noticed the fire in time to save them. If my dad hadn't tried to get into business, maybe . . . But no matter how many scenarios might have made things different, none of them mean it's the fault of anyone besides the people who did it. Full stop. You can pout over other things, but you can't pout over that, because it's not true."

I scuffed my shoe on the packed dirt. "Has anyone ever told you you're the worst at pep talks?" I mumbled.

Elodie raised her light to see farther down the passage. "You know what I used to tell myself when it would get bad?" she said. *"You made it through this, and you survived.* It's way more than most people have been through. That means you can do anything."

I clutched the strap of my bag tight.

"You're a survivor. I'd never wish it on anyone, but you're just like the rest of us now. Welcome to the world's worst club."

I turned away from her, pretending to look at something on the wall. I blinked a few dozen times, dissipating the heat behind my eyes.

Just ahead, Stellan stopped short. When I saw what he was looking at, my heart jumped, and my head cleared.

There was faint orange light coming from the tunnel ahead. If this was it, I didn't have to panic anymore. If this was it—

I realized halfway there what *it* was.

"We're back to where we started." Stellan's voice was a mask of calm.

"How is that possible?" We hadn't been going in one big circle. We'd made a bunch of turns, some sharper than others. And yet, here we were. The afternoon sun outside reflected in the water pooled beneath the fountain. "We must have missed something." I headed back down the corridor, my light bouncing erratically around the endless smooth dirt. "A turnoff. A door."

"We didn't miss anything." Jack jogged up beside me. "I was paying close attention the whole way."

"You saw those ruins." Elodie caught up with us, too. "You see whatever this weird tunnel is. There's no way it means nothing. We'll just have to go around again, watching more carefully."

"And if we don't find anything this time?" Stellan said.

"Give up if you want," Jack snapped. "The rest of us won't."

"So what you're saying is that the rest of you have a death wish."

I grabbed Stellan's arm and dragged him down the tunnel. "We'll take the front this time," I called over my shoulder.

"Not that I'm complaining," Stellan whispered loudly, "but I'm not sure this is the most appropriate time to sneak away and make out. Though there is no shortage of dark corners in here . . ."

"Quit antagonizing him," I whispered once we were out of ear-shot. "It's not helping."

"It's also not untrue." Stellan looked casually down at his arm. I hadn't realized I was still holding on to him. I let go.

Talking to Elodie had taken my panic down a notch. There was no way Stellan would allow her to do the same for him, so maybe it was my job. "I get how you're feeling." It was hypocritical of me, but I went on, "And I know *safe* is a relative term these days, but we're okay right now."

Our lights made a halo of white on the dark ground. "*Are* we, though? Really?" His face was barely illuminated, but I could see his eyes darting around, still searching, despite his protests. "I'll forget for a moment that one of the few people I trusted has been lying to me for years, and that I've been working for the same group that killed my family. But as much as I've been trying to, I can't forget that this, right now, is *exactly* what I've been afraid would happen since we discovered the thirteenth bloodline. That the Circle would find a reason to turn on us. You don't get on the Circle's bad side. You just don't."

"Maybe once we find—"

"The thing is," he cut me off, "it's not just my own life I'm risking to save the people who want to kill us. Where do you think they'll turn once someone remembers that I have a sister? So there you go. *That's* why I'm having a hard time following this dead end further than is logical. Is the psychoanalysis finished?"

This all sounded too familiar. Too much like how I'd been feeling for a long time. Everything he'd ever known was wrong. He didn't know whom to trust. He didn't say it, but I could see the flashbacks hitting hard, too. From the hospital. From Elodie's story of her own family's deaths. It was torturing him not being able to see Anya safe with his own eyes. This spiral into the carefully constructed snarky persona he was so good at playing was his version of my panic attack. "Maybe we could get Luc to go check on Anya," I said.

He exhaled. "I don't want to draw more attention to her than I need to," he said quietly.

"Just because I'm asking you to control yourself doesn't mean I don't understand," I told him. "I very much do. I'm worried just like you are, and I keep thinking there's something I should have done, too. Like maybe I should have just gone to Lydia in Jerusalem and let the rest of you get away while you could. Or—"

Stellan let out an exasperated groan. "I suppose *this* is why I do have to be around for the rest of this treasure hunt. You know, when the Saxons were parading you around like a show pony waiting for the highest bidder, I had a plan to get you out of every one of those places, in case your dear father decided that was the day he was going to put his foot down and force you into something."

"You *what?*"

He ignored me. "I thought I might not have to worry about that kind of thing with you no longer in captivity. Please don't make me save you from unnecessary martyrdom and get us both killed in the process, okay? This quest is trying enough as it is. Are we finished here so we can get back to work?"

I felt like I had whiplash. "I didn't say I was ever actually *going* to turn myself in. And what do you mean you had a plan to get me—" He sighed. I scowled. "Okay. Fine. Once we've done what we have to, I'm free to do stupid, dangerous things to my heart's content. You can yell at Elodie and talk out whatever you need to with Jack and go get Anya. You can leave all of this behind forever if that's what you want. But for now we finish this."

He cut his eyes to me, and quickly away. "Fine."

"Thank you."

We slowed to let Jack and Elodie catch up. For a few minutes, we inspected a divot in the wall here, a root across the path there. I couldn't stop glancing over at Stellan. I knew he had stayed nearby while we'd been on our tour of Circle suitors, but I'd thought it was only to make sure we didn't try to cut him out of the equation. I hadn't realized he cared what happened to *me*. When I darted another glance at him, he quickly averted his eyes. I hung back and walked with Elodie.

"Question," Stellan said. "I know you all want to save them, because apparently you're the most altruistic group of people in the world. But do you actually still want to be part of the Circle once this is done, if they'll take you back?"

It was a good question. One I hadn't entirely figured out the answer to yet.

"Do you *not* want to?" Jack asked.

As much as I'd taunted him about it before the initiation, I knew Stellan had only wanted the power being the thirteenth could bring so he could feel safe and know Anya was happy and secure. So much for that.

Stellan turned to walk backward in front of us, tapping his chin in an exaggerated fashion. "Let's see. So far, our *destiny* has involved divulging every personal detail of my body and my life so the Circle wouldn't murder me for being a traitor. Then letting them think we'd be their puppets—and now we're fugitives. I suppose the prawns at the party the other night were good, though, so that brings it up to . . . two out of ten stars for the thirteenth family experience. Would not recommend."

"Hilarious," Jack deadpanned. "What you really mean is that as soon as things stop being easy you're ready to quit. Because loyalty means nothing."

I sighed. Maybe it was Jack I should have lectured. Or maybe trying to keep anyone from fighting right now was futile.

"Excuse me?" Stellan said. "Talk of *loyalty* from someone who was literally spying on his girlfriend for the enemy?"

I cringed. There was a shuffle, and a bang, and Jack's light fell to the ground, illuminating the two of them from below. Jack had Stellan against the wall, his forearm pressed across Stellan's throat.

Stellan glanced sideways at me, with a smile and a shrug that very obviously said, *He started it.* Then he shoved Jack. I had to jump out of the way to keep from getting knocked down.

"Don't." I took a step forward. Elodie held out a hand to block me. The boys ignored me anyway.

Jack grabbed the front of Stellan's shirt. "I know you never liked being a Keeper, but you had an obligation. You still do."

"Well, you're doing it all wrong right now," Stellan said, low in Jack's face. "A Keeper's not allowed to lay a hand on family members, you know."

Okay, so this was definitely not about the fact that they'd both kissed some girl.

Jack panted hard, the shadow of his chest rising and falling. He would normally never make a scene in front of people like this. Now, though, he shoved Stellan into the wall. "And a *family member* isn't allowed to leave the Circle."

Suddenly I saw what the rest of the world must see in them. They'd been trained to be this aggressive and violent since they were children, but I saw it so infrequently; it was unfamiliar and feral and frightening. I backed off another step.

"The Circle isn't everything," Stellan growled. "If you believe they are, you're just going to continue to ruin your own life and everyone else's."

I watched Jack's fingers curl into Stellan's shirt, his jaw twitch. "I haven't—"

"Oh really? You felt so guilty about being with Avery that you betrayed her to the Circle. You felt so guilty about Oliver Saxon's death that you turned on me and Elodie."

Elodie hissed in a low breath, and I held mine. Oh.

"Do you remember that?" Stellan went on. "You were practically my brother until you decided not to be my friend anymore. It wasn't your fault what happened to Oliver, and it certainly wasn't mine."

There were some things between them I'd scratched the surface of, and there were plenty I knew nothing about. But I did know Jack blamed himself for the death of Lydia and Cole's older brother. He also, to an extent, blamed Stellan and Elodie and the relationship the three of them used to have for being a distraction that led to the tragedy. If that's what this was about, it had been building for *years*. Since they were younger, more naive, less broken. And since they were smaller and less powerful and couldn't actually kill each other.

Jack's biceps strained with effort, whether from holding Stellan off or holding himself back, I couldn't tell.

"It's not my fault that I'm this thirteenth bloodline, either," Stellan said, strained. "And it's not my fault—"

Stellan glanced at me, and then Jack did, too. I wanted to melt into the wall.

"For years you've been blaming other people and hating yourself for bad things that happened." Punctuating his words with shoves against Jack's chest, Stellan said, "It is not. My. Fault."

Jack punched him.

Stellan staggered backward, bracing himself against the wall. He worked his jaw back and forth, and then he laughed. *Laughed.* Jack might actually kill him.

I started forward again, but Elodie grabbed my arm.

"I'm just sorry you're stuck with us when you'd rather be with a real Circle family who plays by the rules." Stellan stalked toward Jack again. He might have been laughing, but the fists balled at his sides said something different. "I guess it *is* my fault that I wanted someone around who I used to trust."

And then I realized it. As much as all of us had been afraid of losing people we cared about lately, Jack and Stellan thought they'd lost each other years ago. They'd both suppressed the feeling for so long that it only took a spark to make it explode.

Love and hate. They weren't opposites.

Stellan shook his head slowly. "I thought maybe one day you would wake up and see that blind obedience is not the same as doing the right thing," he said. "I guess not. But that means you, of all people, cannot talk to me about loyalty."

Jack flew at him, and slammed him into the wall hard enough that his head bounced.

I sucked in a quick breath, but another sound drowned it out.

A loud crack sounded through the tunnel, and Stellan's arms pinwheeled—then he fell backward through the wall, pulling Jack with him.

CHAPTER 11

I rushed to the destroyed wall to find Jack scrambling off Stellan, who lay on his back in a pile of bricks, blood trickling down his temple. They had knocked a person-sized hole into what appeared to be an older, mustier tunnel.

Elodie peered over my shoulder as I climbed through the hole. The air was damper in here, and sour. I coughed, and pulled my shirt up over my mouth and nose as Stellan stood and brushed dirt off his palms.

"If we're supposed to go in there, wouldn't there be some kind of sign?" Elodie said suspiciously. "There's nothing to indicate we should knock through a piece of the wall and traipse inside."

Stellan picked up his flashlight and peered into the darkness.

I picked up one of the bricks. They were about the size of modern red bricks, but a good deal thinner, and rough hewn. They could have been two thousand years old. I scratched at the mortar on the edge of the brick with my fingernail, then smacked it against the nearest wall. It shattered easily.

"Why would anyone make a wall of an underground tunnel out of something that'd break so easily?" I wondered out loud. "Unless . . ."

Elodie reached through the hole and plucked a piece of the brick from my hand. "Unless it was meant to be broken." She thought for a second, then said, "Come here."

She shined her flashlight on me, picking up my necklace, with its thirteen loops, and studying it. "It's a Gordian knot," she said. "I hadn't realized it before." Down the tunnel, Stellan's footsteps stopped.

I picked the necklace up off my chest and held it out. "What's a Gordian knot?"

"It was one of Alexander's tests."

Stellan came back, the hem of his shirt pulled up to wipe his face. He dropped it back onto his chest, and the streaks of blood across it looked eerie in the dark. "Legend said the Gordian knot was impossible to untie."

"The oracles prophesied that whoever undid it would be the king of the world," Elodie agreed, with a quick glance at Stellan. He'd spoken directly to her with no animosity in the words. It was a step. "And when Alexander realized that there were no ends to the knot—"

I squeezed my necklace hard. "He undid it by slicing it in half." I remembered this from history class. I had never connected it to my necklace, or this quest. I looked from my necklace to the hole in the wall. The larger tunnel hadn't been a circle. "It's a Gordian knot," I said. "The whole tunnel is. That's why we ended up back where we started. There's no way into the inner chamber—"

"Except to go straight through the wall," Jack finished. He was flexing his fingers, but dropped the hand to his side when I looked his way, like he didn't want me to see that he'd hurt himself on Stellan's face.

"I guess that's our sign." Elodie climbed through, and we set off into the mouth of the tunnel.

This passage was much smaller—just wide enough for us to go single file—and cut roughly out of dirt. It was also descending rapidly. Roots snaked down the walls and across the path, and the farther we went, the wetter it got. My cheap sneakers were caked with mud.

At the front of the line, Jack paused. As we caught up to him, we saw why: a drop-off of at least five feet, with a pool of water at the bottom.

"I feel like I need to mention that these old tunnels were sometimes booby-trapped," Elodie said. It was barely a whisper, but still felt too loud in the confined space.

"Napoleon got through here, and he's the one who must have sealed it back up," Jack said. "I don't think he would have done that."

"Be careful," I whispered.

He glanced back at me and nodded, then swung himself down into the pit with a splash, sinking up to his knees in water. On the other side, he pulled himself out using tree roots as handholds and Elodie followed.

Stellan splashed down into the hole. Jack looked back over his shoulder. "Help Avery," he said.

"Obviously." Stellan reached for me. He met my eyes, then quickly looked away again.

"What?" I thought again of what he'd said earlier.

"What do you mean, *what*?"

"Nothing. Never mind." I let him help me down and boost me up the other side because the hole was deeper than I was tall. I could have sworn his hand lingered a longer than necessary on my back on the other side, but when we'd scrambled to standing, he just gave me a nudge down the tunnel and followed close behind.

It was eerily quiet, the only noise the damp squishing of our clothes. I felt my shoulder brush the cool, wet wall, and shuddered when I had to wipe a film of spiderwebs from my face. The tunnel narrowed and shortened, so we had to crawl. It opened into a wider clearing a few minutes later, and we stood up one by one, shaking out our limbs and looking around. And then we saw what was on the other side of the clearing.

Our lights shining ahead seemed to fall off into nothing. The tunnel dead-ended into open air.

We made our way slowly to the edge. It was pitch-black. Jack brought his light up, and drew in a sharp breath.

"It's a pyramid," Elodie said, barely louder than a breath.

The rocky sides of the chamber went straight down. But when I looked more closely, I saw tiny steps carved into the side, starting just below the ledge. On the floor of the chamber, about two stories below us, a small, gleaming white pyramid rose out of a pool of water.

My breath caught in my throat. The tomb of Alexander the Great, and his mother. It had to be.

"It's—" Elodie whispered, then cut off. From below came a sound we never would have expected to hear in the world's most famous lost tomb.

Voices.

CHAPTER *12*

There were two people talking down in the cavern. Judging by how muffled they were, they must have been inside that pyramid.

They were the voices of a boy and a girl. Voices we knew.

Lydia and Cole Saxon.

"How the hell did they get here?" Elodie hissed. The chamber must have had other entrances. But that wasn't what she was asking. How did they know *how* to get here?

I'd been waiting to confront my siblings for so long, but now I was paralyzed.

"We have to get down there before they get what we're looking for," Stellan whispered. "And then put a bullet in their heads and end this whole thing."

Jack motioned us all back to the tunnel, where we could whisper without being heard. "You're not going to want to hear this, but we can't kill them." Stellan started to protest, but he went on, "I know some of us might be leaving the Circle, but not all of us are. And I doubt any of us want to give them another reason to hunt us. Right now, the Circle believes the Saxons completely and thinks we're monsters. If we ambush them and kill them without a trial, that'll only confirm it. The only way is to capture them and bring them to the Circle."

I felt my hands curl into fists at my sides. That was so opposite how I'd felt for so long. He was right, though. "Okay," I said.

Reluctantly, Stellan and Elodie nodded, too. We tiptoed back out. Jack pointed his light at the stairs. They couldn't be more than a foot wide and six inches deep, cut right into the rock wall, with no handhold, and certainly no railing.

Elodie pushed to the front and pointed down. Jack lit her way.

"Be careful," I breathed, and she swung off the edge and onto the top step a few feet below, so just her head and shoulders stuck up above the ledge.

Our lights bounced over her, like strobes in a club. Stellan followed her. Trying my best not to think about the sheer drop into darkness inches away, I got on my hands and knees and lowered myself down. Stellan held on to my waist as my toes touched the top step, and, like he knew I wasn't entirely comfortable with it, kept his hand on me while Jack dropped above us until all four of us were in a line again, and down we went, step by narrow step.

Halfway down, Elodie came to a sudden stop. She brought her arm to her mouth, racked by silent coughs. She bent over—and then suddenly she was slipping, her arms pinwheeling in the air.

Stellan grabbed her. I grabbed him. My arm was ripped out of Jack's steadying grasp, but he snagged my waist, leaving the four of us locked together in a precarious chain.

I could feel Jack's heart pounding against my back. Stellan leaned on the wall for a second before he looked up, his face inches from mine, and I realized my fingers were digging into his shoulders, right over his scars.

I jerked them away. "Sorry," I whispered.

He shook his head with a bit of a smirk, as if to say, *That is the least of our problems.*

Elodie looked back at us. "It's slippery," she mouthed, unnecessarily. Stellan put a finger to his lips and we listened for any sign Lydia and Cole had heard us. They were still talking inside. None of us let go of each other the rest of the way down.

The bottom of the stairs disappeared into water. Jack waded into it as quietly as he could, and where I'd expected to slosh through it at knee height, he sank in all the way to his shoulders, and I could tell it went deeper. He glanced up and shrugged silently. We'd have to swim.

We all deposited our phones in a plastic baggie Elodie had with her, and I held my bag aloft as we waded down the steps into the cold, murky depths.

The pyramid was bigger than it had looked from above. It was sticking out of the water at least twenty feet, and who knew how far it went beneath. It was built of silvery-veined white marble that looked like it hadn't been touched for a very long time. With our flashlights turned on it, it seemed to be glowing in the dark pit.

"This is actually it, isn't it?" Elodie breathed, treading water.

But this wasn't the time to marvel at history. I gestured around the side of the pyramid.

When we reached the back, the first thing we saw was another set of steps just like the ones we'd come down. That must have been how Lydia and Cole had gotten in. And nearly at the top of the pyramid, a dim yellow light shined through what looked like an open door. Stellan raised his arm silently and pointed, and we swam to him to find another set of stairs leading up the pyramid's slanted side.

At the top of the exposed steps we all paused, dripping and shivering, getting our weapons ready. We'd capture Lydia and Cole.

We'd figure out what the cure was and give it to Elodie, just in case. Then we'd destroy the rest of whatever it was so Lydia and Cole had no chance of taking it.

"Don't hurt them," Jack whispered, warning. "We take them alive."

He held up a hand, then pointed, and we all burst through the door.

CHAPTER 13

The twins were standing on a raised platform with two boxes on it. They looked up, actual surprise registering on their faces. This was the first time I'd seen them in person since my mom died. My hands knotted into tight fists again.

There were lanterns at their feet, illuminating them and the box they were standing over—which I realized now had to be a casket— in a warm light that shined back from all sides. The entire inside of the pyramid was plated in gold.

"They're getting smarter," Lydia said to Cole.

"Hands up, Lydia." Jack pointed his gun at them, and Elodie and Stellan did the same. "Both of you."

Lydia smiled. "Though not that smart. We have the cure now, and you don't."

"Easily remedied, as soon as you're dead." I couldn't tell whether Stellan was just threatening, or whether he'd decided to disobey Jack after all. I wasn't sure which I hoped was true.

The twins kept their hands up as we came down the stairs. The gleaming gold on the walls and floor reflected our flashlights, giving the space an eerie, shuddering glow. As my eyes adjusted, I saw that the walls weren't bare. They were covered with shelves. And the shelves were stacked with all kinds of things: pots, statues, cylinders that I guessed might contain scrolls. Next to me, Elodie had her gun on the twins, but kept glancing away to stare up at the walls in awe.

"I'd stop if I were you." Lydia shook one of her hands, and for the first time, I realized she was holding something. "Cole," she said, and my brother flicked a lighter. Whatever was in Lydia's hand went up in flames. She dropped it on the floor. "There went the cure. Oops."

Stellan cursed and ran down the stairs, but the piece of papyrus was already ash by the time he reached it.

The rest of us followed. The golden floor was slick underfoot, but perfectly dry, even though we had to be below water level now.

Lydia held out her hands. "Shoot us and you'll never know what it said! It's only in our heads now."

I started to say some things I'd probably regret, but Jack cut me off. "What *happened* to you?" he said.

Lydia's big, dark eyes shifted to him. She had her hair pulled back in a tight ponytail, and she and Cole looked more alike than I remembered. "Excuse me?"

"How did you become these people?"

"Us?" Lydia asked incredulously. "The traitor is asking what happened to *us*?"

"Jack has always been loyal to you," I protested. Even at the expense of his relationship with me. Somehow, that made me want to defend him more, even though I wasn't sure why he'd chosen right now to bring it up.

Lydia ignored me, her eyes still on Jack. "I thought you might be coming back to the right side, but you weren't. It was all for her in the end," she said, inclining her head at me. "Of course it was. Everything revolves around her."

Jack took a step closer, toward Lydia's side of the casket, pulling her gaze with him. "Avery has *nothing* to do with you killing people."

Cole was still peering into the casket, his hands still above his head like he was barely interested in the proceedings around him. I wondered not for the first time just how much of this he actually cared about, and how much was simply an excuse to blow things up and kill people. I suspected there was more of the latter than any of us wanted to know.

"What was it that made you into this?" Jack said again, holding Lydia's gaze, his gun trained on her forehead.

There was a subtle movement from the other direction, and suddenly, I understood. Jack hadn't just picked this moment to point out the twins' moral failings because he was upset. He was distracting them. Without a word passing between them, he and Stellan had made a plan.

"I've defended you for so long because I thought that, despite everything, you were a good person," Jack went on. I wondered how much he believed what he was saying. I didn't think he was this good an actor. "I wanted you to be a good person."

Lydia's shoulders fell, just a little, and she gave Jack a sad smile. "No, you didn't. You never actually cared."

Just then, there was a scuffle and Stellan was holding Cole, one arm around his neck, the other pointing a gun at his head.

Lydia whipped around. "No!" she screeched. "Cole!"

"Tell us about the cure or he dies," Stellan said. "I think you know I will have no problem at all shooting this idiot."

"How do we know you'll let me go once we tell you?" Cole choked out over Stellan's arm.

"My word," Jack said, and then looked at Stellan. "You will let him go. We're Circle. It means something. It means we're not them. We don't kill our own."

Lydia's eyes were glued to Jack's. I thought I saw tears in them. "I believe him," she whispered.

Stellan shoved the gun harder into Cole's head. "Then what is it?"

"It's her," Lydia blurted out, gesturing to me. "Avery, the cure is you."

CHAPTER 14

I scowled at her. "You mean I'm the *virus*. My blood. We already know that."

"No." She started to lower her hands, but a gesture with Jack's gun made her change her mind. "The virus, as we know, is both of you, together." She glanced between Stellan and me. "But your blood alone is the cure."

"*What?* That makes no sense."

"Because everything else about the virus is so scientifically explicable?" Elodie said. I guess she had a point.

"Poetic, really," Lydia said shakily, her eyes darting from me to her brother, still held prisoner by Stellan. "We should have known Olympias would do something like that. She makes her son's line important, and makes sure that a girl has just as much power. And then she gives the girl the ace in the hole. She knew how little the Diadochi valued women, so she made a woman the most important piece of the puzzle. You're the key to everything."

She turned to Stellan. "I told you. Now let my brother go."

"How do we know you're telling the truth?" Jack said.

"I think she is," I answered. She was crafty, but she wouldn't risk Cole's life. I knew that much. "That's all it said?"

Lydia nodded.

I held up my hand, and my knife. I never understood why, on TV, people who needed blood always cut straight across their palms. I made a tiny cut on the back of my hand, and the blood welled up.

Elodie was standing beside me. "Um." I held my hand out to her.

"This is not weird or unsanitary at all," Elodie murmured, but she dragged her finger across my hand and put it to her lips. We all watched her. After a second, she shrugged. "I don't feel any different."

I crossed to Jack and held my hand out to him, just in case. He took a drop of blood, too. I looked down at the cut welling up on my hand. My blood was death—and it was life. The cure we'd been planning to destroy to end this was *me*.

"Please," Lydia said. She was still watching Cole fearfully. "Jack. You promised."

I wiped the blood on my wet jeans.

"Let him go," Jack said.

Stellan paused for a second, then shoved Cole away from him so that he smacked into the casket. "Hands in the air," Stellan growled.

Lydia sagged with relief, turning to Jack with tears in her eyes. I'd noticed it before, but it punched me in the gut now: she was completely in love with him. He was looking at her like he wanted to let her rot in jail forever, but she absolutely worshipped him. She probably had for a long time. I wondered if he'd realized the power he had over her.

And then I'd come along. As much as the *family member and the help* thing was a worry, Jack had been mine immediately in a way he had never been hers. In the way she'd always wanted. And our father had paid the kind of attention to me that she'd never get. I was the one the Circle treated like a celebrity. I got everything she'd ever wanted without even trying. Without even wanting it.

And still, for a long time she'd just wished I'd be her sister. I did believe that.

What I *couldn't* believe was that I was feeling in any way sympathetic toward Lydia. All those cracks opening in me in the past few days were letting in things I would never have expected, and I understood her better than I should. Especially now that I knew that feeling of responsibility for the people I cared about.

My sister and I were so much alike in some ways.

Stellan shoved his gun into Cole's back. I didn't have the same almost-lukewarm feelings about Cole.

"You're going to answer for what you've done," Stellan said. "Whether it's me who puts a bullet in your head or someone else in the Circle, it will happen." He started to shove Cole off the platform, but then he grabbed his arm again, pulling him along so he could glance into the open casket, and then at the other, still-closed one next to it.

For just a second, he met my eyes. The open casket was Olympias. The closed one was, if we were right, Alexander.

I took the few steps up to the platform. Inside the open casket was a human shape, covered entirely in gold. Obviously the twins thought this was Alexander. Anyone would, if they didn't know.

Elodie came up beside me, stared at the gold shape for a moment, then turned to the second casket. I did, too. Jack and Stellan each pushed a Saxon twin ahead of them to stand at its foot.

Elodie and I looked at each other, then pushed it open.

Inside was a wooden box. And in the box was a jumble of desiccated bones, arranged into a vaguely human shape, missing one femur. That must have been all Napoleon was able to do when he returned the bones here. This was the body of the world's greatest conqueror, decayed the same as any normal man. Fought over for so long, desecrated so many times, and finally returned to rest.

Cole wrinkled his nose. "Who's that?"

The four of us glanced at one another. Elodie closed the top of the casket gently.

Jack and Stellan steered the twins off the platform. Lydia squinted back over her shoulder like she understood something had happened but wasn't quite sure what. Elodie and I ignored her and turned back to Olympias.

Her arms were crossed over her chest, and the tube that must have held the scroll with the cure lay beside her, open and empty. Scattered around her body were jewels and baubles of all colors and shapes, shimmering in our flashlights, and on her head rested a gold diadem, its center, above her brow, forming a sharp point.

Elodie pulled out her phone to take pictures from every angle. "There is so much history here." She gingerly picked up a piece of jewelry from the casket, and looked around. "The Circle's been looking for this their whole existence." She stood up accusingly, and turned to the twins. "How did you find it?"

Lydia just shook her head. Cole laughed.

"It doesn't matter right now," Jack said. "They're not going to tell us. Let's get them out of here before they have a chance to call backup."

Cole laughed again, then spit right on Jack's shoes. "You'll never get out of here alive. We have people waiting outside. They'll kill you." He turned to Lydia. "I don't know how we ever got a Keeper who was so gullible."

"Walk," Jack said, obviously trying to hold his temper. They pushed the twins up the stairs. I started to follow. Elodie lingered on the pyramid floor, taking in as much as she could in the short time we had. I knew we'd send people back to look—and come back to look ourselves—when we could, but it was hard to see all this and just *leave*.

"It's true," Cole went on from partway up the stairs. "Just the fact that you think we *changed*. We didn't change. We've always done what had to be done, haven't we? You were too stupid to see it. We even used you to do it."

"Cole," Lydia warned. "No."

"What do you mean?" Jack said.

"I bet you still, after all this time, believe that what happened to Oliver was your fault. Well," he said, correcting himself, "it *was*, technically. Instead of doing your job, you were kissing my sister. This one," he clarified, nodding at Lydia, "since there are enough of my sisters you've kissed that we have to specify."

I remembered that, too. On top of the drama with Elodie and Stellan, Lydia had kissed Jack the day Oliver Saxon died.

Jack was rigid. "Keep moving," he snapped. We had stopped at the top of the stairs, at the small platform just inside the door, and he pushed them out and down the stairs, toward the water.

"We could have terminated you for that. I was all for it. Lydia was nice enough not to, since she'd done it on purpose. You've always been too soft when it comes to the Keeper," he chided Lydia. "You're just lucky he's even softer."

"Wait." I came up behind Jack and squinted into the dark at Cole. "What do you mean Lydia did it on purpose?"

"Only because I wasn't told what was going to happen," Lydia said under her breath. And then, louder, "Cole, that's enough."

Jack was blinking down at them. Below, Stellan had stopped, too, so we all waited just above the water. "Are you telling me . . . You're not saying *you* killed your brother."

"Of course we didn't kill him. We—" Cole rolled his eyes at Lydia's intake of breath. "Fine, *I* just let it happen, but everyone later realized it was for the best. We'd been in an alliance with some other families for years. Our brother wanted to stop it, so instead, he was a martyr. It primed the Circle for what's happening now. And it just happened to work out that Lydia wanted to make sure the Keeper stayed around. She didn't have him under her thumb anymore. It was easy enough to let him believe it was all his fault, then act like we forgave him so he'd have to be loyal to us."

Jack just stared at Cole. "You killed Oliver and let me think it was my fault. You killed Avery's mother. You killed *Fitz*."

"Well . . ." Cole squinted into the distance. "Probably not *quite* yet, but . . ."

I had to have heard him wrong.

"Cole, no," Lydia pleaded once more, but it was too late. It was way too late.

"What do you mean by that?" Stellan sounded lethally calm.

"How stupid are you?" Cole said. "How else do you think we got here? The old man can hold up to a surprising amount of torture, but everyone snaps eventually."

My lungs were collapsing. I couldn't breathe. "Fitz is alive?"

Cole shrugged. "Barely."

It only took a second, but I *did* realize what was happening. I didn't try to stop it.

Jack swung his gun away from his guard on Lydia. And he shot Cole Saxon in the head.

CHAPTER 15

Cole dropped like an abandoned puppet, falling into the water. Lydia screamed, the sound reverberating around the cavern. And she kept screaming as she abandoned any pretense of being a good hostage, throwing herself into the water by her brother. She kept screaming as Elodie emerged from the pyramid and ran down the stairs.

I'm glad it's this dark, I thought desperately. Seeing that would have been worse.

Lydia took a breath, and then she screamed again. The sound was chilling, grating, scraping my nerves and my heart and my insides raw.

Still screaming, Lydia pulled her bag out of the water and rummaged in it. I wanted to tell her, *You can't save him, this isn't something you bandage up and come back from,* but Elodie was grabbing us all, and only then did I realize that Lydia had a gun in her hand. We were on the steps—we had nowhere to go.

Stellan recovered first and took a shot in Lydia's direction. Her screams stopped and I thought he'd hit her, but I saw a shape swimming away under the water.

We'd splashed in, too. "We have to take her with us. We have to get her," I yelled, but I cut off when a gunshot reverberated in the cavern, whizzing so close to my face that I gasped.

"Where is she? Where'd she go?" Stellan and Jack both took shots back the way we'd come, but the shooting didn't stop. We were as likely to get hit as we were to hit her.

"We have to go!" Elodie urged again over the screams. "We'll catch her somewhere else!" We swam around the edge of the pyramid as fast as we could. Lydia was still screaming, and still firing, but without light, the shots were all over the place. We ran up the narrow stairs, and were almost to the top.

I barely heard the shot before I felt it.

I couldn't think. I couldn't see. The only thing was the pain, the searing, like my arm was being prodded with a hot poker, and the realization in the same second—she shot me. I'd been shot.

I felt arms around me, pulling me. I realized I was screaming, and then I was splayed out on the ground, Elodie leaning over me with a light, her face terrified, then relaxing.

"It's her shoulder. It'll be okay," she said, from far away. "Avery." She shook me. "I know it hurts like hell, but you're going to be okay. We have to go."

Hands came around my face. Stellan. "Breathe," he said, and placed one of the hands on my stomach. "Breathe into my hand."

I did. I sat up. Another bullet ricocheted into the clearing from below, and we all ducked. "Go," I said through clenched teeth, and dragged myself into the low tunnel.

Each time I jostled my arm, it was like the bullet was hitting me again. Stellan scooped me into his arms the second the tunnel was tall enough to stand in. Elodie tied her soaking wet jacket tight around my shoulder, and then we were all running, down tunnels, out through the pile of broken bricks, stopping at the bottom, where the last rays of the late-afternoon light poured in.

"Let me go first," Jack said. "We'll leave through the museum— avoid those guards out back in case they're Lydia's."

I made Stellan set me down and tried to concentrate on the plan.

"Shoot through the lock . . . " I heard, and then Jack was going up the stairs, yelling something, and then we were all running, Elodie mumbling into her phone to Mariam, me trying not to trip over my own feet, dizzy. I knew vaguely I hadn't lost *that* much blood. I was going into shock. I forced my focus ahead.

Jack shot through the lock on the back door of the museum and kicked it open, and then we were running straight through the same exhibits we'd seen earlier. There was still a metal gate pulled down over the front door, and Jack shot out the padlock on that one, too. Elodie hauled it up, and we all ran to the open door of Mariam's cab. Jack pushed us all inside, and through my haze, I saw armed guards rounding the corner.

"Jack," I called. Stellan turned just in time to grab his arm and haul him into the van. They both flopped across me, just ahead of a gunshot that pinged the car where Jack had been.

"Go!" Elodie screamed. It wouldn't be that easy. Mariam wouldn't know how to drive like this was a getaway car. She'd probably be too shocked to do anything. I was about to yell at Elodie to get in the driver's seat herself when the cab took off. Elodie heaved the sliding door to the van closed, and yelled, "Lose them. Hide us."

We screeched around a corner, and then another. I caught glimpses of Mariam's furrowed brows as she watched for pursuers in the rearview mirror, but she wove quickly and expertly through the tiny streets until we were on a freeway, wedged between a bus and a truck piled high with scraps of wood, with at least six other vans that looked just like ours.

Elodie, crouched by the door, put her head in her hands and then looked up at us. I was draped across Stellan's lap, blood soaking through Elodie's jacket on my shoulder. Jack had pulled himself partly off of us, but he and Stellan were holding on to each other. Elodie threw herself at us, landing on top of the pile in a four-person embrace, her face buried in my neck while mine was smushed into Stellan's, and I didn't even know whose hands I was clinging to, but I was clinging hard.

"It's just a deep graze, but it needs stitches," Elodie said a few minutes later, when we'd all calmed down enough to think. She was examining my shoulder. "One of us can do the stitches, but we need supplies . . . Mariam, do you know anyone who works at a doctor's office?"

Mariam's eyes were huge in the rearview mirror, but she was still driving. "My friend's brother cleans the floors at an office of a . . . a doctor for the skin?"

"A dermatologist. Perfect. The office will be closed—can he get us in? We'll pay him a lot of money, and I promise he won't get in trouble."

After making a short phone call, Mariam steered us off the freeway.

We huddled into a small, dim exam room at the dermatologist's office. Elodie injected my shoulder with a numbing solution, and then left Jack to clean it and stitch it up while she and Stellan went outside to talk to a certainly traumatized Mariam and probably to have a long-overdue conversation themselves. As much as we'd been at each other's throats since Jerusalem, the past couple hours had begun to knit the four of us back together.

I stared up at the dark wall, decorated with curling posters showing the stages of skin cancer. Jack closed the door, crossed the room to where I sat on the exam table in a circle of light, and pulled me into a careful but bruisingly tight hug. I hugged him back with one arm, burying my face in his shoulder. "Are you okay?" I murmured.

He pulled away. "Am *I* okay? You're the one who's been shot."

"I know, but you—" He'd just killed someone he'd been charged with protecting his whole life. He seemed strangely calm. It probably hadn't sunk in yet.

"Yes, well."

I glanced down at where his hands were still resting on my waist. He did, too. He cleared his throat and let go of me, picking up the needle he'd already prepared for my shoulder. I felt a tug as he put in the first stitch, and looked down at my shoulder, watching him loop it through my skin and tie it off. I never thought I'd be able to watch something like that without it bothering me. I never thought I'd be comfortable with a lot of the things I did now.

"Avery," Jack said quietly, "he's alive."

It took me a second to realize he was talking about Fitz. The feeling of something *good* happening wasn't one I was used to anymore. I was having a hard time wrapping my head around it, especially since being happy about anything felt wrong when so much was still grim. Fitz was alive, but he'd been being tortured. I'd just seen my half brother killed. My mom was still dead. The juxtaposition of emotions was enough to make my head spin. "Yeah."

"We can get him out."

"I know. We thought for so long—"

Jack nodded and threaded the needle again. "It's like . . . suddenly

I don't even care that he's Order." He paused, and I could see him judging my reaction. I just sat quietly and let him go on. "I still don't like that he's lied to us, the same as with Elodie. But . . . I thought I'd gotten him killed. I thought I'd gotten Oliver Saxon killed. I'd forgotten how it was not to feel so terribly guilty about those things."

"Jack—" I reached out for him, and he shook his head, pulling the thread through my skin with a tug.

I sat back down and watched him string another piece of thread. I couldn't help but think about the first time he'd done something like this, when we'd practically just met, and I'd been stabbed at Prada. I let myself look at him like I had then: this boy who was almost intimidatingly gorgeous, but also quiet and kind. Who, for some reason, had taken an interest in me. Now he was just as handsome as ever, his dark hair still damp from the tunnels, the same intensity burning in his gray eyes, his drying T-shirt clinging to him.

Jack looked up to find me watching him. His eyes searched mine. I had the sudden feeling that this was supposed to be the part of the story where I realized I was wrong, and everything was forgiven. Where, after detours, Jack and I found our way back into each other's arms, where we realized we were meant to be all along.

"Can I tell you something?" He finished the stitch and set the needle down on the tray. When he turned back to me, there was a calm on his face I'd never seen. "I feel better about Fitz, and about Oliver. I still feel terribly guilty about what I did to you."

"Jack—"

He shook his head. "You don't need to do that. We both know it was bad. We both know you haven't entirely forgiven me, and I understand why. I'd like to try to explain just a little. I wasn't lying when I said that it was all for you. I thought going to the Saxons like that was the best way to keep you safe."

"I know—"

"But it was also because I thought it was the right thing to do. What Stellan said wasn't wrong. I had never done anything as terribly wrong as wanting you like I did, and giving in to it, and I thought I was making up for it in some way by doing the right thing then. I've thought about it a thousand times since—what the right thing really means. Stellan was wrong about *that*. I'm not a daft child. I know I don't actually have to ask their permission to think."

"I know. He knows, too. We were just all in a mood."

He picked up the needle again. "The point is that I do care about doing what's right by you. I care about you very much."

"I know," I whispered, and the feelings I'd been suppressing for so long rushed back in even stronger. How much Jack had done for me. How much I'd cared about him, as a friend and as a lot more. That version of us was simple. It was naive. It was sweet. I missed it. And I *had* forgiven him.

So why wasn't I jumping on this perfect moment to tell him so? To tell him that I wanted us to get back together?

The moment I posed the question, the answer hit me so clearly I couldn't believe I hadn't seen it earlier.

I thought Jack and I had broken up because of his spying for the Saxons. I thought if I forgave him for that, things would change between us. But well before then, I'd been annoyed with his making my decisions for me, protecting me when I didn't want protecting. That was really what had driven me away from him. I'd thought he'd started acting differently. But I was wrong. Jack hadn't changed.

I had.

When we'd first met, his looking out for me had been exactly what I needed. He was safe. Caring about him didn't feel like throwing myself off a cliff like so much of this new life did.

That's why I'd fallen for Jack so hard, so fast. He was exactly what I'd wanted, back when I was a different person. And now he wasn't. Not in that way.

It seemed so obvious. What we used to have was sweet and happy and nice. And we would never be back there.

I knew he wouldn't push me on it. If I changed the subject, he'd let it go. But I couldn't keep doing that.

"I care about you, too." I paused, looking up at the open cabinet of medical supplies, steeling myself. "Can we talk about something? About us. I know we haven't really had time to think about it—"

He was leaning close enough to my shoulder that I felt him tense. "Oh, I've had plenty of time to think about it."

I bit my lip. He was right. I'd been avoiding this conversation because I hadn't wanted to deal with clarifying my own feelings, and that was cruel of me. "I guess I just mean that don't know about you but clarity in *something* sounds good right now. So, um. I really do care about you a lot. But I don't think we're going to get back together."

He froze, like he was surprised I'd said it so bluntly. I was a bit surprised myself. "Right. Of course. I'm your Keeper. And even if I wasn't, I did something unforgivable."

"That's not why." If that was the only problem, we'd be back together already. I still *did* care about him. Part of me even still wanted to be coddled and looked after. But a bigger part of me didn't.

"The truth is," I said, studying the scrapes on my hands, "I'm not the same person you asked to prom in Minnesota. I really do care about you so much, and what we had for a while was—I'll never forget it. But I don't think we'd work like that anymore."

As much as I was sure this was the right thing to do, I braced for his reaction. He'd get over it eventually, but right now, I expected him to mumble something noncommittal and finish my stitches in awkward silence. But he said, "Have you really just given me the 'it's not you, it's me' speech?"

There was a lightness to the words I wasn't expecting at all. He looked up and smiled a little, bringing out that adorable dimple that had always seemed out of place on someone so serious. Since when did Jack make jokes?

He really was the perfect guy. He just wasn't perfect for me in the way I used to think he was. I was weaker around him. And softer, and probably nicer. But that wasn't who I was anymore, for better or worse. Sometimes, the story didn't turn out how you thought it would.

It's not you, it's me was surprisingly accurate. "I'm sorry," I said quietly.

Jack shook his head and opened a bandage. "One more thing, though. Perhaps it'd be less awkward to put it out in the open."

I knew exactly what he was talking about, of course.

"Are you and Stellan . . ." He trailed off.

"No," I said, and wondered why, for just a second, I felt like I should qualify that. Probably because we *had* kissed that time. But it seemed unnecessarily mean to bring up right now, and I did know one thing that was irrefutably true. "You and me were—are—our own thing. It had and has nothing to do with him." Whatever pull I had to Stellan—*destiny* or otherwise—and the relationship I'd had with Jack had always felt like entirely separate things: two parallel tracks rather than a collision course.

Jack smoothed on my bandage and threw away all the wrappers left on the sterile tray. "Okay. I hope, though . . ." He shifted uncomfortably, and then said, quickly, "I hope you two can take care of each other. I know there are things only you understand. He needs it, too."

I blinked at him, surprised. If it were anyone else, I might have thought he was being sarcastic, or trying to manipulate me somehow. But I knew Jack really meant it.

He took a deep breath and let it out. When he looked back up, he looked . . . at ease. More than he had in a long time, and I felt terrible for not doing this earlier. Jack hated gray areas. Now things were black and white again.

"Jack?" I slid off the exam table, the thin sanitary paper crinkling under me. "I know I'm the one who's been antisocial lately. But I don't want you to just be our Keeper. I hope we can still be actual friends."

He smiled. "We've been friends since we were eight years old and thought each others' names were Allie Fitzpatrick and Charlie Emerson. Yes, we can still be friends. Would you like to throw in an *I love you but I'm not* in *love with you* for a trifecta of cliché breakup lines?"

"Oh." I felt myself flush. "I—"

He opened the door for me. "Avery, I'm only joking. Let's go figure out how to save Fitz."

We met back up with Stellan and Elodie and made a plan for the night, and for tomorrow. The combination of painkillers and the numbing injection had finally made my wound feel okay, and the stitches looked good, so Elodie took a handful of the supplies, cleaned the room so no one would know we'd been there, and pressed a huge wad of bills into the hands of the boy who had let us in. And then we were back on the road, out of Alexandria. We had a plan about Fitz, but there was no way we could fly out of here right now—Lydia would have the Saxons watching everywhere. So we were going to spend the night in a nearby town and regroup while things got set in motion behind the scenes.

The van's fabric seats were damp, and it smelled like blood. I couldn't believe Mariam hadn't dumped us out on the side of the road yet. I guess the fact that we obviously had a lot of money to pay her went a long way. Elodie had talked to her while I was getting stitched up, and had learned a lot. Mariam had four sisters and two brothers, and her taxi was their primary source of income since her dad had gotten sick.

"Thank you, Mariam," I said. I felt like I had to talk quietly or whatever spell had gotten us all out alive would be broken. "I'm sorry about all the blood. I'm sure Elodie told you already, but we'll give you money to replace your car."

The smile she gave me wasn't even hesitant. She grabbed her phone from the middle console and turned it to me. "This is you?"

It was a paparazzi photo of me and Stellan at some airport somewhere. "Oh," I said, startled. "Um—"

"Don't worry, she's known the whole time," Elodie piped up. "She kept it quiet even before I asked her to. We're fine."

"Thank you," I said to her again. I'd thought we could trust her, but it was nice to have it confirmed that we didn't have to worry about talking in here. Mariam glanced from me to Stellan with a broad grin before she turned back to the road. Stellan widened his eyes with a shrug.

Jack and Elodie sprawled in the far-back bench seat, with Stellan and me in the middle. Elodie was still coughing, but it hadn't gotten worse, and Jack had never shown any signs of illness.

Out of the corner of my eye, I could see Jack watching Stellan and Elodie, as many emotions flitting across his face as there had been in that room with me. Over the past few days, the three of them had learned a lot about one another.

Jack turned to stare out the front window. Elodie was working dirt out from under her fingernails with a knife. We were on a smaller road now. Mariam's van had no air-conditioning, and the wind whipped through the open windows.

"I remember the first time I met you two," Stellan said. There was a subtle shift in the car as Jack and Elodie's attention turned to him. "Bishop had to save me."

I glanced back at Jack. The kids from the Saxon and Dauphin households used to train and do their schooling together, back when the families got along. That was how they all knew Fitz, and each other.

For a moment, I wasn't sure Jack was going to respond, but then he said, "I just made some people back off. He didn't exactly need *saving*." It was like they were telling the story to me. "He was at least a foot taller than me—"

"And I was crying like a toddler," Stellan said. "I'd just been tossed into this child boot camp. I couldn't speak a word of English."

And his family had just died. He'd been ripped away from his baby sister. He was in incredible pain. I remembered all that from when he'd told me his version of this story. He didn't mention it now, though.

"Not like being friends with me helped him much," Jack quipped from behind me. "I was Fitz's pet. They all hated me."

"They hated him because he was better than they were. He was picked early as one who could become Keeper." There was a surprising warmth in Stellan's voice.

"And he was the miracle child," Jack agreed. "We were—"

"Feared. Admired. Revered," Elodie cut in. "Resented." The boys didn't protest.

"I practiced my English," Stellan said. "I taught them Russian—taught *him*, I mean. I always wondered how you picked it up so quickly." He frowned at Elodie, but there was no malice behind it.

She shrugged. "And I made them accept me as part of their little in-crowd by beating them both in fights. Of course no one knew Fitz had been training me."

"We thought she was some magical warrior creature," Jack said.

"I was," Elodie retorted, and beside me, Stellan smiled for the first time since we'd learned she was Order. Something passed between the three of them. An acknowledgment of things they maybe hadn't admitted. A forgiveness.

I knew where the story went as they got older. They'd all stayed close—including and despite their various romantic entanglements—until Oliver Saxon's death, and then it had fallen apart. Until I'd shown up and thrown everything up in the air again.

Elodie curled on her side and tucked her head against the van's musty seat. She yawned so widely, I could see her back teeth. Jack was blinking, too.

We were all quiet, the sounds of the road and the music Mariam had low on the radio a blanket of noise muffling any more thoughts. Soon I glanced back to see Jack breathing deeply, asleep with his arms crossed over his chest. Elodie snorted in her sleep.

"She always insists she doesn't snore," Stellan whispered. "Now you can back me up."

I smiled, then pulled out my phone. It was hard not to be obsessed with the news, even though nothing major had happened the last couple times I'd checked. That wasn't the case this time. Since we'd been at the doctor's office, another attack had been reported. I inclined the phone toward Stellan. "China," I whispered. A government building. Only two people had died, but that didn't matter. The Chinese media was blaming it on Japan, and saying there was more to come. Their military was taking to the streets to stop the terrified looting in Beijing and Shanghai and dozens of smaller cities. "That doesn't fit with religious extremism," I said.

"The conflict between China and Japan is old, too. They seem to be stirring all the pots they can."

"Does that mean the Wang family is collaborating with the Saxons, too?"

"It's possible," Stellan whispered. "They could have told the Wangs and the Melechs and anyone else that for the price of a few deaths and some chaos in their territories, they'll have a position of power in the new Saxon regime. And if they're blaming it on Japan out in the world, they're probably blaming it on the Mikados in the Circle. Probably saying they're in league with us."

I flipped through more. Riots in Jerusalem. Half the EU considering following the UK and closing borders. People in surgical masks picketing outside a government building. And this was just over these small attacks.

What would happen if the Saxons had more of the virus? What would happen if they had both that and the cure? I glanced down at the bandage on my shoulder.

Life and death, all in my blood.

When Olympias had said on the clue that *a woman holds all the power* now, she hadn't just been referring to how she herself physically held the secrets in her tomb. She'd been referring to me. The girl of the bloodline, with the power to destroy them, and to save them.

It was far more power than I wanted.

"The scientists are getting closer to finding a way to deactivate it in our blood," Stellan whispered. "Elodie has already told Nisha what we found out about the cure, and she's working on it." Nisha was our main contact with the crew of scientists. "And they've learned more about my blood, so maybe that'll help."

I looked up to see headlights from an oncoming car slant across his face. "Yeah?" We'd changed into clean clothes before we left the city, but we hadn't had a chance to shower, and we were all grimy. Stellan had pulled part of his hair back with a rubber band from the clinic. If I'd thought he looked stereotypically Euro-hipster normally, this was a whole new level. To my surprise, I didn't dislike it on him.

"I got a report about it earlier. They found some of Olympias's writings. She used to say she created Alexander's blood, that she *made* him what he was. They still don't know exactly how she did it, whether scientifically or . . ." He trailed off.

Not that I believed anything about our situation was supernatural, but I could see how people back in Alexander's day might have believed the rumors that his mother was a witch.

"But however it happened," he went on, "she said she gave Alexander's blood incredible regenerative properties. She implied that it was resistant to disease, and that wherever on the body there's enough blood near the surface, it could be impervious to surface wounds."

Goose bumps rose on my legs. "Walk through fire."

"Blood, near the surface of the body." The wind ruffled the part of his hair that was still down.

"Your heel," I remembered. His heel was the only part of his body that looked burned in the way a normal burn would look, and he said it had taken much longer to recover. "The Achilles' heel. There's so little tissue there. Less blood at the surface, probably?"

"So more opportunity to be injured and not heal. That's what I thought, too." He leaned back, fingers to his mouth like he wished he had a cigarette.

"The Great," I said. He inclined his head. Invincible. Indestructible. To some extent, at least. "Does that mean some kind of ancient genetic engineering? Is that possible?"

"These days there is biotechnology, and a science called epigenetics that has to do with how genes express themselves, but we don't have anything like this . . . We're not necessarily at the peak of all knowledge now, though, like people tend to think we are. Who knows what was possible then."

We looked out the front window again.

"What if they can't deactivate it?" I said, unable to hold it back anymore. "Now, if they capture us, they have everything they need. And the only way to destroy the cure . . ."

"No," he said. I'm sure we'd all thought it, even if no one would admit it. How much was one girl's life really worth, when the alternative was this terrible?

My own grubby hair clung damply to my neck. I pulled it back. "I'm not saying it should be Plan A, but if it's me or half the world? Do the math."

"We're going to figure something out," he said firmly. I almost believed him.

For a while we stared out the window, watching the miles go by and the headlights approach and zoom past. Driving in a musty van toward the unknown felt like half my childhood. Funny that that was comforting now, when I started off every one of those drives in tears over yet another last-second move. By a couple hours in, though, my mom would always make it better. She'd stop at a gas station, we'd buy whatever weird regional snack we could find, and we'd sit in the parking lot and speculate about our new home.

I wasn't used to these intrusive memories being *nice* ones. I felt Stellan looking at me. I told him what I'd just been thinking. "And she'd do what she always did when I was upset. She would . . . pet me. Just rub my back, or my hair, like I was a scared puppy. I always calmed down. Is that weird? I don't know why I just told you that."

He shrugged and stretched his legs into the space between the driver's and passenger's seat. "I don't know why I tell you a lot of things."

"I could have saved her," I whispered. "The cure is my blood. I was right there."

"You didn't know," he said.

"I loved her so much."

He pulled his feet back in. Headlights from an oncoming car slanted across his face. "I know."

"You don't." Outside was flat as far as I could see, dotted with shadows I knew were scrubby bushes, and lights in the distance. It was like voicing one of the concerns I'd had since the tomb, and then letting myself talk about my mom, had opened a floodgate. Or maybe it was Stellan. I had a definite tendency to overshare with him in a way I never did with anyone else. Maybe Jack was right and the two of us understood things no one else really could. "I had no other family. We weren't anywhere long enough for me to find people I cared about, and if I did, we left them. She was all I had, and even though I loved her, I spent a lot of time resenting her for that."

Out of the corner of my eye, I saw Stellan turn in his seat to watch me.

"I'm sorry. I know that sounds whiny and that all you guys had childhoods so much worse; this doesn't even compare." I had barely let myself think these things, but now I couldn't stop. You could say things in the dark that weren't okay in the daylight, I guess. Studying the broken headrest of the passenger's seat in front of me, I went on. "When she got kidnapped, I felt so horribly guilty, and at the same time, I almost *blamed* her. I couldn't help but wonder what would have happened if she'd told me the truth so I wouldn't have stumbled into it blind like I did."

I squeezed my locket so hard, my fingers hurt. "When we got her back, I didn't even take advantage of the time I had with her. I think I was still a little angry. And now she's dead. My mom is *dead*. I should be able to just be sad like a normal person, but I can't." Jack saying it on the bus had made me realize it. If I was just sad, everything would be so much easier. "I feel guilty because it was my fault. And angry because it was partly hers. And then *so* guilty again, about being angry."

Stellan started to say something, but I wasn't done. "And on top of it all, I feel so disgusted with myself over everything. Over how I feel about my mom. Over how I don't even feel bad that Cole is dead. He's my half brother, and he's dead, and I'm glad, and that's disgusting. I can't believe I feel those things. I don't even recognize myself."

Before I even realized I was shaking again, Stellan's hand was gently cupping the back of my neck, his thumb running over my hair. "Like this?" he said quietly.

I tensed. I should want him to stop. I didn't. "Yeah."

"Is this weird?" he said after a second.

"Yeah."

"Good weird?"

I nodded.

"You don't have to keep making up ridiculous excuses like panic attacks to get me to touch you, you know." One side of his mouth tugged up. "All you have to do is ask."

"Shut up," I whispered, but he didn't stop petting my head, and I didn't tell him to. The shaking calmed. For some reason, I remembered that night on the train from Paris to Cannes. He'd had a head injury, I'd helped him take care of it. The next morning, we'd woken up accidentally wrapped together in my bed, with Jack sleeping next to us.

I glanced to the back seat at Jack and Elodie's slumbering forms. "So have you talked to your sister again?" I said, changing the subject abruptly.

His fingers paused. "Before we went into the tunnels. They're at the safe house. They're fine." He gave a wry smile. "The nanny told me to stop calling so much. I was making Anya nervous."

I pulled my knees up to my chest. "I'm glad she's okay."

He nodded. His hand trailed off my back and he turned to stare out the window. I realized he'd never answered the question of how he knew what a panic attack looked like, and exactly what to do. I realized I'd been doing a whole lot of talking about myself.

"Hey, are *you* doing okay?" I said.

He didn't turn around. "Never better."

"I was serious when I said you could leave. Not that you need my permission." I remembered the very first time I'd learned he even had a seven-year-old sister. The tattered photo he kept in his wallet of the tiny, scarred blond girl. The reason why he became part of the Circle in the first place, and the only reason he cared about the power that being the thirteenth line could bring. It wasn't fair to him that now he was so caught up in it that he hadn't run when he had the chance. It wasn't fair that he had to be here now rather than ensuring that she was where she should be. He *should* leave. "Once it's safe again, you can take Anya and go."

I thought he might answer. But just like when I'd mentioned it in the tunnels earlier, he didn't say a thing.

CHAPTER 16

Everyone disappeared into separate rooms off the same hallway with nothing but a wave and quick plans for the morning. Tomorrow, we were going to get out of Egypt and rescue Fitz. I stayed watching all their doors for a few seconds before I shut mine.

My room was sparsely furnished, with a heavy wooden armoire, a stiff-looking sofa, a bed, and a thin rug over the brick floor. A stick of incense had been lit and sent up thick, sweet smoke.

I took a shower—cold, because I couldn't figure out how to get the water to warm, or maybe there wasn't a way, since this was not a fancy hotel—and flopped onto the bed, pulling the thin quilt over me.

Every part of my body ached. It wasn't just the bullet wound—it was the stiffness from sitting on the bus so long, the blows from the explosion, the knot on my elbow from falling out of my chair deceiving the guard at the hospital. It all caught up at once, and I thanked Elodie a million times over for the painkillers she'd grabbed.

I stared up at the ceiling fan, which was turning lazily. We were just off the lobby, and outside my door, footsteps clomped back and forth on the brick floor. Someone made a comment in Arabic, and someone else laughed. When we'd walked through the lobby, it had smelled like mint tea, and I realized it did in here, too, over the incense.

I lifted my head. A silver pot of tea with a slim metal cup and a small dish of some kind of pastries—fried dough balls soaked in a syrup—sat on the nightstand next to the single lamp. The proprietor must have delivered it as we were checking in. My worn-out heart thumped at the kindness of the gesture, the way it made this insignificant place feel more like home than anywhere had lately.

Home. What would that mean for me now? Earlier, it had sounded like Jack planned to stay with the Circle once this was all over—but now that he was a Keeper who had killed a family member, everything was a lot more complicated. Elodie, I assumed, might go back to the Order. Stellan would almost certainly leave the Circle as soon as he could, though he hadn't confirmed it. He hadn't said much the rest of the drive, actually.

I let my eyes drift closed, playing over everything we'd said in the car. It had been so long since I'd really talked to anyone. I'd isolated myself from all of them lately, but being without Stellan had been especially hard, I realized. Instead of making me more stressed, talking to him made me feel stronger. The last time we'd talked like that was probably at that bar in Cannes, right before we—

My eyes flew open.

I stared up at the wooden beams of the ceiling, but the picture wouldn't fade.

Maybe after shutting everyone out for so long, I just wanted somebody to hold me and comfort me. But if that was the case, I would have turned to Jack earlier rather than breaking it off with him, right? I knew it wasn't just that. If I was being honest, I'd been hyperaware of Stellan ever since that kiss at the Melechs'. I had no idea why. It had been a fake kiss that had made me panic. Not exactly the stuff of romance novels. And yet. No matter what, it wasn't something I wanted in my head, not least because recently, those thoughts led to other, uglier ones.

I grabbed the second pillow and pushed it over my face like it would block out the images. I pictured every fancy dress I'd worn that had ended up torn or bloodied or burned. I tried to remember all twelve Circle families' mottos and symbols. I started the alphabet backward—and around *R*, there was the memory again, kissing him on the steps of a bar in Cannes, under a green striped awning, at Colette's villa. Us with Colette not long after that, in Paris, right before—

I was only under one blanket, but it was stifling. I shifted restlessly.

There were more footsteps outside, and they stopped. There was a light tap at my door. I bolted upright, and my first thought was to feel guilty about what I'd just been thinking. The second was to grab my gun, just in case. I padded on bare feet across the cold brick and said, "Who is it?"

"It's me," Stellan said.

I had known it would be.

I set down the gun, unlocked the deadbolt and the chain lock, and opened the door. The lamp on my bedside table cast only a dim glow, and he stood silhouetted in the lobby light.

"Did I wake you up?"

"No," I said.

"How is your shoulder feeling?" His accent was thicker than usual.

"Hurts."

He was chewing on his lower lip, looking different from the person who had just been kissing me in my head. He'd grown more gaunt recently. His eyes looked tired. Sad. A little broken. They had for a while, and I just hadn't noticed. Probably because all of ours did.

But he looked—oh God. He looked *good.* He was wearing a new T-shirt he got from the mall earlier and tracksuit pants that were too short for him. His hair was down again, and wet like he had just showered. He looked so much better than I wanted him to look. I had the distinct impression that, for maybe the first time ever, I was thinking impure thoughts about him and he wasn't reciprocating.

"I lied. I'm not doing entirely okay," he said, without looking up from the floor. "Can't sleep."

I was a terrible person.

I opened the door all the way, and he hesitated, then came inside. I glanced down the hall and locked the door behind him.

"Worrying about Anya, or something else?" I said quietly, trying to make up for what I'd just been thinking.

"That. And everything I told you in the tunnels. And—"

"Flashbacks from the hospital?" I asked, remembering my hunch. "Or from other stuff?"

He looked surprised. "Yes, actually. And—"

"What?"

"You."

I was quiet. Yes, we'd been friendly earlier, but I didn't want to hear that he was feeling this way because of anything to do with me. I didn't want to feel better knowing he was in my room right now. I didn't want to be looking at his mouth and realizing I'd been looking at it all day. I didn't want to need him, even if it was just for purposes of distraction. I didn't want him to need me at all.

"You make me feel too many things," he said abruptly. He crossed to the window, pulling back the heavy curtain to look down at the street. "I had gotten good at blocking it all out. And ever since you got here, you've made me feel all these things, and some of them aren't good."

I couldn't do anything but blink at him, taken aback. I felt my heart pounding in my bullet wound.

"I don't mean it's your fault." He dropped the curtain and paced in front of the carved wooden armoire, both his hands in his hair. "I don't know why I said that."

I stood in the middle of the room, my feet cold on the brick floor. "But some of them *are* good?"

I didn't know why *I'd* said *that*.

Stellan stopped pacing and looked up. He crossed the room in two long strides, taking my face between his hands, obviously warring with himself. The side of him that had nuzzled into me in the hospital because someone was showing him a tiny bit of kindness. The side that had been a huge pain since Jerusalem. The side that, when he couldn't sleep, had decided the thing to do would be to come to my bedroom.

He let out a long, shaky breath. "Yes. Some of them are good."

My hands found his chest. It was just about the hardest thing I'd ever done not to reach up and kiss him.

And then it wasn't, because I was doing it. I was stretching up on my tiptoes and pulling him closer, and he responded so quickly, I knew he'd been about to do it himself if I hadn't. There was no should-we, shouldn't-we, no trying to pull away, no trying to stop.

That kiss for the Circle hadn't counted. This, as far as my body could tell, was the second time we'd ever kissed. More deliberate than the first time. Much more complicated.

I wasn't sure who led us to stumble across the room and onto the stiff sofa, and it didn't matter. I didn't know how I ended up with my knees on either side of his hips, my hands running through his hair, damp and smelling of unfamiliar soap.

I let myself get lost in it and my focus narrowed down: his lips— his hands—my skin. Just like it had after the bomb in Jerusalem: live-survive-escape. Just like after my mom—

Screams. Thundering of a stampede of footsteps out of the room, but too late. The metallic smell permeating that room, hands slick with blood.

The memory broke and I was left blinking at Stellan's concerned face.

I pushed away. Stupid. What did I expect would happen if even *thinking* about kissing him triggered it?

His eyes shuttered. He dropped his hands from where they were tangled in my hair. "It's okay. I'll leave."

I couldn't even pretend. That's how much of a lie it would have been. "No. Don't."

He rested his hands by his sides, his face wary, confused. "What's wrong?"

"Nothing." I rubbed both hands over my face. "I don't know. It's stupid."

He gestured for me to go on.

"All the stuff I told you earlier. It doesn't just make me feel weird about Lydia and Cole and my mom . . . It's all tangled up in you. Us. Not that there is an *us*. I don't mean—" I felt myself flush. This was a ridiculous conversation to be having anytime, but it was especially mortifying while I was straddling him. I continued in a rush, "Just the first time we did this, it was only a few days later—" I shrugged helplessly.

He linked his hands on top of his head and leaned back into the sofa. "Are you saying you think our kissing each other that night had something to do with what happened?"

"No. Of course not. I mean, not exactly," I said, because he was right. That was crazy. "It's just that if I'd been paying more attention those days"—I tried to explain—"or if I'd let my mom persuade me to leave the Circle . . ."

"Is this why—I thought—" Stellan's hands moved tentatively back to my thighs, his thumbs making circles. "When we kissed at the Melechs'. Or when we were dancing, or anytime I hold your hand. You tense up. Is it because you associate that with . . ."

So he'd noticed. Of course he'd noticed.

I shrugged. But then I whispered, "I don't know. Maybe. Yes."

He looked off into the dark over my shoulder. "I'll stop kissing you if you want. It doesn't mean I have to leave. We could just talk."

My fingers clenched in his shirt. My nails were ragged, one of them torn at an awkward angle. Every time I moved my left arm, my shoulder burned. I was exhausted. I should just go to sleep. I *shouldn't* want to do anything that made me feel this panicky. What I should want and what I did want were annoyingly at odds right now. "No," I said in a tiny voice. "Don't. Please."

His lips twitched up. "So are you using me for some kind of desensitization therapy, then?"

"I don't know."

The look in his eyes was still complicated, but he didn't resist when I pulled him to me by the shirt and kissed him again. It wasn't long until the bad memories started knocking against the place where his lips touched mine. I pulled away. The corners of the room were all shadows, too heavy for the single lamp to extinguish.

Stellan's hands rested on my waist. "*Kuklachka*—" He caught himself. "Avery."

"It's okay. I know you don't mean anything offensive by it. I kind of miss it."

His eyes sparked. *"Kuklachka,"* he breathed again, lower and rougher.

"I'm sorry. It's stupid. I know us kissing didn't actually cause anything. It's just—"

"It triggers something in you. I know. It's not stupid. It's . . . inconvenient." He ran his palms down my arms. "Can I propose a theory? I wonder if you think you *shouldn't* be doing this and that is what's causing this reaction."

"What do you mean?"

His thumbs stroked my palms. "I mean, it's okay to feel the things you were talking about earlier. Grief doesn't just mean *sad.* The anger at your mother, the guilt—it's not wrong. It doesn't mean you're betraying her. It's okay that you were thinking about things other than her when it happened, and it's okay that you are now. It's normal. It's even okay to feel . . ." His eyes fell to my lips. "To feel good."

I found myself shaking my head. I hadn't felt anything near happiness or peace since my mom died, and for good reason. I couldn't just go on like normal, pretending everything was okay when nothing would ever be okay again. Who pictured their mother dying while kissing a boy and wanted to keep kissing him anyway? There was obviously something terribly wrong with me.

"Or maybe I'm wrong and it's just an association. In which case—" He looked around. The side table between the sofa and the bed was within reach, and he poured tea into the little silver cup. He took a sip. And then he pulled my mouth to his.

Mint. The taste of it was stronger on his tongue than the scent of it was. Surprisingly sweet. As thick as dessert. I deepened the kiss.

"Think about mint tea instead," he murmured when we paused. I could feel all ten of his fingertips through my leggings.

"What?"

"Make a new association. When you think of kissing me, think of mint tea instead of . . . other things."

"You're planning to do this often enough we need a new association?" I whispered.

He traced the curve of my hips. "If we're ever in public again, we might have to kiss occasionally. It might as well not be painful for you."

I rolled my eyes, but pushed away anyway, self-consciously. "We're destruction, remember? I don't think mint tea will change that."

"Our blood may be." He took another sip of the tea, set it down. "This is not." He kissed the corner of my mouth lightly. "This is not." A kiss on my jaw, on the opposite side. "When you think of this—" He pulled at my bottom lip with his teeth, and I let out a shaky breath. "You will no longer think about ruin and grief. Now it will be here. This room. Mint tea. Incense."

I breathed in the sweet, spicy scent; every one of my senses shivered at the heat of the tea and the cool of the mint on his lips. When the screams echoed in my head again, I tried to ignore them. "So this is how you get over something?" I whispered.

"No," he said, suddenly serious. "And at some point we'll get you better help than I can be. But while you're in survival mode, you do what you can."

A door slammed in the lobby—real this time, not in my head— and we both startled. I knew I wasn't the only one who needed more help than a few kisses could be.

"I'm scared of it happening again, too," I whispered, watching the door, watching him. The tension in his jaw when he'd first showed up here tonight had come back. "I was so afraid Elodie—and it would be my fault. I'm scared *all* the time."

He blinked a few times. I could tell I'd hit a nerve. "I know."

"I hate this."

He drew my face back around to him. "I know. Let yourself not think about it right now."

"I don't think it works that way."

"Maybe it could, just for now, if you let it." He reached to the table again. Instead of sipping the tea this time, he dipped his little finger into the plate of pastries, tasted it. "Honey," he said, pleased.

"Why?" I asked.

"Why what?"

"Why help me?" I said awkwardly. He had plenty of his own demons, as I could see. I didn't know why he'd want to come near mine. "There's no border crossing to ruin here."

I understood him showing up at my door. I understood me kissing him, him kissing me back. It was all a part of this strange, shifting push and pull of attraction between us. It was becoming increasingly less clear-cut, but I still understood it. I didn't understand all this unnecessary kindness.

He leaned his head against the back of the couch. "I suppose I like making you feel better."

I looked down at us wrapped together. "I admire your sacrifice. Very noble."

He nodded gravely. "I take my job seriously, even if it's difficult." Just like my own teasing, it was a little shakier, a little more lost than the words implied. "Really, I think helping you makes *me* feel better. So what I'm saying is it's selfish in every way."

"Well, if it's helpful . . ."

He grabbed my hips and pulled me tighter to him. "Thank you for *your* sacrifice, then," he murmured, nuzzling into my neck, and I almost giggled.

Maybe the flashbacks *were* because I thought I shouldn't feel happy. And maybe I kind of thought that was true. But that didn't change the fact that I *wanted* this. I did. Everything had felt so terrible lately that maybe he was right and I was allowed just a tiny bit of something that didn't. And the past few hours had been not-terrible. He had listened to all the troubling things I was thinking and didn't look at me like I was crazy and never once did anything well-intentioned but infuriating like suggest I leave this quest to someone else for my own good. Plus, doing this right now gave me something to concentrate on besides sadness and fear. And yes, it just felt good.

His T-shirt still had creases from the store running down the front. I traced my finger down them, felt his chest rise to my touch. Rather than letting it trigger a memory that led down an ugly path, I made how warm and solid and alive he was tether me to the here and the now. Not all over the world, not in Paris on the day my mom died, not earlier in the tomb. *Now.* This room. Safe. At least for the moment.

Stellan dipped into the dessert again, then picked up the plate to hand it to me. Instead, I took his hand. I pressed the pad of his finger between my teeth, felt the honey thick and sticky on my tongue.

His eyes went dark. He set down the plate. Then he dabbed honey across my mouth and took my sugared lip between his.

"Honey," he murmured roughly against me, "and mint. Let that be all this is."

He took another sip of tea and I drank in the sweetness. Another, and I arched against him as his lips tingled coolly at my collarbone.

I worked on thinking only about the way this felt, cozy, hazy, almost peaceful in the dim room, his thumbs ghosting across my hip bones and mine sliding under his shirt.

And maybe I didn't want us to need each other, but I needed this. I let myself sink into it, sink into *him*. And slowly, softly, as sweetly as the honey on his tongue, everything else fell away, and I let myself—for tonight at least—not feel bad about feeling good.

CHAPTER 17

In the morning, I woke up alone and staggered sleepily out of my room. Elodie was already in the lobby, drinking what I could tell from the scent wafting from it was thick, sweet mint tea.

I blinked at the pot for a second. That association thing was supposed to work in the other direction. *Kissing* means *think of mint tea.* Not *mint tea* means *think of*—

"Are you just going to stand there?" Elodie said.

I sat, hugging my arms around myself. If I was going to feel like this every time I smelled mint, that would be seriously inconvenient.

"Feeling all right?" I asked Elodie.

She rolled her eyes without looking up from the newspaper. "Yes, your miracle blood has rescued me from death's door." She glanced up, then did a double take. "Oh *really?*"

I surveyed myself, alarmed. My clothes were wrinkled, but so were hers. She certainly couldn't tell what I'd been up to last night just from that. I relaxed. "What?"

Elodie rummaged through the bag at her feet and pulled out a makeup compact. She tossed it to me with a smirk. "Go look in the mirror and do something about that, if you want. Nothing to be embarrassed about as far as I'm concerned, but you might disagree."

I knew I hadn't been sleeping well, but were the circles under my eyes *that* bad? I clicked on the light in the bathroom, and—*oh*.

There was a dark purple bruise the side of a quarter at my collarbone. When I pressed on it, it was tender. I was certain it would taste like mint and honey.

It wasn't like it had taken long to pack up this morning, so I sat in the hotel lobby, picking at the breakfast buffet: a bean dish with flatbread, cheese, eggs, and sliced tomatoes and cucumbers. We'd be leaving shortly. It was possible we could have gotten on a commercial flight from Egypt—the borders weren't as strict here, and the Circle might not be watching as closely as they would have been out of Israel. But we didn't want to risk it. Luc had sent one of the Dauphins' planes for us, and it would be here in a couple of hours. This way, we wouldn't have to show passports leaving Egypt or arriving in France, and there would be no record of where we were.

When the Dauphins learned that Luc had let fugitives into their country, they might not be happy, but Luc was good at doing things without his parents knowing, and we hoped to be hiding somewhere in Paris by the time they found out. Ideally we'd stay there long enough to regroup and learn more about the cure from our scientists.

Our scientists who, Elodie had reluctantly admitted, were Order. There had been a moment of renewed tension when we realized the Order had had our secrets all along, but Jack of all people had urged us to keep an open mind, and even to agree to meet with them and see what they could do for us.

I had so many questions, and most of them started with *why*. Why did Fitz go to so much trouble for the kid of a fellow Order member? Why weave the threads of my life together with Jack's, and Stellan's, and even Elodie's?

If they cared enough to help hide me for years, why didn't the Order save my mom?

The thought made my chest feel tight again.

Jack was on the phone with Rocco, going over the plan we'd made last night. Our first instinct had been to go to the Saxons' and break Fitz out ourselves, but Elodie had talked us out of it. So we'd been in touch with Rocco. As we'd suspected, the entire focus of the Saxon household right now was on Cole's death. We hoped this meant Fitz would not be high on their list of priorities. Rocco would be breaking Fitz out and smuggling him to Paris. It seemed too simple, but in this case, simple was probably best.

I glanced up when Stellan emerged from his room. His eyes found me immediately, and his step stuttered. It made my pulse stumble, too. Not because I was nervous about seeing him, but because I really didn't want it to be awkward.

He glanced at Jack, then strolled across the room to survey the food on the table behind me. "Morning," he said evenly, one eye on Elodie, who was sitting on the couch nearby, texting. "Did you have a good night?"

I watched him. "Fine. You?"

"Not bad." He glanced up from the bread he'd just put on his plate, and a smile pulled at his lips. He reached out a thumb to graze the spot on my collarbone that I must not have covered as well as I thought. "Oops," he whispered, but there was no remorse behind it at all.

I took a quick look to make sure Jack's back was still turned. "If you did it on purpose, that's obnoxious," I whispered. He held up his hands to proclaim his innocence.

The tension left my shoulders. We were going to be okay. Which was good, because it was nothing. I was attracted to Stellan, and I had been for a long time—I could no longer deny that. The feeling was obviously mutual. And in times of extreme stress, it seemed to boil over. Which was fine. It wouldn't be a big deal.

He sat down next to me and bit into a slice of cucumber. "Can I use your phone?" He couldn't find his. Mariam thought she remembered seeing it in the van, but apparently it had been lost between some cushions, or maybe it had fallen out when we'd stopped at the doctor's office last night. I handed him my phone and walked away to give him privacy while he talked to Anya. I couldn't help but watch him, though. Talking to her was the only time I ever saw him smile in a way I knew for sure wasn't fake.

A couple of hours later, we got out of the van on the tarmac of a private airport near Alexandria. We all hugged Mariam good-bye and sent her off to her family with enough money for them to live on for a year.

As we climbed the steps into the plane, ready to head back to the place closest to *home* for all of us, I asked Stellan, "So if you left, where would you go? Does Anya want to live at the beach or in the mountains? Or maybe a big city?"

I said it jokingly, but he didn't smile. He drummed his fingers on the railing. "It seems like to stay away from them, you always have to keep moving."

He was right. Even if we were no longer wanted criminals, the Circle doesn't let you leave. It wouldn't be easy. And that meant learning not to call any one place home. "Yeah. That's what my mom thought, too."

I fell into a seat. Stellan sat across the aisle.

"What about you? Would you think about leaving again?" he said. It sounded casual, but I could tell he'd been thinking about it as much as I had.

I looked out the window at Jack and Elodie, who were still on the tarmac talking to the pilot. "I don't know. If the scientists can't do anything with the virus and the cure, I guess it might come down to killing myself or hiding for the rest of my life. Hiding doesn't sound so bad when you think of it that way."

I saw Stellan wince a little at that. "Would you would *want* to leave, though?"

I remembered that night at a bar in Cannes again. *You want to be wanted*, he'd said. He'd been right. *You want control.* Right about that, too.

I remembered further back: washing my hands in the sink at Prada. Blood on my hands, the first time of many. "I don't think it matters anymore what I want."

"It's not the only thing that matters, but it'll always matter. It's your life."

Was that really even true anymore? "Would *you* want to leave if what you wanted was all that mattered? If you didn't have to think about things like safety and duty?"

Stellan thumbed open an air-conditioning vent by his seat. "My father . . ." he said. I tensed. Stories of family were seldom good with this group. "He made the best gingerbread. Families in our neighborhood actually bought it from him around the holidays."

"Gingerbread?" I said incredulously.

"Gingerbread." Stellan settled back, crossing one ankle over the opposite knee. "He did all the cooking and cleaning and sewing, and taught me."

"You *sew?*"

"What, you don't?" He smirked, but then he turned to look out the window. "That's what I want, eventually. What I used to have with my family. That's what—"

"That's what aches," I said quietly. *Toska*. The *ache*. That dull sense that something's missing.

"Yes."

Outside, Jack and Elodie started up the steps. "Gingerbread and sewing," I said. "So what you're telling me is that you want to be somebody's grandma."

"Luc's grandmother carries a tiny dog and a flask of scotch everywhere she goes. I think I could handle that."

Jack and Elodie came down the aisle and settled into seats nearby and told us what they'd just heard. Rocco had found out where Fitz was. It looked like this was actually going to work. Suddenly, I felt nervous again.

As the plane took off, I checked the news. Lots of countries were working to calm the panic, and it was obvious which news outlets were Circle-controlled by the kinds of headlines they had up. Non-Circle outlets weren't interested in being reasonable. The whole Internet seemed to be sharing some article speculating that the virus was actually the result of government testing, a disease that had reacted with GMO foods to become deadly or something like that. It linked to another article about how vaccines were designed to make us susceptible to it, and a million other conspiracy theories, most still not as crazy as the truth.

We thought it might start World War Three if the Circle took sides between us and the Saxons. Turned out the only side being taken was against us, but there was plenty of chaos anyway.

I put my phone away and watched a movie in French with subtitles I didn't actually pay attention to. Jack and Stellan both stared out the windows of the plane. Maybe everyone else was more nervous than I realized, too, because we all jumped when Jack's phone rang halfway through the flight.

Rocco had broken Fitz out. Fitz was on his way to Paris safely.

It was done.

There was no angry Dauphin welcoming party at the airport. No one had noticed the plane missing, Luc said, and we should be fine as long as we disappeared now.

Disappearing was the plan. Fitz had made it to Paris before we did. Someone in the Order owned a boat that did dinner cruises on the Seine, and if we met there, we could be certain no one would see us.

Our cab pulled up at the bridge where the boat was docked. The four of us made our way down the stone steps to the river's edge, which would usually be full of picnickers and joggers and glamorous women smoking cigarettes on their lunch break, but now was eerily quiet.

We found the right boat, and the door at the top of a carpeted gangplank swung open.

I froze in place. Fitz was thin, and his eyes looked sunken behind his glasses, but the smile that lit his face was exactly the same as I remembered.

I hadn't really cried since just after my mom died. I hadn't let myself. But as Fitz came down the ramp and pulled me into a hug, I burst into tears.

CHAPTER 18

The boat was long and thin, with an upper and a lower deck, both set with long strings of dinner tables. For now, we were the only people here. The rest of the Order would meet us shortly.

Elodie found me tissues and water, but I was still sniffling as I hung back and watched Fitz. He and Elodie talked Order business. He hugged Jack and murmured a few things, and Jack glanced at me and smiled.

Then Fitz clapped Stellan on the back and asked about his sister. Stellan was cordial, but I could tell he was still feeling guarded. As glad as I was to see Fitz, I understood. I'd built Fitz up as this mythical faux-grandfather for years. I remembered the last time I'd seen him. Mr. Emerson, our jolly next-door neighbor. He'd helped us pack up our moving van in Boston. And then he'd hugged us good-bye—and for years after that, he was in my life only via post-cards, letters, and the occasional phone call. I should have known this person who cared enough to stay in touch all these years wasn't just a random neighbor.

There was part of me that, now that we had an adult we actually trusted again, wanted to throw everything at his feet and beg him to tell us what to do. The other part felt like nothing I'd ever known was quite real, and I should be cautious.

The five of us made our way to a table on the lower deck.

"My brave girl," Fitz said, with a hand on my shoulder. Back home, Fitz didn't have any kind of accent that I remembered, but now his voice was lilting, light. An Irish accent, maybe? Yet another thing to ask. Yet another piece of the puzzle. "I'm so sorry, love. Your mother—"

He took off his glasses and wiped his tired eyes with the back of his hand. He'd arrived in Paris a couple of hours before us, and had had time to clean up and get settled, but he still looked rough, with a dark bruise across one cheek and his glasses taped together at the hinge. I thought of Lydia and Cole in Egypt, and how they'd gotten there. I didn't want to think of the injuries on Fitz I couldn't see.

"My brave kids. I've wondered so many times whether all of you would be friends if your worlds collided." There, again, was that uncomfortable tug on my stomach, of just how much our lives had been steered to get us here, not just by Fitz, but by my mom, the Circle, the Order. I suddenly felt close to tears again. I didn't exactly feel upset—just confused. Overwhelmed. Guilty—again—for feeling anything but what I should feel, which was relief that we were all here and remorse that my mom wasn't.

Jack answered a call and warned us to be careful—apparently the Saxons had gotten word of the Dauphins' plane's movements and knew we were in Paris. They were stationing Rocco and some others here to try to find us, but they had no more intel than that. They didn't seem to know yet that Fitz was gone.

We asked Fitz about Rocco's breaking him out of the Saxons', and he told us that story, along with an abbreviated version of what had happened since he'd been imprisoned. He'd tried to break out on his own twice early on, he said—he'd been at the Saxons' before, and knew a little about the inner workings of the house because my mother had been an Order plant at the Saxons' for years.

I gripped the table, and Fitz turned to me. "I have much to tell you about your mother, Avery." He glanced around the table. "In fact—"

He cut off when the boat's door swung open and half a dozen people came inside. I took a last swipe at my eyes with a tissue and stood to greet the Order.

Each member of the small group gave Fitz a hug, then shook hands with us and found a seat at the table. Most of them were adults, but a couple of girls were just slightly older than us. One of them, with sleek dark hair and a gold stud in her nose, looked familiar.

"Were you at the Rajeshes'?" I said.

She nodded. I recognized her now, in the same heavy dark eyeliner she'd put on me while Lydia and I were getting ready for the dinner where I'd met Dev Rajesh for the first—and only—time.

"I have been assigned to the Rajesh home for years," she said. Her voice was quiet but confident, with a soft accent. "After recent developments, I got a new assignment. I have been speaking with you on the phone about the experiments. My name is Nisha."

This was Nisha, who had been experimenting on our blood for weeks? I could barely choke out a hello. Elodie sat next to her and took out a list of questions she'd come up with on the flight. I settled back into my chair. Fitz stood behind his seat on one side of me, and Stellan sat at the other. He'd been observing silently since the Order came in.

"Will any more of the group be joining us?" Jack asked, taking his own place across from me.

The Order members looked at one another. Fitz cleared his throat. "That's one of the things we need to tell you about our organization. There is still one of us in every Circle home. Some of them are here today, but some are at their assignments. Other than that . . ." Fitz paused. "The people in front of you are actually all that's left of the Order."

Some of the meager group gave small nods.

Jack shook his head like he wasn't sure he'd heard correctly. "The people in this room . . . plus a few others hiding in Circle households, doing nearly nothing?" he asked. "You mean to tell us that's the entire Order?"

"We used to be more," Fitz said. "There was a clash with the Circle a few decades ago that decimated our ranks, and we haven't recovered."

Half the questions I wanted to ask immediately went out the window. I saw now exactly why they hadn't mobilized to rescue my mom. They were barely staying afloat as it was.

Fitz took a seat. "I know that's surprising, but just because we don't have numbers doesn't mean we don't have insight. And I know you have much to report."

He introduced us to the Order members and gave a brief run-down of how he knew us, and what we were to the Circle. "And this is Avery." He looked down at me. "Sweetheart, I've thought for a long time about how I might tell you this."

A kernel of worry took root in my gut. Did I not already know all the secrets there were to know?

"This is not the ideal way to do it," he went on, "but I believe this is important for everyone here to know. Some of you will remember Claire. Avery is Claire's daughter." All around the table, people sat up straighter, shooting alarmed glances at me. "Which means," Fitz continued, "that she's my granddaughter."

I couldn't possibly have heard right. "Your what?"

"Your *what*?" Elodie echoed.

Fitz nodded at her. "You never knew Claire. I didn't want anyone here to make the connection."

Across the table, Jack looked nearly as shell-shocked as I felt.

"How—" The boat was barely moving, but the chair under me felt unstable. I pressed my palms to the tabletop. "What?"

"I'll tell you everything. I promise." Fitz sat and squeezed my hand where it rested on the table. "I just couldn't keep it a secret any longer."

I tried to pay attention to the Order members around the table introducing themselves, but I couldn't think about anything but that word. *Granddaughter.*

It can't be true, I wanted to say, but of course it could. It explained everything. Why Fitz would have cared about us—and why he went to so much trouble to learn about the mandate. Why my mother trusted him.

I glanced over at him. Now that I knew . . . he had my mom's eyes. Clear and bright and green. I hadn't noticed when I was a kid. I hadn't noticed so much. Now that I knew, it was even harder to stop the flood of memories. Some were nice: movie nights and holidays, how we ate Sunday brunch together every weekend and my mom would read us our horoscopes from the newspaper. Some were strange. I remembered a conversation I'd overheard one night, when my mom had asked Fitz whether he thought I should be home-schooled. I remembered the day we left Boston—it was the only time we moved that my mom cried. She tried to hide it, but I heard her after she thought I was asleep that night in the hotel. Because she hadn't just been leaving behind a friendly neighbor. She'd been leaving the only family she had, probably because something had just happened that had made them decide it was no longer safe to stay. She was terrified and didn't know whether she'd ever see him again.

A foot touched mine under the table, and I blinked back to the present. Stellan raised his eyebrows in a silent question. I nodded. *I'm fine.*

The boat had started moving, and we were cruising slowly around the back side of Notre-Dame. I tried my best to tune back in to the conversation.

"We're not surprised to see this turmoil happening," a middle-aged woman with close-cropped black hair I'd vaguely heard introduce herself as Hanna was saying. "Every one of the Circle's messes in the past centuries has been for a reason. Yes, the wars do tend to be over some petty infighting, but they also have a purpose: to change the power structure of the world to the Circle's advantage. After World War Two, the United Nations was formed. It was an obvious way for the Circle to give themselves very public power while looking like it was for the good of the world."

"The UN was also formed to bring peace within the Circle," Jack pointed out.

Fitz nodded. "In the same way, I believe the Saxons *created* this current crisis to seize power for themselves while assuring the Circle they'll bring peace. Dictators throughout history have done the same thing to wrest power away from anyone weaker."

I couldn't argue with him. We knew that was exactly what they were doing.

Elodie filled them in on our search for the cure, and what we'd found. Nisha took over from there. "Since we last talked to you, we have discovered something more about Mr. Korolev's blood." She glanced at Stellan. "We believe it has to do with how the virus works."

Stellan sat up straighter.

Nisha explained to the rest of the Order what had been in the report Stellan had told me about, about how his blood seemed to heal him like it did by replicating certain compounds far more rapidly than was normal. "After learning this and learning that Miss West's blood is the cure," she finished, "we believe that the basic mechanism could be that the virus itself is only in *her* blood, but in very small quantities, and that *his* makes it multiply out of control and become dangerous."

Elodie was nodding along. It did make a lot of sense. The boat went under a bridge, and we were plunged into darkness for a moment before reemerging into the light. We were coming up on the Louvre in the distance.

"How does that help us?" Jack asked.

"We're not sure yet," Nisha conceded.

"What we're afraid of," Elodie clarified for the Order, "is that the Saxons will capture them for more of their blood. The attacks—though they've been devastating—have so far been small, but if they get more—"

"And they have the cure for themselves in case of disaster, negating that logical argument against releasing it," said a man with a thick beard.

Elodie nodded. "Exactly. And now they know it infects more than direct Circle. If they release it on a larger scale, it could not only cause mass casualties, but throw the world into even more chaos. Of course, there's always the possibility they'll just kill the Circle directly, too."

"We'd love to eliminate the virus," Nisha said. "But since it is in their bodies, and there is therefore no way to destroy it directly, we've been attempting to find a way to make it inactive in their blood. Without success . . . so far."

"And if it continues to be, these two will have to disappear, and hope they can stay out of the Circle's clutches for the rest of their lives," the Order man said. "Or to be even more safe—"

"Yes," Fitz cut in sharply, not letting him so much as voice the other possibility. "One idea is that Avery and Stellan would stay on the run from the Circle. From the Saxons and their allies."

Stellan's foot pressed into mine again. I pressed back.

"I have to ask," Hanna said, "is there a reason why there hasn't been a targeted attack on the Saxon family to remove that threat?"

I glanced at Jack, who was looking at his hands folded on the table. Elodie reminded everyone that the Circle's code was very clear on what happened to anyone who attacked a member of another family, and that's why we had decided not to kill Lydia and Cole in Egypt. Jack squeezed his hands together so tightly that his knuckles went white. We still didn't know what the Circle would do about his killing Cole. The anxious knots in my stomach tightened even more.

"If an Order member were the one to commit the assassination, you'd get around that," Hanna was saying.

"The Saxons have not been easy to find," Elodie said, "probably for that exact reason. Our contact inside their home hasn't actually seen any of the family members for weeks."

"And," Fitz said, "we know they have allies. Evil has wide roots. Taking out Alistair and Lydia is no guarantee of safety."

"So why not go wider?" Hanna asked. "The Order does not generally use violence, but I think we can all agree these are extreme circumstances."

Across the table, Jack's mouth pressed into a hard line. Any statement that started with *We don't usually, but* was suspect.

"It's certainly something to consider," Fitz agreed. "Sacrifice a few for the good of the world."

"With this virus," Hanna said, "it could be a targeted strike. Cleaner than bombings or assassinations—the world is already afraid of the virus. A string of 'accidental' infections, and then we claim we found the cure and it's all over."

I leaned forward, cutting them off. "If I'm hearing you correctly, you're suggesting we kill the whole Circle? That's exactly the opposite of what we've been trying to do."

"Sweetheart, no, of course it wouldn't be the first choice," Fitz said. "We're simply running through our options."

This was exactly what we'd been afraid of when we'd found out Elodie was Order. I glanced across the table at her. She was inspecting her hands, but the crease between her brows said she wasn't behind this plan, either.

We weren't just being naive, were we? Was this something we should be considering?

"Maybe we wouldn't have to eliminate *all* of the Circle," another man across the table said diplomatically. "I'm sure you have some allies you'd want to keep safe."

"So we base our tactical engagements on who's nice to these kids?" Hanna said. "That's a slippery slope."

I tried not to think about every fantasy I'd had about a knife in Cole's chest. In Lydia's heart. I felt no remorse about Cole's death, and I was probably a terrible person for that. But as much as I wanted revenge, I couldn't imagine playing God and doing a preemptive strike against anyone who could eventually be a problem.

I'd let myself hope the Order would have real solutions. Not just another set of evil schemes.

I pushed my chair back from the table with a scrape. "I'm sorry. I need a few minutes."

I went up the stairs from the lower deck to the open upper deck and found a bench along the railing. We went under a bridge, and the Eiffel Tower appeared, reaching high into the cloudy sky. I took deep breaths of the summer afternoon air, and I didn't turn around when I heard footsteps behind me.

"So it appears the Order would like to either get rid of us or use our blood to murder people. That sounds oddly familiar . . ." Stellan settled beside me.

I propped my feet on the railing and watched the wake come off the boat. "So maybe we will have to leave all this behind. If we haven't been able to do anything and this is the only alternative the Order can think of . . ."

I shuddered, but before I could even tense up too much, I felt Stellan's fingers pull through the tips of my hair.

"We could all go," I said. "Elodie and Jack, too."

Stellan paused, working through a tangle. "The thing is . . . if we're leaving the Circle to keep them from using our blood, we couldn't be in the same place, could we? You and I couldn't, at least. It would defeat the purpose."

"Oh." I wasn't sure why I hadn't realized that. I wasn't sure why it made me this much more tense. "Right."

Our boat rocked in the wake of a passing, nearly empty tourist boat. I glanced downstairs, where the Order were still talking. Earlier, I'd been excited for this meeting. Now I didn't want to go back down there.

Another set of footsteps came up the stairs, and Jack poked his head onto the upper deck. "Mind some company?"

Stellan dropped his hand from my hair. "Come on up. We're discussing mass genocide."

Jack cringed, but he came up behind our bench. "If the Order isn't going to be much use, we'll just have to figure it out ourselves, won't we?" He squeezed my shoulder and then, after a short hesitation, clapped a hand on Stellan's, too. "It'll be all right."

Stellan and I glanced at each other, and I reached up to squeeze Jack's fingers back. "So what do we do?"

"First order of business will be to keep the cure away from them, same as before. Knowing what the cure is changes the method, but the objective is the same," Jack said. I scooted over and he sat on the other side of me. "I was thinking about it a lot on the plane, and I think the second thing for us to do will be to work on the Circle. Make them believe us. If the Circle turns on the Saxons, maybe *they'll* stop them, or at least help us."

"Not that I disagree," Stellan said, "but Lucien has been trying to tell them the truth and he's getting nowhere. It's not that easy."

I watched the boats moored to docks along the Seine.

"That's why we need something more than our word against theirs," Jack said. "I don't know what that is yet, but I think that's what we work toward."

Fitz came onto the upper deck. His eyes looked tired, and his sweater looked two sizes too big. "Here you three are." He turned to Jack, then to Stellan. "May I speak with Avery for a few minutes?"

Jack nodded and stood. Stellan nudged my knee. "Okay?" he mouthed. I nodded, wishing I could ask them both to stay. I moved to one of the smaller tables on the deck, and Fitz joined me. The boat was turning, heading back toward the Eiffel Tower in the other direction.

"I'm sorry that upset you. I understand how you feel," Fitz said. "No one wants to see this end in more death and destruction—not even me, in spite of everything."

I nodded, though I wasn't really sure that was true for all the Order members. "Everything's just a little . . ."

"Overwhelming?" Fitz sat across from me. "I'm so sorry we weren't able to tell you earlier about who I was to you. It's been one of my biggest regrets that I wasn't able to be part of my grand-daughter's life."

"Why weren't you?" I said quietly. And then I amended it, to be fair. "You were. You were one of the only people who was ever part of my life for more than a few months. But why couldn't you . . ."

"Your mother and I tried. That's why I lived near you for as long as I did. It was an experiment. But with my own ties here—it was too dangerous."

I realized I was nervous. I'd wondered for so long how my life got to be the way it was, and now that I was about to find out, I wasn't sure I was ready. I nodded anyway. "Go on."

He told me the story.

Like the Circle, the Order started their operatives young, he said, and membership often ran in families. My mom had been assigned to the Saxon household when she was fifteen years old. "I blame myself for what happened then," Fitz said. "But here you are, so I can't regret it."

He hadn't realized my mom was falling for Alistair Saxon un-til it was too late. The Circle took the prohibition against family members being romantically involved with the help seriously, as I knew, and he had never considered that my mom would get involved with a member of the Circle, either. But Alistair was different. Even Fitz saw it. He wasn't like his older brother and his father. He was reasonable, and saw the Circle for what it was. He wanted more for them, and for the world. He was *good*. But then his brother and father were killed, and everything changed. He came into incredible responsibility overnight, and in such a way that he felt a threat to his family he'd never believed in before. They blamed the Order for the deaths, when in reality, it wasn't true. But that incident changed the Circle, and it changed Alistair.

My mom would have ended the relationship at that point, Fitz said, but it was too late. She was pregnant with me. She confided in some Order members, and it was a mistake. Every one of them wanted her to end the pregnancy. She refused. But then she found out I was a girl.

"And because of what we knew about girls of the Circle, and what you'd mean if you did have the gene, it changed things. Still, your mother was determined to keep you," Fitz said. "I helped her come up with a plan. She told everyone—both the Order and your father—that she'd lost the baby. And then she disappeared."

From up on the riverbank, a siren got closer, and I tensed, wondering what had happened now. It passed.

"Once you were born," Fitz continued, "and you did have the violet eyes your mother and I were hoping you wouldn't, we knew it was unlikely I'd be able to be a real part of your lives."

I'd been mad at my mom for a long time for running from this, and it was all to keep me alive. And here I was, in the same position, considering doing the same thing. Doing the bare minimum to keep my own blood from being the end of the world, and then washing my hands of everything to do with the Circle. Disappearing, just like she did.

I rested my elbows on the white tablecloth and my head in my hands.

"And that was when I began my research," Fitz said.

I glanced up. Jack, Stellan, and Elodie were by themselves on the lower deck now, talking in a tight knot. At this point, this was no longer just my story. And even if it had been, I wanted them here.

"Just a second," I said, and called them upstairs. Stellan sat next to me again, and Jack and Elodie seated themselves on the other two sides of the table. I caught them up on the quick version of my mom's story, and then Fitz went on.

My mom had been young, and naive, and optimistic, he said. She thought she'd be able to keep me from this world forever. Fitz, knowing that might not be true and that my life and freedom would be compromised, was determined to help. "So I began researching what might actually happen if Avery were discovered. All I knew at that point was what the Circle knew. The mandate would produce a weapon, supposedly against the Order. The girl with the violet eyes was the key, which was why we couldn't let such a girl exist."

"Wait," Jack said. "What do you mean you couldn't *let* a girl exist?"

Fitz studied his hands. They were cut up, his fingernails filthy. "It was one of the Order's most important tasks inside Circle households. We'd keep watch on the families."

"You mean spy on them," Jack cut in.

Fitz inclined his head. "And advise in ways that led to the most favorable outcomes. Our people are high up in many households. Some of them are Keepers."

Shock flitted across Jack's face. Elodie shook her head at him.

"We couldn't let any of the twelve families have a girl with violet eyes," Fitz continued, "so we didn't. The methods have changed over the years. Just this past century we were able to isolate the genetic marker and make sure no baby girls with violet eyes would be born at all if we kept up with our duties."

"Genetic engineering? Like what Olympias did to Alexander," Stellan said.

"Like how she created the healing properties of your body, yes," Fitz said. "Impossible, but true."

Elodie cut in. "Going all the way back to Olympias, the

Order has been advanced scientifically. We've lost some of what she knew—she was remarkable. But yes, the lack of that modification on Avery's mother is what allowed Avery to exist."

"So you're saying Alistair was the only person in the history of the Circle to sleep around with someone he wasn't supposed to?" Stellan asked.

I kicked him under the table. He just shrugged.

"Of course not. The Order operative in the household tries to keep an eye on that. And it's not guaranteed that any Circle child will have the purple eyes anyway—it depends on the mother's genetics, too, which is why many Circle marriages are arranged. But between that and the fact that the Order member in the household does their best to prevent it . . ."

"But my mother *was* the Order operative in her household," I said.

He nodded. "I'm sure there have been other slipups, but until relatively recently in history, the world was not so connected. No Internet. Much less travel. A girl like you could have lived out her whole life without anyone noticing or caring about her eye color."

I thought about the other girls through history who could have been in my position if things were different. How easily things could have been different for *me*.

"Finally, I discovered Napoleon's research," Fitz said. "It was the breakthrough I'd been waiting for. I learned about the thirteenth bloodline, but I still didn't know how they'd be connected to Avery and her well-being. So it became about finding that bloodline. I'd just begun to come to a new hypothesis about it, from a different interpretation of Napoleon's diary, when, on an off chance, I heard about Stellan and his sister."

I saw Stellan's throat bob with a hard swallow.

"I thought there was no way it could be true," Fitz told him, "but you were the closest thing I'd had to a development in nearly a decade. I had the Dauphins take you in."

For a few seconds, the only sounds were the boat's motor and the distant sounds of traffic. "So it's true. I was a science experiment," Stellan said, his voice too even.

"Yes," Fitz said matter-of-factly. "When I first brought you in, it was so I could study you. Elodie came to me around the same time, and I had her placed in a position not only to do the Order's work in the Dauphin home, but to keep an eye on you."

It was exactly what Elodie had told us.

Stellan sat forward, resting his arms on the table. "Do you know who killed my family?" he said, his voice so level that if I couldn't feel his foot bouncing under the table right now, just inches from mine, I wouldn't know it bothered him at all.

"I'm sorry," Fitz said. "I wish I did."

Stellan nodded tersely.

I crossed my legs and brushed his calf with my foot. He glanced at me, and I felt the bouncing of his foot slow.

I honestly wasn't sure whether I was only offering moral support or whether it was more. The more anxious I got, the more I found myself longing to go back to last night, in my room in Egypt. For a few hours, we hadn't thought about any of this. We hadn't analyzed, we hadn't planned, we hadn't made decisions. It was the first time in a long time I'd felt anything but terrible.

Stellan glanced at me again. I wondered whether any part of him was thinking the same thing.

"So when did you find out about the virus?" I said.

Fitz shook his head. "I didn't. All I knew for certain at the point when the Saxons took me is what I've told you. It had crossed my mind before, what I'd do if something like that ever happened, and if you, Avery, were ever in danger. I had only minutes to implement that plan, though luckily I'd hidden the diary earlier, and I knew Avery had the necklace. You all took my decades of research and brought it to its end in record time."

"What about me?" Jack said quietly to Fitz.

Fitz turned his chair to face him. "You had nothing to do with it, Charlie." I'd forgotten that Fitz had actually called him that—it wasn't just made up for me. "You were around the age of my own grandchild, whose life I couldn't be a part of. As you got older, and you proved yourself to be smart and loyal, I grew attached to you like you were my own family. I found myself hoping that, one day, I'd be able to introduce you two." He took off his glasses and wiped them on his shirt. "You all came to me in different ways, but I consider all of you my grandchildren. And here you are: all together."

Jack held his phone in a stranglehold and stared at the table. Elodie looked at each of us in turn. Stellan laced his hands together, chewing his lip. There it was: all of our stories. I felt like in some way, we were all hoping for a miracle in our pasts that would make everything better, or a miracle from the Order to tell us what to do. We'd gotten neither.

Jack heaved a sigh and set down his phone. He met my eyes across the table with a tiny shrug, like he'd just been thinking the same things I had. I nodded. He turned to Fitz, and so did Elodie.

Almost unconsciously, I shifted closer to Stellan, and my foot twined around his ankle, just above his boot. He looked down. A few moments later, Jack and Fitz pushed back from the table and made their way to the railing. Elodie pulled out her phone.

The second no one was looking our way, Stellan murmured, "Are you *trying* to make it hard to concentrate?"

Hard to concentrate on the bad stuff? Yes, I guess I was. I shrugged. He smirked. A little of the hopelessness lifted. There were worse things than friends who flirted as stress relief.

"I'm being supportive. Like you were with petting my hair. I'm not sure how this is any different," I whispered, and then I thought of something. "Or is it? Does the thing with your blood—" I cut off. That was about to sound different from how I meant it.

"What?" He shifted closer, so my toes ran up his ankle.

"Never mind."

"Now you have to tell me."

Elodie's phone rang, and she stood to take the call. I watched her go. "I was just going to ask whether, besides making your scars hurt, the thing with your blood makes the rest of your skin more . . . sensitive? In a bad way *or* a good . . ."

I trailed off when I glanced over to see Stellan's eyebrows up at his hairline. He cleared his throat. "So you're *definitely* trying to make it harder to concentrate."

I elbowed him. "And that's why I wasn't going to—"

I was interrupted by Elodie rushing toward us.

"How long ago?" she was saying. "No. No, no, no. Get the doctor— well, have him do something *more*!" She yanked me to my feet, then said into the phone, "We're on our way."

Dread curdled my stomach. "What?" I stumbled after her.

"Luc," she said, pulling me down the stairs. "They've infected the whole Dauphin family."

CHAPTER 19

It's a trap," Jack said. Our boat was cruising as fast as the motor could take it back toward the Louvre. We'd thought about jumping out and getting a cab, but it wouldn't have been any faster.

"We know," Stellan said shortly. He would run through a wall of gunfire for Luc, and right now, our blood was killing him. Nothing was going to stop him from getting in there.

Monsieur Dauphin had collapsed immediately. He was dead. Luc and his mother weren't. We'd seen at the sites of the other attacks that there could be a few minutes' difference in how long it took people to get infected—we could only hope against hope we'd get there in time.

"The Saxons will have people outside," Elodie said. "They'll grab you. They'll grab Jack if they see him, too, because of Cole. It'll have to be me. Who has a water bottle?"

I pulled one out of my purse, and Elodie dumped the water over the side. "Give me some of your blood. I'll go in the front. You guys go in one of the side museum entrances. I doubt they have enough people to watch them all."

Elodie pricked the inside of my arm with her knife, and I let the red drops slide down the inside of the bottle.

We leapt off the boat before it had fully stopped and sprinted up the stairs to street level. Elodie ripped off her wig and stuffed it into her bag to throw the Saxon people off, and took off across the courtyard.

Stellan started to run across the street himself, but Jack grabbed his shirt. "Elodie has the blood. It'll be worse if they catch you two. Walk calmly. Blend in."

We joined a crowd of tourists crossing the street, and then Stellan steered us down one of the arms of the museum and to a service entrance, where a security guard stopped us. Stellan barked a few words in French, and surprised, he opened the door. Once we got inside, we dropped the pretense and ran, through a corridor of offices, some loading docks, and what looked like an art preservation lab. When we hit the Dauphins' suite of rooms, Stellan bounded ahead up the stairs, and Jack and I followed.

I burst into Luc's bedroom to find Stellan stopped short and Luc sitting on his bed, blinking at us, Elodie beside him.

I grabbed Stellan's arm, my legs going weak with relief. We weren't too late. Stellan ran across the room to kneel by Luc, speaking to him low in French.

Elodie got up. "I gave them both your blood." It had been less than ten minutes since we'd gotten the phone call. "Madame Dauphin is in the other room. They didn't infect the baby. I saw what I thought were a few Saxon guards outside. I got past them, and I told the Dauphin security to be on the lookout."

I let Stellan speak to Luc alone for a few minutes before I staggered across the room and dropped onto his bed. "Hello, *chérie*," he said, his eyes haunted, voice strained. "This is exciting, isn't it?"

"Luc, I'm so sorry—"

The door burst open. A woman who must have been the Dauphins' doctor, judging by the stethoscope around her neck, said something in frantic-sounding French. The whole room froze, then turned wide eyes on Luc.

"What?" I said. "What's going on?"

Elodie ran to us, dropping onto Luc's other side. "Madame Dauphin," she said. "She's dead."

We all crowded around Luc: the doctor, stethoscope in her ears, listening to his heart. Elodie clinging to his hand. Jack pacing at the foot of the bed, chewing a thumbnail. Stellan stood next to me, silent, rigid. I slipped my hand into his, and he squeezed it so tightly I winced. It had only been ten minutes since we'd heard that Madame Dauphin had died, but it felt like a lifetime.

"Why isn't the cure working?" Elodie barked at the frightened doctor. It was the third time she'd asked.

For the third time, the doctor stammered something in French that I could tell meant *I have no idea.*

Suddenly Luc blinked a few times fast, then swayed like he was dizzy. He caught himself before falling onto the bed, his eyes rolling back and slipping closed. We all froze.

"More blood," Elodie said, frantically grabbing for my arm.

"We must have missed something," Jack said. "Could Lydia have lied? Or could it be that you have to inject the cure rather than ingest it? Or—"

Luc coughed. Everyone went silent. We all knew what came after the coughing.

Stellan fell to his knees, his hand ripping from mine. "No," he whispered.

Elodie's hand clapped over her mouth, her face frozen in a mask of shock.

No, I echoed in my head. We'd *found* the cure. Please, please no—

Luc coughed again, harder this time, rattling in his chest. A sob escaped around Elodie's hand. I couldn't move. I couldn't breathe. I'd seen this a thousand times in my nightmares. I stared at Luc's slim, angular face, just waiting for blood to stream down his cheeks. For the next cough to be red.

His eyes fluttered, and I stared, horrified.

And then he blinked—and opened his eyes. He looked at Elodie and squinted, then pulled himself to sitting. He coughed again, and it turned into clearing his throat. He shook his head like he'd just woken up. "What happened?" he said.

He wasn't bleeding. That wasn't how this worked. Once any symptoms hit, it was over. It didn't ever reverse. Not in the cases we'd seen personally, and not in any of Nisha's research.

Something weird had happened to Luc—but it hadn't turned into the full force of the virus. He was alert now. *Alive.*

Somehow, the cure had worked for him when it hadn't for his mother, even though Luc had more Circle blood.

A sob tore out of Elodie's throat, and she threw herself on Luc. My legs were shaking, and only then did I realize Stellan was holding me against him as he kneeled, his arm around my waist. My knees gave out, and I fell into his lap on the hardwood floor.

He hadn't died. We hadn't killed Luc.

The door to the room burst open, and Colette came in, her voice frantic in French. She ran to Luc and Elodie soothed her, telling her what had happened. We all waited a few more minutes, making sure Luc didn't relapse, but he seemed to feel fine. We had no idea why. The din built as everyone threw out theories. It turned into a wall of noise until all I could hear was the rasping of my breaths and the shaking in Stellan's, his chest rising and falling against me. Neither of us was contributing to the conversation. It kept playing in my head—Luc's cough. The second his eyes cleared again. One of my hands had Stellan's wrist in a death grip, and his thumb was stroking mine. I turned to him, and the anguish on his face made my other hand clench in his shirt.

Luc was okay, but we weren't. The way I'd been feeling on the boat earlier washed back over me.

Luc cleared his throat. "Water?" he said.

"I'll get it," I heard myself say. My eyes didn't leave Stellan's.

I must have been telegraphing exactly what I was thinking, because he said, "I'll show you how to get to the kitchen."

We got to our feet and strolled out of the room and silently down the carpeted hallway.

As soon as the stairwell door shut behind us, plunging us into darkness cut only by the weak green light of the SORTIE sign, Stellan spun and pinned me to the wall. We hadn't said a word, but that made it even more explosive, setting a match to every nerve in my body at once.

This kiss was the opposite of sweet and careful. There wasn't enough of his mouth to keep mine happy, my hands couldn't find enough of his skin. It was the physical manifestation of panic and terror and relief so bone-deep it made us feverish and wild.

I didn't know what was wrong with us. This was an absurd thing to be doing.

I didn't care.

My head fell back against the wall and every rational thought—every worry I had wanted to forget earlier, every bit of the horror show of the past hour—fled my mind.

I came back to my senses some time later, when a breeze made me shiver. I was propped on the handrail, my legs locked around Stellan's waist. I pulled away and he gave me a dazed smile that was a world away from his earlier distress.

This was like a *drug*.

I shivered again and he rubbed my arms. "Cold?"

I looked down. My tank top was drooping off one of my shoulders, Stellan's hands warm on my skin. "Where'd my sweatshirt go?" I whispered. I looked over his shoulder to find it in a heap on the next landing down. "How . . . ?"

He shrugged and laughed, low and rough.

I blinked myself back to reality. I felt so much clearer, more alert. I'd been upset with myself about being distracted after Cannes, but *this* was the type of distraction that would help me concentrate and calm down and feel like a human being. That was helpful. "We should probably go back. Make sure everything's still okay."

"They would have let us know if it wasn't," Stellan said, but he dropped one last kiss on my lips and then set me back on the floor. I reached up to smooth his hair, and he loped down the stairs to grab my discarded hoodie. He held it out with a teasing eyebrow raise.

"Don't look at me like that," I whispered, shrugging it on. "You're the one who took it off me. *And* you're the one who told me to do something for stress-relief. This is as good a hobby as anything. A temporary hobby at that, if you're leaving."

If I hadn't been watching him closely, I might not have seen his face change. Just as quickly, he went back to normal. "I'm flattered you'd choose me over knitting," he whispered.

We ran down to the kitchen and grabbed an armload of water bottles. Maybe I hadn't really seen that pause. This whole time, Stellan and I had been a story for the Circle, and now we were a distraction for ourselves. That was what this was. It was not—

It *wasn't*. Not least because that wasn't something my heart could handle right now. The occasional instance of kissing-for-fun-and-stress-relief was one thing. *Liking* somebody was another, especially under these circumstances. Especially *him*. It wasn't that.

I made a point to walk a couple feet farther away from him than I otherwise would have.

When we got back to Luc's room, Elodie grabbed the water out of our arms with a frown. "I was starting to get worried you wandered into the clutches of the Saxons."

I was about to reply, but then I looked behind her and did a double take.

"Oh. Right. Rocco's here," Elodie said. "I'll explain in a minute."

Rocco was crouched by Luc's bed. Holding Luc's hand. Luc looked around self-consciously.

Elodie took the water to Luc, and Stellan and I were left gaping. "But Rocco had a thing with the Emirs' *daughter*," I whispered.

"And that means he couldn't be interested in Luc? How . . . limiting," Stellan whispered tightly. "That's not what confuses me about this situation."

"Remember when Luc was talking to Rocco without us and we all thought it was weird?" I whispered. Stellan nodded. Elodie gestured, and the two of us followed her to the balcony, where Jack was already waiting. We weren't far from the balcony of the room I'd stayed in when I first got to France. Below us, the Louvre courtyard and the Tuileries Gardens spread in either direction.

Stellan wouldn't take his eyes off Luc and Rocco just inside the French doors.

"Lucien only just told me on the phone last night," Elodie whispered. "It *wasn't* the Emirs' daughter Rocco had a relationship with after all. It was Malik."

Malik Emir had been the first to die in the string of assassinations the Saxons blamed on the Order. It had happened before I even knew the Circle existed. "Everyone thinks the Emir Keeper and their daughter got caught and Laila had to terminate him herself, right?" Elodie said. "That *is* what happened with Rocco and Malik—but Malik promised Rocco he'd let him escape. Rocco loved him, and he believed him. But Malik decided he couldn't let what happened between them get out for the sake of his reputation, and tried to kill him instead. Rocco fought back, and in the scuffle, Malik was accidentally killed. Rocco ran."

"That's where Rocco got the scar," I whispered.

Elodie nodded. "The Emirs covered it up, but the Circle was suspicious. The Saxons found Rocco somehow, learned the real story, and it seems like that was where they got the idea to commit these assassinations and blame them on the Order. The Circle was primed for it. For a while, Rocco thought the Saxons were good-guy vigilantes. It didn't take him long to realize he was wrong. And then we found him."

I stared at them through the glass doors.

A lot of things went through my head: Rocco had faced just as much tragedy as any of us. But was there any chance he could be using Luc? Could he hurt him if he got that close? And I realized suddenly why relationships between family members and staff were forbidden. And I also remembered how recently I was in that exact position.

I glanced up at Stellan, and he just shrugged. It'd be pretty hypocritical for us to police Rocco and Luc having a secret relationship, even if Rocco was working for us. "Okay?" I said.

Elodie sighed. "I told Lucien you'd be fine with it. I thought he was going to have a heart attack when he admitted it to me, but I reminded him that you two, of all people—"

"So what now?" I cut her off.

Elodie had spoken with the Dauphins' security, and they were tightening their safety measures around the Louvre. There would also be a lot to deal with regarding the Dauphins' deaths. We still had no idea why the cure had worked for Luc and not Madame Dauphin.

Jack leaned back on the railing. "About that. Earlier, Nisha told me more about what they've been researching. Seeing what happened with the cure, I had a thought. We never saw the original wording. We just know Lydia translated it as that your blood is the cure. But there are rather a lot of shades of the idea of remedy, or treatment. What if this one didn't mean antidote, like she thought? What if it was . . . *vaccine*?"

The idea rolled around in my head. It only took a second for it to make sense. "Nisha said my blood is the one that has the virus, and Stellan's just makes it replicate out of control. So that could make sense. Aren't a lot of vaccines essentially a mild version of the disease to prime the body against it?"

Elodie was nodding along. She pulled us inside and we shared the theory.

"Avery, have you been putting your blood in my food?" Luc said. It was a little too bright, a little too fake-cheerful. Considering his had just parents died, then he'd nearly died himself, I was shocked he was doing this well.

Wait. His *parents*. Monsieur Dauphin. What I would always associate with him was—

"The wedding," I said. Luc raised his eyebrows. "When we were supposed to be married. Part of the ceremony was cutting our hands and putting them together, remember? You had my blood all over you. If you accidentally wiped your face, or put your own cut into your mouth, you could have ingested it."

Stellan was pacing at the end of the bed, wearing a path on the hardwood floor. "But Elodie was infected—"

"Maybe I was never infected at all," Elodie said. "I could have actually been coughing from dust. I'll have the doctor examine me and see what she thinks."

"What about your mother?" Stellan asked me. "If your blood is a vaccine—"

Wouldn't I have vaccinated her at some point, too? But I shook my head. "Before I met you guys, I was not covered in blood nearly as often as I am now. If my mom was ever cleaning up a cut for me, I'm sure she would have washed her hands immediately after, and it never would have—"

I had to stop before that train of thought went too far, or I'd panic again.

"If it's really a vaccine, would Luc have gotten slightly sick like he did?" Stellan said, still testing the theory.

"Sometimes you can get a vaccine for say, the chickenpox, and still get a mild version of the chickenpox, right?" Elodie said. "And it's not like this virus is normal anyway. Something kept Lucien from dying. That's the important part. We should get Nisha to start testing it. If it really is a vaccine, we could get it to the Circle. That might even clear our names, and get them to help us against the Saxons. I'll call her right now."

An hour later, we'd done all we could for Luc, and left him to handle family things. As I set the table, my thoughts tried to wander. I wasn't the one who deserved to be upset right now, but being around this much death—

A shiver passed through me. I really was feeling calmer after that little stairwell rendezvous earlier, or I wasn't sure I'd be okay. Now I was helping Colette assemble some snacks in one of the Dauphins' sitting rooms so we could eat and make a plan about where to go from here.

Elodie came into the room. "Happy news," she said, spreading her arms. "The doctor says I have bronchitis."

I let her take a cookie from my hand. "Are you kidding me? That's why you've been coughing?"

"I'm supposed to drink lots of fluids and take some cough syrup. She said it's relatively common in the month after the kind of surgery one gets from being shot in the abdomen, but I swear, it was that bus. Traveling with the masses could kill a person."

Colette snorted, and handed me a bowl of fruit I was just setting down when my phone rang. I grabbed it out of my bag, checked the number, frowned. Why was Stellan calling me? Colette had sent him to get coffee mugs just a couple of minutes ago.

The door swung open and he walked into the room.

That's when I remembered. "Your phone," I told him, showing him my screen. "Maybe Mariam found it."

"Answer it," he said, setting the mugs on the table.

I picked up. "Hello, sister," said a girl's voice on the other end.

It took me a second longer than it should have. "How do you have this phone?" I said to Lydia. I put the phone on speaker.

"I found it in the tunnels in Alexandria." Lydia's voice sounded entirely too light. Singsong. Creepy. She was up to something. I'd worry she was tracing the call, but she knew where we were already. "I was disappointed, though. There aren't even sexy text messages on here. How boring you and your *husband* are."

Stellan pulled out the chair next to me and sat. The whole room was listening now.

"So, have you saved the lives of the poor Dauphin family yet?" She didn't know that the cure didn't work. Stellan and Elodie both glanced down the hall to where Luc was, like Lydia might have someone here waiting to kill him.

"I knew there was a chance you'd avoid my people there, you know," Lydia went on.

My throat tightened. "What do you mean by that?"

"When are you going to understand that I am always one step ahead of you? Finding this phone proved very useful. Say hello, love."

Away from the phone, there was a whimper, then a little girl's cry of pain.

Stellan jumped up so fast his chair fell over. He ripped the phone out of my hand. "Get your hands off my sister!" he roared.

"Too late!" Lydia chirped. "I have this adorable little girl with me now, and you'll only get her back if you do exactly what I want you to do."

Stellan yelled something in Russian. Jack and Luc and Rocco ran into the room, alarmed.

I grabbed the phone back. "You crazy bitch. She's a little kid."

"All I want is you, Avery. You and that boy of yours. Is it really worth all these people you supposedly care about getting hurt? Come alone—just you two. I'll know if you try any of your little tricks. I'm in his hometown. *Ciao*."

She hung up. Stellan was staring at the phone, frozen. Then he blinked half a dozen times, and flipped the table. I recoiled, avoiding a flying loaf of bread. A jar of jam shattered, throwing sticky bits of glass everywhere, and a puddle of coffee spread across the hardwood.

Stellan walked straight over the mess, his boots leaving a sticky red trail, and ripped his arm away when Elodie touched him, his hands on top of his head like he was trying to physically hold himself together.

"The virus and the cure," Elodie murmured. "If they thought they had both, they'd be unstoppable. If they have you—"

I nodded, watching Stellan pace in the hallway, then storm back inside. Jack approached and Stellan tried to throw him off, but Jack shoved him against the wall. He got in Stellan's face, murmuring something low and intense. Finally, Stellan stopped struggling. After a few more seconds, he grabbed Jack's shoulders, touched their foreheads together, and crossed the room to right the table he'd flipped over.

Colette was standing hesitantly over the mess of food, watching him. Elodie approached cautiously. "You can't go there. At the very least, she'll take your blood and lock you up. Or kill you, since there are probably others of the thirteenth bloodline out there who wouldn't give her so much trouble."

Jack nodded.

"The Order will help you," Elodie said. "We can send in a team."

They were right, of course.

Stellan set a block of cheese back on the table, then the empty metal coffee pitcher. "No," he said. "I'm going. Alone. It's the only way to save her."

I crouched by him and picked up pieces of glass. We *should* let the Order go. Even if it meant Anya might die, which would be very possible if we didn't obey Lydia's orders. One little girl's life for the Circle? Maybe the world? It shouldn't be a question. Just like it shouldn't have been a question that *my* life wasn't worth the potential for the destruction it could cause. There were so many *should*s.

Stellan and I locked eyes in the late-afternoon light. All the same things passed between us that had earlier this afternoon on the boat, and in Mariam's van in Alexandria, and in my room in Egypt. Whatever this meant, whatever *we* meant, however this ended up, we were on the same side now, for better or worse. "Not alone," I said. "I'm going, too."

CHAPTER 20

A few hours later, we were on the Dauphins' plane. I'd left lots of vials of my blood for the scientists to research the vaccine while we were gone. So someone would *have* the vaccine, just in case the worst happened in Russia. But I had to believe we'd be okay. We had a plan—to get Anya back, but maybe something more, too. Jack had come up with a way for us to take advantage of a terrible situation.

Stellan was wearing a path from window to window. Even when we hit turbulence on the approach to landing, he kept pacing, looking out the window, blazing as bright as the sunset outside. The flirty, half-broken boy was gone. In his place was the version of Stellan who could tear a person in two without blinking. I kept having to remind myself that he contained both those things.

When we hit a particularly rough patch of air, he looked down to find me watching him, and slowed. "I'm sorry," he said gruffly. "I'm scaring you."

"No," I said. On the contrary, the glimpse of how he looked when he loosened his grip on his usual restraint—I hadn't been able to stop watching him. He would do anything for the people he loved.

Just like Lydia Saxon would. In his hands, though, I knew that power might burn hot, but it would never turn ugly.

I was right all along. Power *was* a knife edge: wanting it, coveting it, getting it.

Longing was a knife edge. The ache for power, for family, for love.

I heard Stellan's voice that night at the bar in Cannes. *You want to be wanted. You want control. Say it.*

I had. I'd wanted it. I'd wanted him. All of it—the power, the wanting, the fact that he'd been the one who had seen that in me—it swirled together into this *thing* I still felt when I was around him. It was the same reason I felt so comfortable telling him things I'd never tell anyone else.

Stellan walked back and forth, back and forth. I scooted over to one side of the love seat, deliberately. He hesitated, then sat. I held out my hand. He took it.

For a second, I was back in the Dauphins' stairwell, tangled up in him. We'd already made our plans; it would be easy to give in to that pull again right now, allow us a few minutes of respite from thinking. From *feeling*. Turn to him, kiss him, touch him—that's what would make sense to do right now in this friends-with-benefits arrangement we seemed to be cultivating.

But I didn't. I held his hand tight the rest of the flight. I kept holding on as we touched down on the tarmac. And then, together, we walked down the stairs to his hometown.

It was abandoned.

Stellan told me he'd grown up in a suburb of the city Elodie had mentioned. He hadn't been back here in nearly a decade, and he didn't know it had become a ghost town.

The car we were in had to drop us at the end of the street because there was too much debris to drive farther. None of the streetlights worked, but the moon was almost full and bright enough to see everything. What looked like construction materials were scattered everywhere, and bushes grew up through cracks in the street, the only spots of life in an otherwise bleak landscape. The paint on all the buildings was peeling like burned skin, most windows broken out and glass scattered over the street. We stepped over a graying pink teddy bear with little sprigs of green growing out of its eye sockets, and I felt Stellan shudder.

I gripped his hand tighter. We passed a church, spires reaching to the cloudy sky and topped with domes oxidized to green, and then we saw it. There were footsteps in the thick layer of dust. Recent ones, judging by how little dirt had settled back into them.

Stellan stopped still, staring at the footsteps' path. "I thought that might be where she'd go."

He set off jogging down the street. I caught up. "Where?"

"My old apartment building. And if I'm right, that means she knew where that was. Which might mean—"

Which might mean the Saxons were the ones who had set the fires that killed his and Elodie's families, too.

The footprints in the dirt outside the apartment complex told us we were right. We turned on the flashlights on our phones.

"Whatever you do, don't leave my side," Stellan said. "What she wants is to capture us. You, particularly."

"I know."

"If she tries to take you, I'll kill her."

I stared at the foot-tall weeds growing through cracks in the asphalt and felt the weight of my gun in my hand. "I know. If she touches you, *I'll* kill her."

He glanced at me sideways. "I know."

The front door to the complex hung heavy on its hinges, and Stellan gave it a push. It opened into a small lobby with a broken tile floor, a narrow staircase, and a bank of mailboxes covered in what looked like a decade of dust. From either side, a hallway faded into darkness. The dust on the floor was disturbed in every direction, so we couldn't tell which way she'd gone.

We crept to the stairs, and I looked up to see them winding around and around. Down here the stairwell was nearly pitch-black, but it got lighter as they went higher. There was a wrongness to it I couldn't place. I saw a tremor go through Stellan, but we crept up the stairs. Three flights up, I saw where the light was coming from. Off the stairway landing, the building's front was normal and intact, but the back had been charred to nothing, letting the moonlight in.

I knew where Stellan had to be leading us. His family's apartment. There was more left of this floor—the hallway was still here, and some of the apartments still had their doors, and even parts of walls. Many of them, though, opened straight into the night, that ghostly silver light filtering in.

Stellan stopped in front of one with no door at all, glanced behind us, then tiptoed inside, his gun drawn.

The room was nothing more than a blackened box. The wall between it and the next apartment over was partially intact, but the outside wall was gone, and the top branches of a tree outside had woven their way in, its leaves snapping in the breeze.

Stellan stood frozen in the doorway. It was eerily quiet, but Lydia's voice echoed in my head. Always one step ahead. And to do that, she preyed on our weaknesses. She knew Stellan wouldn't risk Anya. Apparently she knew before I did that I wouldn't let him come alone.

She didn't know that she had a weakness, too, even now that Cole was dead. She didn't know we'd exploit it. We just had to get through this.

I rested my hand on Stellan's forearm. "She brought you here because she knew it would bother you," I murmured.

He nodded hard and kept going. The next room was slightly less burned. In the corner I could make out what looked like an armchair, facing a huge box of a TV on a dresser. Closer, a charred baby's crib, covered in bright green moss, half the wall between the rooms collapsed over it. The far half of the room was gone. It was like time had stopped the night of the fire, leaving everything in this building untouched.

Stellan whispered something in Russian that could have been a curse or a prayer. We picked our way over burned debris into a bathroom where inches of brackish water sat in an unburned claw-foot tub, and exposed electrical wires rained from the ceiling.

"She's not here," he said under his breath. "She has to be here." Then, "Lydia!" he shouted.

So much for trying to sneak up on her. I grabbed him, his face in my hands. He tried to push past me, and I shook him, like he'd done to me at the border crossing. "Stop," I ordered in a whisper. "She's doing this on purpose to make you panic so you'll make a mistake."

His eyes flicked from me, to the door, to me. "Okay, yes. I'm—"

Finally, there was a sound. But it wasn't my sister. It was his.

Stellan's whole body tensed. He shook my hands off. "Anya!" he yelled.

The scream came again, its echo bouncing against Stellan's voice.

Stellan took off running. "Lydia!" he bellowed.

I chased him until he came to a sudden halt in a dim vestibule. Another set of stairs led down in one direction and up in the other, where otherworldly light filtered inside. I could see Stellan shaking with the effort to hold himself back, but he waited for me and gestured: *up or down?* Anya screamed again, and both our heads shot up.

Halfway up the stairs, everything went to hell.

There was a bang, and the wall next to me exploded. Stellan ducked, yanking me with him. I hit the filthy stairs on my hands and knees, looking up to see four shadows on the landing above us. We knew Lydia likely wouldn't have a huge security force with her.

Stellan plowed forward into them. He grabbed one, throwing him over the banister. He hit the ground two stories below with a thud, and didn't move. Stellan grappled with the second one, holding his body between himself and the third, who looked frantically for a clear shot, and a fourth, in a black baseball cap, who hung back. I hoped Stellan remembered the plan in his current state.

Anya's voice rang out again in frantic Russian.

"Lydia!" Stellan bellowed. "Let her go!"

I hunkered against the wall, waiting for an opening where I might be able to help, but Stellan didn't need it. He snapped the neck of the guy he was holding with a quick twist. As he yelled a string of something in Russian—calling to Anya or cursing at the men, I wasn't sure—he shoved the body into the third guy and, grabbing the barrel of his gun, wrenched it from his hands and smacked him in the head with the butt of it, felling him immediately.

I jumped up and grabbed the back of his shirt before he could attack the fourth guy. He was wearing a black baseball cap with a bandana under it, just like Rocco had said he would be.

While we were in the air, Rocco had been communicating with the one member of Lydia's team he trusted. We couldn't be certain of his loyalty, but it was the best chance we had. Now he dropped his gun to his side and raised his folded hands to his forehead in the Circle's gesture of respect. "Omar?" I mouthed. He nodded. "Are there any more with you?" I whispered. He shook his head.

"Lydia!" I yelled. "All your guys are dead. Give us Anya and we'll let you live."

She didn't answer. I pushed on with the plan, still holding on to Stellan. He was barely holding back from charging up the stairs right now. I pulled my phone out of my pocket and flipped on the recorder. "What is this even about, Lydia?" I called. She didn't answer. We crept slowly up the stairs. "You kidnapped Stellan's sister to get us here for our blood. That I understand. But I still don't understand why you're doing any of it." Still nothing. I went on, "Why attack the Circle, first with all those assassinations, then with the virus? Why blame it on us? Is it all really just for power?"

"If you say it in that way—*just* power—you still don't get it," she finally called back. I could tell by her voice that she was still a couple of flights above us.

I gestured to Omar, pointing him to the end of the hall, where we'd seen another stairwell.

"Why, then? Why do you think you deserve to be the ones to rule the Circle?"

"God, Avery. You've never even tried to understand," she spat. "We're the only ones who aren't afraid to do what we have to to keep our family, our country, the *Circle* safe. We're going to make the Circle great again, like we used to be, with our family at its head. It's not about power at all. It's about family. Our family. Your family, too, if you'd actually ever cared about your family."

We were getting closer to her. I held up the phone, wanting to capture everything she said. "It turns out I don't believe in sacrificing other people's families for my own family's gain," I yelled.

"That's where you and I will always be different," she said.

Stellan growled like a feral animal. I knew that was the last straw, and we had what we needed. I let go of him, and he took off up the stairs.

When I caught up, he was on a circular landing. This floor was different. Here, too, one side of the building was gone, but the other led to what looked like a bathhouse, with sinks along one side and small rooms to the other.

Stellan ran to the first door on the left hallway. When he turned the knob and found it locked, he yelled something in Russian and slammed his gun into the window that took up most of the door, shattering the frosted glass. Nothing. He ran to the next, and the next, smashing it. "Stop," I called, running after him. "She's not here."

"There is no *stop*," he roared, and smashed not his gun but a bare fist through the last door. He turned, blood dripping from his hand. "Lydia!"

Where was she? We were at the top of the building. Through the collapsed wall, I could out see over the ghost town below.

Stellan ran down the only place still left to go—the hallway—and I had no choice but to follow. I held my gun ready, praying Omar had made it here to back us up.

The hall dropped us in a small wooden room. A sauna. It smelled like rot and something sickly sweet. Stellan coughed. "Lydia—" he said, and coughed again. And then I coughed.

"Get out of here," I said. "Mold. Or something—"

Suddenly, I felt the floor dip beneath me.

I stumbled.

She's knocking down the building, I thought. *That* was her final play. She'd trap us—but the walls were moving, too. Not falling, just bowing inward, rolling.

I swayed. Stellan's footsteps running across the floor, his face in mine. My legs collapsed, and he caught me.

"Avery," he called, from far away. His blind rage had blinked off, just like that. He was terrified. For *me*. My head spun.

"Kuklachka." His voice dragged my mind back. I tried to stand. I couldn't stand.

Another jolt. Stellan shaking his head, blinking. The floor coming up to meet us as he collapsed, too.

She's drugged us, said a small, confused voice in the back of my mind. *The virus? No. Some other drug. That's why she brought so few people with her, because she knew she had this. One step ahead—* And then, *She'll only capture me. She'll kill Stellan.* Everything in me shattered into panic. In my head, he had a bullet through his heart. In my head, blood was streaming down his face, just like my mom's. *Get up,* I shouted to him, but only inside my head. *Run. Leave me here. If you're not okay, I don't know if I can—*

And then Stellan and I were lying on the floor staring into each other's eyes, but I didn't know why. There was something I should do say think his eyes were so blue, blue with gold and that meant something, I knew it, but now I only wanted to touch his face. My hands wouldn't move.

He blinked, trying to talk, but it was a wisp I couldn't catch. Just his eyes, his eyes watching me fall, like his heart was being ripped out. Mine too. He'd always understood me so well, I felt like he had one hand inside my chest.

I looked down. He *did*.

We were standing in a bright room, bursts of candy pink and lime green and electric blue and orange. Vines growing on the walls, dust and sunlight, moss and the thick, rich scent of mint and honey.

Stellan had his fingers curled around my heart, still throbbing, dark blood dripping from his fingers to the floor, a gaping hole in my chest. He looked at it like it was something beautiful, precious. And I—

I had his. Cradled in my two palms, warm, raw, just pulled out of his chest. "No," I whispered, to him, to me, to both. "Put it back." I couldn't be responsible for this. It was too much. And I couldn't trust someone else to hold my heart in their hands either, not after everything. It had been broken and patched together too many times; it was too fragile now. But I'd let him, hadn't I? I remembered now. I'd let him hold it. *Given* it to him, even. And he'd given me his. It pulsed in my hands, *beat beat beat,* all color and warmth and life.

"No," I said again. He looked up at me, all blue eyes and dappled sunlight. *I can't lose you. You have part of me in your hands, and you will take it with you. The best thing is to put it back.*

Please. Put it back.

I thought it was warm in here, but I was getting cold. "Put it back," I whimpered again.

There was a sharp intake of breath, and a jolt. I was blinking up not at the warm filtered light of the room with the vines, but at the night sky, and Stellan's face. "Put it back," I murmured again, shivering.

"Kuklachka," he said. I felt him set me down and lean over me. He was running his hands over my face, my hair. I reached up to cup his jaw, felt the scratch of stubble under my fingers. That warm room. Where were we? A name broke through the fog. "Anya," I said, my voice cracking.

"Omar," he answered, and I knew that was good.

And then I was awake, and I was sure of it because my head hurt, and my throat hurt. She'd drugged us. It had been a dream. Or a hallucination. My heart in his hands. I wanted to put it back in, sew us both up, pretend it hadn't happened. It was written all over his face here in the real world that he thought I wasn't okay and that his heart *had* been carved out just now. Mine had been, too, thinking Lydia could have caught him. He gathered me against him and pressed his forehead to mine, and we held each other, warm and alive, my lashes blinking against his cheekbones, while the stars spun overhead.

I can't feel this way about you, said the voice inside my head, admitting it even to myself for the first time.

"I can't *not* feel this way about you," he answered. "I've tried so hard."

Had I said that out loud?

A shout, and Stellan looked up. "I knew she'd follow *us,*" he said. "I sent Omar with Anya in the other direction."

I sat, unsteadily, then tried to get to my feet. The edges of my vision fuzzed again, and then there was nothing.

The next time I opened my eyes, I knew where we were. The plane. I was on a couch and Stellan was on the one across from me, watching me openly. A little blond girl slept curled in his arms. The roar of the engines and a slight shake told me we were already in the air. Safe. Away.

Stellan was still staring, like he wasn't quite sure if I was really awake. When I blinked a few times and lifted my head, he closed his eyes and murmured something under his breath.

I sat up, and he leaned forward. "Be careful. You might still be—"

Anya whimpered, and he cut off.

I stood, gingerly, and grabbed the edge of the couch when a wave of dizziness hit. My bag was still across my chest, and I dug out contact drops.

"Are you—" he said, but his sister made another noise and he got quiet, looking down at her like he was cradling a poisonous snake instead of a skinny blond child with bandaged knees sticking out from under a dirty blue dress.

He didn't know what to do with her, I realized. Even the way he held her wasn't familiar, but stiff and awkward. I was surprised at first, but then I realized. He'd spent his whole life protecting Anya, but none of that time actually being her brother. He probably didn't know much more about kids than any of us did.

He glanced up at me, back to Anya again, like one or the other of us might disappear. I felt suddenly self-conscious. I looked down at my hands, expecting them to be coated in blood. It was a dream, I reminded myself. A hallucination, and an especially melodramatic one at that. Was the rest of it a dream? Had I really woken up outside, staring at the sky?

Then everything that had happened before we'd been drugged finally broke through the fog. "Lydia?"

"She got aw—" Stellan whispered. Anya stirred again, and he got quiet. "She got away," he mouthed.

So Lydia was still alive. I wasn't sure how I felt about that. "Omar?" I mouthed back.

He nodded to the back of the plane. We were bringing Omar with us, because it wasn't like he could go back to Lydia. So it had worked. We'd planned to lure her to us, and Omar would take Anya as far away as he could before she figured it out. Us being knocked out was a wrench in the plan, but Stellan must have woken up faster than she'd anticipated.

I stole a glance at him, and the too-open way he was watching me made my pulse stumble. Had we really said those things, or was that in the dream, too? If we had, did it count?

I hugged my arms around myself, and when I touched my shoulder, it hurt more than usual. I looked down. There was a new bandage on it.

I looked up at Stellan quizzically. He cut his eyes to the bar counter, where a first aid kit lay open. I still didn't get it until I peeked under the bandage and saw a fresh slash across the healing bullet wound. And then I noticed a small puncture in the crook of my elbow, like there had been a needle there. She'd taken our blood while we were passed out—both in the medical way that made more sense and by slicing us open, just to be mean. She'd probably taken a lot. That's why I was so dizzy.

Stellan turned a tiny bit to show me his back. His shirt was soaked through with blood. I crossed the cabin, and he winced when I pulled on his collar to find a slash across his back, too.

Even with his scared little sister to take care of, even with his own wounds, Stellan had bandaged me up.

I stared down at his back, covered in blood. *If she tries to take you, I'll kill her,* his voice said in my head. And, *You make me feel too many things.*

I let out a long breath, then crossed to the bar and felt Stellan's eyes on me as I gathered up the bandages and wet a bar towel with warm water. I brought them to the couch. He hesitated, then shifted enough that I could reach his back.

I tried to reach down his collar, but the wound was too hard to get to, so I tugged on the hem of his bloody shirt.

He cautiously extracted one arm from under his sister. Anya's hair was stick-straight and pale blond, with one tiny braid woven through it. Through the blond wisps across her face, I could see scars just like Stellan's, stark even against her pale cheek.

I pulled at his T-shirt, working it off over his free arm with his help, and then over his head. He shook his hair out, and I let the shirt drape over his opposite shoulder.

When I could finally see his whole back, my breath caught. Lydia had cut him right across his scars.

He glanced back at me quizzically. I picked up the towel and cleaned the area as gently as I could, careful not to get his blood near my own cuts, just in case. I might not even need to do this. He healed so quickly. But I wanted to. Everyone should have somebody to put them back together when they need it.

Maybe that was why I couldn't stop feeling like I did about him. Maybe two broken people who put each other back together over and over made one whole. Because that's what it felt like sometimes. Like all we did was patch each other up.

I patted some antibacterial spray on the wound and spread a line of bandages over it, then picked the towel back up to clean off more of the blood. Instead, I found myself staring at his back. The scars, the two tattoos—the Dauphin sun at the base of his neck, and a sword running all the way down his spine. I touched the hilt of the sword, between his shoulder blades, with the very tips of my fingers.

I knew the muscles under my fingers weren't from hours spent in the gym. They were from the same places his scars were. From fights, from running, from wins and losses.

I walked my fingers down the tattoo, gently. Stellan tensed.

How much must it have hurt to have gotten this done over the scars? And what did it mean? He wasn't Jack. He didn't *like* being a Keeper. Why he had gone to this much trouble and pain to have a weapon tattooed onto him?

I remembered something he'd said when we'd just met, right after he'd stabbed the man who had tried to kill me on the Prada floor. *It takes more effort to kill with a dagger. You have to do it on purpose. Guns make it too easy.*

Maybe that's what this was. It was something that was his, not theirs. A personal rebellion against the Circle, and against his own pain.

I tried to stop myself. I *tried*. But despite my best intentions, I touched my fingers to my lips and pressed them to his back.

I could see the side of his face. His eyes had fallen closed, and now they fluttered open.

"We are both," he breathed. "Destruction. Salvation. Both."

I'm in love with you, answered a voice inside my head.

I stumbled back a step.

He looked over his shoulder, brows creased. I could only stare at him, dumbly. The thought had short-circuited my brain. Oh God. I was in love with him.

I'd barely let myself consider whether this could be a little more than just kissing, but just *a little more* was never going to happen. I'd probably skipped over that long ago. Now it seemed so obvious. This was why shutting Stellan out after my mom died had felt so terrible, and why having him back in my life now felt right. He had become my best friend, my confidant. He calmed me down and made me better, and I also wanted to make out with him all the time. What did I *think* that meant?

I was in love with Stellan.

"*Kuklachka,*" he whispered, because I was still staring at him, the dark circles under his eyes in that too-pretty face from too little sleep and too much worry, the small, concerned crease in his forehead. "Are you okay?"

I nodded hard, because what else was there to do? No, I was not okay. *I can't feel this way about you* suddenly meant so much more.

After we do what we have to do, you could leave suddenly meant so much more.

Confusion danced across his face. For once, he couldn't tell what I was thinking. He reached for my hand. "Come here," he mouthed.

I looked down at the towel in my hand, not finished yet. "Please," he breathed.

He scooted carefully down the couch and I climbed up, tucking my feet under me and letting him gather me against him with his free arm. I tucked my head against his chest. I could hear the steady beat of his heart, smell sharp, coppery blood on his skin.

Anya startled, but settled back down with a whimper, curling into a ball so her little blond head rested against *my* shoulder. I heard the tiniest catch of Stellan's breath, enough to tell me he'd noticed, small enough to tell me he was pretending not to care. He pressed his face into my hair. Our breaths mingled with Anya's slow, even, sleeping ones, and a few minutes later, when Stellan's cheek touched my forehead, it was wet.

CHAPTER 21

From the plane, we'd sent the recording I'd made of Lydia to Elodie and Jack. Within an hour, the whole Circle had heard it. Some families said that we'd fabricated it. Some were calling for the Saxons' heads. It felt like we were back to where we were just before the initiation, but that was a vast improvement. Even if the Saxons did now have the virus and what they thought was the cure, if enough of the Circle believed us and started paying attention to where the threat was really coming from, we might be able to stop them.

Anya was sitting at the far window of the car, her face buried in a stuffed gray-and-pink mouse we'd bought at the airport and her hand in her brother's. I was trying not to stare at her—she had been an abstract idea for so long, and now here she was in the flesh, looking like a regular, overwhelmed seven-year-old girl. She didn't speak any English, but I'd been giving her encouraging smiles since she woke up. All she'd done was stare at me, her huge blue eyes with a gold ring around them exactly like Stellan's.

For his part, I kept catching him watching me, curious and thoughtful, like I was something to unlock and he didn't have quite the right key. He was sitting in the middle, his long legs splayed to fit in the small backseat. I was far too aware of the spot where his thigh rested against mine, of the roughness of his hand when he touched my arm to show me that the entire area around the Eiffel Tower had been cordoned off, police surrounding it.

I loved him. *I love you*, I said experimentally in my head. Oh God.

I hadn't thought it would be possible. I was too scared of caring, way too scared of losing, especially now, when losing him was such a real possibility. And no matter what, there was no way I could feel this strongly about *Stellan*. Because I used to date his ex–best friend. Because he wasn't the kind of guy I should go for. Because while I was thinking about his tongue in my mouth, my mom died. Because we were supposed to be married. Because we were the end of the world.

Apparently none of that mattered.

All this time, I'd been telling him I was okay with him leaving me behind. That he *should*. And I was right. I glanced over at Anya again, the scars crossing her delicate face a testament to how hard a life she'd lived already. She didn't deserve to be forced into the world of the Circle now.

I knew then that I couldn't tell Stellan how I felt. *Take care of each other. Take care of each other.* It echoed in my head. It wasn't like I thought he was in love with me, too, but I knew he did care about me. Anything I told him would just make him feel even more guilty about leaving when the time came. Better to let him believe I was happy with our temporary "hobby."

My phone rang. I forced my attention back to the present. "Hi, Lydia," I said, unsurprised.

"I have your blood." I wasn't sure whether I should be more worried or less at how calm she sounded. "Plenty of it."

"The Circle knows what you did," I countered, unable to keep the triumph out of my voice.

"And some of them even believe it," Lydia said.

"We've won, Lydia," Stellan cut in. "We'll make the rest of the Circle believe us now that we have you on tape. They will no longer let you get away with this." I hoped that was true.

"Hello, Avery's fake husband—but maybe real boyfriend?" Lydia mused. "There has to be some reason you'd risk your life for his sister. Poor Jack. How does he feel about being relegated to third wheel?"

"What do you want, Lydia?" I said, avoiding Stellan's gaze. We drove over the river. The Paris streets were even more empty than yesterday, only a scattering of people waiting to cross at the light in front of Notre-Dame.

"You're welcome for not hurting your sister, Avery's boyfriend. I'm not the monster *my* sister says I am."

I don't know what I'd expected Stellan to say, but it wasn't a quiet "Thank you."

"So I'm calling to tell you," Lydia said, "that this is your fault. Things were going to be fine, but by turning the Circle on us, you've ruined everything. Now I have to clean it up, and that annoys me. I hate having to resort to threats. It's so crass."

"Threats?" I said. Anya whimpered and pulled her hand away. Stellan must have squeezed it.

Lydia sighed. "The only way to ensure our family's safety—and therefore the whole *Circle's*, like I tried to tell you—is to have the Circle behind us. They were getting there rather well on their own, but now that's changed and we've got to give it a push. Since we know this virus infects anyone with a trace of Circle blood, we could wipe out half a city with a snap of our fingers. And the Circle knows it. So now, if they don't cooperate, their people pay."

Stellan made a strangled noise. "Lydia—" I said.

"The Circle will see eventually that this was the only way. They'll thank us. But until then, you've made us be the bad guys, and I really wish you hadn't."

"Lydia! You don't have to—"

"Good-bye, Avery."

"How are they doing it?" I said the second we reunited with Jack and Elodie. I tossed my bag onto the table in the Dauphins' sitting room and threw myself into a chair.

The Saxons had made their threat to the Circle. Bow to their authority, or have your territory obliterated by the virus. So much as a hint of interference from us or anyone else and they'd pull the trigger immediately.

"I suppose they'll make up some kind of treaty that everyone will have to sign, giving them full control over the Circle. They've called a meeting for tomorrow evening, giving the families a day to get everything together. They haven't said where the meeting is yet, except that it's somewhere in Europe," Elodie finished before I could ask.

"There's no way the Circle will sign that," I said. The Circle only cared about the Circle. About their own family, in particular, and their power. They wouldn't give it up to save the lives of regular civilians.

No one argued with me.

I squinted at the morning sun through the window. We'd been in Russia and flying all through the night. At least we'd gotten a few hours of sleep on the plane. I rubbed my forehead. I couldn't stop thinking about talking to Lydia. How does a girl—someone so much like me—turn into this?

Stellan came back into the room. The Dauphins' nanny was still here, caring for Luc's orphaned baby brother, and Stellan had taken a few minutes to get his sister set up in another one of the rooms in the nursery.

"So if we can't stop the release of the virus," I said, "we'll have to stop the virus from killing people. We have the vaccine. How fast can we get it out?"

While we were in Russia, the science team had confirmed that the theory about my blood being a vaccine was true.

"The problem is scale," Elodie said. "Because of its regenerative properties, a single drop of the virus diluted in millions of gallons of liquid would still be lethal."

"Like if they were to put it in a city's water supply," I said.

Elodie nodded. "Or aerosolize it. For the vaccine, though? It takes a drop of your blood per *person*. Even if we drained you dry, it wouldn't be enough to vaccinate a single Paris neighborhood, much less the whole world."

I pushed up my sleeves. It suddenly felt way too hot in here.

"Um, excuse me." We turned to find Nisha standing in the doorway. She and the entire science team had been based at the Order headquarters here in Paris, but while Stellan and I were gone, Elodie had moved them to the Dauphins' so we'd all be in one place. "I'm sorry to interrupt. We have an idea."

The lab tables and microscopes looked out of place in the Dauphins' ornate dining rooms. On one of the tables, Nisha and the rest of the scientists were crowded around a Plexiglas box with a tiny white mouse sniffing at its corners. I leaned down and touched my finger to the glass. The little mouse nosed at it.

"As you know, we had been attempting to deactivate the virus," Nisha said in her soft accent as we gathered around, "but that has proved impossible so far—and now that the Saxons have your blood, that avenue is closed for the moment anyway. When we learned the cure was really a vaccine, though, we wondered whether we could use the same mechanism of the Great modification in Mr. Korolev's blood to make the vaccine more effective. It looks promising."

Elodie twisted one of her small gold earrings. "Promising how?"

"We are using the Great modification in a specific way to make only the right parts of the mouse's cells replicate quickly."

Elodie was the first to understand. "I thought you were experimenting with altering Avery's blood. Like, in a vial."

"Unfortunately," Nisha said steadily, "it would be impossible to modify the blood once it's already *outside* the body."

All the curtains were drawn, and it was dim enough that it could have been any time of day as we looked at each other over the makeshift chemistry lab. "I don't understand," Stellan said. "You said my blood takes the tiny bit of virus in her blood and multiplies it so fast it becomes deadly. Wouldn't this just trigger that same process inside her?"

"We'd be using what we've learned about the modification, not necessarily your blood, as it were. And we are attempting to isolate certain parts of the cells. Small distinctions, but important. The hope is that it will affect only the amount of *vaccine* in the blood, and not turn into the virus and kill . . . the mouse."

I felt everyone's gaze on me.

"No." Stellan stepped in front of me like he might block me from what they were thinking. "You're not using me to try to turn her into a walking vaccination clinic. Not using what we think *might* be some science from thousands of years ago and that we've studied for a few days."

I glanced out the window to an eerily empty Louvre courtyard. "The vaccine's the only chance we have left, isn't it?"

No one answered.

"The serum is ready," said another of the scientists, approaching the box with a full syringe. I'd seen her at the Order meeting. Half of the Order crew we'd seen at the meeting was here, in fact.

"This is a trial to see whether this mouse can get the vaccine in its blood?" I said.

"Not exactly. The science is complicated. You would be the only one able to grow the vaccine in *your* blood, but these trials give us a better idea of whether the virus will take hold instead. If you wanted to go through with this, we would do trials until we found a version of the serum that did not kill the mouse, and then . . ."

Then try it on me. And either it would work and we'd have a way to distribute the vaccine—or it wouldn't and I'd die of the virus myself.

"Show me," I said.

Nisha nodded. "Subject T-twenty-three. Commencing trial of substance two-point-six," she said into a handheld recorder. She picked up the mouse and injected it with the syringe's contents.

Stellan gripped the Plexiglas. Across from us, Jack and Elodie peered in, too.

When Nisha set it back down, the mouse shook itself, then darted across the box. Darted back. After a couple of minutes, Nisha dropped in a lettuce leaf, and the mouse ran to it, nibbling at the edge. "If it's feeling well enough to eat, that's a good sign," she whispered excitedly.

"How long would it take for it to get infected?" Stellan asked.

"It happens quickly in the mice. We'll have to watch it for a few hours, but this is very promising—"

A bump on the side of the box drew everyone's attention back down. The mouse was stumbling. There was a bead of blood coming out of its ear, bright against its white fur. The other two scientists hurried over. As we watched, the mouse fell on its side, hemorrhaging and convulsing, blood trickling from its mouth. It didn't move again.

Everyone's eyes flicked to me.

"I'm sorry," Nisha said. "We thought we had it."

I pulled my hair back into a ponytail, snapping a few strands of hair caught in one of the new bandages. "Do you need more of my blood for the experiments?" I said, forcing a smile.

We gathered in the parlor again.

"No," Jack said without preamble. "Absolutely not."

It felt like the moments right before a plane took off. You're hurtling along the ground faster and faster, so fast you can feel what has to happen next. Things were careening toward an end.

"Even if they find something that doesn't kill the mouse, we can't inject you until it's been thoroughly evaluated," Stellan added. "Any drug goes through *years* of trials before it's tested on humans."

Jack nodded. For once, the two of them were in agreement.

I watched the dust swirling in the morning light through the window. The curtains in here were wide open. "We've followed the clues for a long time, and this is where they've led. If we were supposed to go to a new place, or solve a new puzzle, we'd do it."

"But this is *not*—" Jack started.

I cut him off. "I could have taken myself out of the equation to stop this earlier, and now the whole world is in danger. It might not be my fault, but it's my blood. I have to seriously consider it."

"And if it doesn't work, it's *my* blood that could—" Stellan couldn't seem to say the words.

Luc had gone to make some calls, and now he came back into the room, Rocco on his heels. As soon as we'd left Russia, we'd given word to Rocco that his undercover days in the Saxon household were over. Lydia would know Omar hadn't worked alone. "There may be another factor to consider," Luc said. "I just heard that over half the families have accepted the terms and plan to sign the treaty."

"What?" We seemed to all say it at once.

"I was surprised as well," Luc said. "It's not all of the families yet, but many of them are giving up their power for their people's lives."

That was something I hadn't expected.

"That's it, then," Stellan said. "If the whole world isn't going to die, we let the Circle fend for themselves. We could leave some of your blood with the scientists, and eventually they may develop a viable vaccine. Or not, and the Saxons run out of the virus at some point. And we wash our hands of it. We *leave*. We go to some secluded island and—" He met my eyes. "We go to two *different* secluded islands. On opposite sides of the world so even if they find one of us, they won't be able to weaponize us. And that's it. That's the end."

"But if they sign the treaty and give all that power to the Saxons . . ." I said.

"The Saxons, for lack of a better term, rule the world," Jack finished.

I twisted my locket. "If we had a vaccine, we might be able to get it out before they sign. Keep half the world from dying *and* keep the Saxons from becoming dictators."

"The Circle aren't that weak," Stellan argued. "They'll fight back, eventually. Diadochi wars were happening even in Alexander's time. Clashes between Circle families aren't new."

"But what if—" I started.

Stellan turned to me. "What if this kills you?"

We all fell quiet.

Elodie sighed. "Until they have something that works on the mice, it's irrelevant. What's not irrelevant is our Monsieur Dauphin here." She ruffled Luc's hair with a sad smile. "We're supposed to be there in an hour, so while we keep praying for a miracle, we'd better get going."

There was a ceremony for when the head of a Circle family died, to pass leadership to the next generation and honor the dead. It was supposed to be performed within a day of the death. Even after Lydia's declaration of war, we carried on with Luc's.

In a normal situation the whole Circle would be invited, but technically, only one family had to be present as witness. Stellan and I sat in the front pew in black clothes we'd gotten from the Dauphins' well-stocked closets. We hadn't talked to each other since the conversation about the vaccine experiment. It hadn't exactly been an argument, but it had felt like it. I pushed a stray strand of hair behind my ear. I had it pinned up, hiding as much of the pink as I could, to look sedate enough for a funeral.

But nothing about this church was sedate.

"This is my favorite church in Paris," Luc had said as we followed him inside Saint-Chapelle. Every wall was stained glass. The late-morning sun turned the cathedral's cool interior into an impressionist painting, blues and pinks and greens dancing over our skin.

Luc stood at the altar with Colette—the only other Dauphin family member we trusted—behind him. He looked so strong this morning. I wondered whether it came from Luc's natural optimism, or whether death was so much a part of life in the Circle that it was always taken in stride like this.

I felt the tension in the inches of church pew between Stellan and me growing as the ceremony played out: Luc chanting low over a book with the Dauphin sun on the cover, pricking his own thumb and tracing the same sun on a blank page on the inside. Tearing out the page with what must be his father's blood on it from this same ceremony, lighting a corner with a candle, and letting it crumble to ash.

At the appointed time, Stellan and I stepped to the front of the church. Colors played over his face like magic, just as they had in my hallucination. I couldn't help but picture him holding my heart in his hands.

He looked up, his blue eyes as big and troubled as his little sister's had been earlier. Without really thinking about it, I took his hand. He squeezed it hard, and guided me through the words I had to repeat as a witness to a new generation of the Circle.

I wondered if we'd ever do one of these ancient rituals again.

If we left, I knew what would happen. Being on the run was a state I understood well. Except now, it looked like I'd be doing it alone. But what if we stayed, and what if I lived? What if this worked? Would they even accept me—*us*, if Stellan stayed, too? The Circle had never liked me much besides the color of my eyes. And even if they did, would it just be a life of being a symbol and living by a Circle code I didn't entirely agree with? Was I crazy to think it could be more?

Despite everything else—or maybe because of everything else—I'd known since our talk with Fitz that there was something else I needed to do in Paris. After Luc's ceremony, we all assembled again at Père Lachaise Cemetery. Luc had pulled some strings.

Fitz was waiting for us at the gates. We wound our way through the city of crypts, and there, under a tree off a cobblestone path on a sunny afternoon in Paris, we buried my mother.

Her grave was beautiful. I knew she wouldn't want to be buried in a Circle plot, or an Order one. We'd lived so many places, none of them felt right, so I chose Paris. My adopted home for now, and the center of all we'd been through. And she'd love the flowers.

It was the only concession I made to an over-the-top memorial. The hundreds of flowers were all yellow, her favorite color. Daffodils and tulips and roses and daisies. Calla lilies and hibiscus and freesia, scenting the air with a perfume so heady, it made me dizzy. My mom would have thought it was ridiculous, and perfect. We threw handfuls of the flowers in after the casket, and left the rest piled around the headstone and surrounding the gravesite like a celebration.

Afterward, everyone else waited a short distance away while Fitz and I looked down at the flowers. For the first time since my mom's death, I really let myself know, deep down, that she wasn't coming back. And she would forever be someone who had had her life cut short trying to do the right thing. And though I'd grown up believing I was a girl without a dad, now I was truly, forever, a girl without a mom.

Fitz cleared his throat. I reminded myself that one good thing had happened recently. I was a girl with a grandfather. With so much else to concentrate on, that one hadn't quite sunken in yet. Fitz drew a book from his jacket pocket. "Happy birthday, sweetheart," he said, handing it to me.

For a second I didn't understand, but then I remembered the date. It was my seventeenth birthday today.

I opened the blank cover of the book and read the title page. It was a hard copy of Napoleon's Book of Fate.

"This was your mother's when she was your age," Fitz said. "For her it was just fun, but she left it behind when she ran with you, and it helped set me down the research path that led us here." He tapped the book with one finger. "Maybe there's something to this fate nonsense after all."

I flipped the yellowed pages. The book smelled like dust and vanilla perfume. I wondered if my mom had consulted it when she'd decided to leave my father and the Circle.

Fitz adjusted his glasses. "You're very much like her. Just as brave and smart. Just as idealistic. I don't think she'd like what your life has become."

I stiffened.

"But she'd be proud of you. I'm proud of you, Avery." He glanced down the path. "I heard about your dilemma. I don't think it will come as a surprise that I strongly encourage you—all of you—to get out while you can. The Circle has already taken too much from me, and from you. I hope you'll realize that your mother was right all along, and that you deserve more than this. I'll help you in whatever way I can."

He kissed me on the temple and strolled down the path to join the others, leaving me alone with the chirping of birds and the distant hum of a lawn mower.

He was right. My mom would hate that I was part of this. I'd come to understand her. She'd run from it not because she was weak, but because she was strong. She'd left her whole life behind—everyone and everything she knew—for me. She'd made the choice she'd thought was best, and because she had, I now had a choice, too. Just like hers, nothing about it was black and white. Not good or evil. Not right or wrong.

I opened the Book of Fate to a page with questions, and my eye lit on one immediately. *Is my intended path the correct one?*

When an Internet algorithm wasn't doing it for you, you were supposed to make a complicated series of marks on a paper, count them, and find the answer. I chose one at random, and turned to that page. *Fight it as you will, destiny will always win.*

I closed the book. Maybe it was true. My mom had run from this, and I'd ended up right back here anyway, like fate was determined to have its way.

I picked up a sprig of freesia and rolled it between my fingers, releasing the scent into the air. I glanced at my friends, and Elodie, watching me, gave a tiny nod and herded everyone down the hill. Stellan was leaning on a crypt, one hand in his pocket and his suit jacket draped over the other arm, and it made my chest hurt. We still hadn't talked. He stood, ready to leave me alone, too, but I let myself catch his gaze and hold it. I wasn't sure what I was trying to say with the look, but it felt too bold, too open, too risky. Too much like everything I'd been denying for too long.

Stellan glanced down the hill, then made his way up the path to me instead. He tossed his jacket over a low-hanging branch, taking something out of the pocket before he did.

I accepted the small paper envelope. Holding the sprig of freesia between two fingers, I opened it. Inside was a picture of my mom and me.

"I'd sent it in to get printed last time we were in Paris," he said gruffly. "It's for your necklace, since the last one burned."

I stared at the photo. It had been taken sometime between Cannes and Fashion Week. My mom and I were laughing, her face bright red like it always got when she laughed so hard she couldn't breathe.

I hadn't remembered this. In my mind, we'd spent that whole time fighting, or worrying. But I was wrong. At least some moments in my mom's last days had been . . . nice. Despite everything.

I clicked open my empty locket and slipped the picture inside. It fit perfectly.

I looked up at Stellan, tried to say something. *Thank you. Why.* The words wouldn't come out.

He nodded, like he understood anyway. I squeezed the locket in my fist.

I hated that my mom would never know the version of me I'd become since I came to the Circle, and that I'd never understand the version of her that had existed before them. But I loved that we'd had the time we had. I loved that even though I had sad, sullen memories of our moves, I also had memories of her drawing me out with Broadway sing-alongs. I loved that copying her when I was younger was why every morning, I drank at least two cups of coffee that were at least half sugar. I loved that, even though I looked so much like the Saxons, it would always be my mom's smile staring back at me from the mirror. Maybe that would make me try to smile more.

I had to look up at the rustling leaves of the tree overhead to stave off tears.

When I looked back down, Stellan was watching me. I held his gaze, and then he wrapped his arms around me from behind without a word. We looked down at the mound of flowers.

I loved him. And not just him—I loved *us.* Our whole little family. Things were hard, but it *wasn't* terrible and sad all the time. Just like there had been in the hard moments with my mom, there was a lot of happiness. This was a life. This was some form of what my mom had always wanted for me. What *I'd* always wanted for me.

Love and hate. Good and bad. Salvation and destruction. They weren't opposites, either. We were both. *I* was both. Maybe everyone was. Maybe that was okay. Maybe we did what we could with whatever we were given.

I let my head rest back against Stellan's chest, the freesia caught in both our hands and the ground in front of us littered with sunshine. Even though this was a funeral, every beat of his heart against my back said *alive alive alive.*

CHAPTER 22

Back at the Dauphins', we gathered awkwardly in the front hall. Even Luc seemed reluctant to enter the quiet, empty apartments after the funerals. But then we heard a bang from up the stairs, and a kid's shriek of laughter.

Luc elbowed Stellan and grinned, and then he ran a hand through his hair, pulling his careful coif back into his usual bedhead. "*Alors*, my first act as head of the Dauphin family will be to invite in the people half the Circle still thinks are their enemy and the other half are afraid of. Sounds right. Everyone come in, make yourselves at home, and I will open some ridiculously expensive wine."

It broke the awkwardness, and I twisted my newly filled locket around my fingers as I followed everyone into what had become our favorite sitting room.

Before we were even settled in, Jack perched on the arm of the couch, his hands in his pockets. "I hate to bring us back to duties so quickly, but I was speaking with Fitz at the ceremony, and he told me something we need to think about right away. We'd mentioned earlier that it was possible the Circle could come back from a Saxon takeover."

Elodie had been lounging on a couch and now she sat up, interested.

Jack shook his head. "Unfortunately it's not a positive. Fitz believes, due to conversations he overheard while he was in captivity, that the Saxons may be planning to assassinate the heads of all the families, when the time is right. And it sounds like once this treaty is signed may be that time."

There was a loud pop as Luc uncorked the wine bottle. "Excuse me?" he said.

"What about their plans being 'best for the Circle'?" I said. "I think that somewhere deep down, Lydia actually believes that."

Jack spread his hands. "I agree, but I think she could easily fit this plan into that framework. If every family was trying to introduce new leadership, no one would have time or energy to mutiny."

"She'd probably call it giving the Circle a fresh start," Stellan muttered.

"I think we've got to assume it's true and try to do something about it, but it doesn't necessarily change—" Jack turned to me. "There's plenty of your blood to vaccinate the families."

"If they'll take it." Luc got down wine glasses from the well-stocked bar while Colette poured. "I've already tried to tell them we have a vaccine, but they won't listen. No one knows what—or who—to believe anymore."

I stood, crossing the room to look outside through the split in the heavy velvet curtains. The streets on the back side of the Louvre were almost empty. This city that had come to mean so much to me was terrified and cowering, avoiding the virus, or the riots because of the virus. Down the block, a group of people in black masks appeared. They smashed the window of a parked car with a pipe and laughed, and I winced. Was that what the world was coming to? Something had to be done. Something had to be done to save the Circle, too.

I heard a knock. I knew even before I'd turned around that it would be Nisha standing in the doorway.

"We have good news," she said, but she didn't say it with a "good news" kind of smile. "A mouse has lived. We have many more tests to do, but to have any chance of getting a vaccine out before the treaty meeting, we would have to do the procedure . . . Miss West's injection, that is . . . tomorrow in the morning." Her eyes softened. "You don't have to decide now."

I felt strangely calm as she left the room. I slipped off my shoes and curled back in the armchair, trying to ignore everyone staring at me.

At first, all I'd wanted was to keep people I loved safe. I understood Lydia in that way. But I'd come to feel responsible for so much more.

I may have been wrong assuming all the Circle families were only out for themselves, but they would need as many people on the good side as they could get. The more I thought about leaving, the more I realized I didn't want to. And it wasn't just to avoid going back to a life of hiding. I'd said I didn't care about power, but maybe I was wrong. If someone like Lydia Saxon could change the course of the Circle, why couldn't I? Why shouldn't I? The more I realized what was there for the taking, the more I wanted it, even if I had to fight for it. Maybe I did have a little of the Circle, of the *Saxons,* in me after all.

"I don't think we should leave." I ran a thumb along the chair's stitching. "We've all pledged ourselves to the Circle in various ways, but more than that, I think we have a responsibility. My mom, the

Circle families we respect, Fitz, the Order—they all just wanted the Circle to be what it's supposed to be. I don't think I can abandon that now. I know it's dangerous. But my mom ran from this to try to keep me safe, and it just made everything worse. Running has consequences, too."

I wasn't my father, letting terrible things happen. But I wasn't my mom either. I don't know if I really believed it was fate that brought me back to the Circle, but I felt like I was standing at the edge of the world, holding it in hands that were no longer trembling. I remembered something my mom had said, way back in Lakehaven, Minnesota. *I know you're afraid of falling, but sometimes you've got to let go.*

"Each of you has to decide for yourself," I said. "But I'm going to stay."

I said it to the group, but I was looking at Stellan. He nodded, like it was what he'd been expecting all along.

"And I'm going to do the vaccine experiment. Tomorrow, I guess." The decision felt right, like I'd come full circle. My existence had caused this. It could be my blood that ended it.

Jack closed his eyes. Stellan watched me stoically.

"If it continues to work on the mice, Nisha said the chances are pretty good it will work on me," I said. "Pretty good is *way* better than anything else we have. You're right that we could save the Circle with what we have now if they'll take it, but for the rest of the world—even if every single family signs the treaty, Lydia is volatile. We need to either stop the Saxons for good, or we need a scalable vaccine. Since the former looks unlikely . . ."

"She's right," Elodie said quietly. "I don't want to admit it either, but she's right."

No one argued this time.

"No matter what ends up happening," Jack said, looking at his phone, "Paris is shutting down. There are protests going on in the square in front of Notre-Dame that are starting to turn violent, and police are advising that people stay inside. Should we go somewhere that's not here?"

"A hotel?" I said, thinking of the mob I'd seen forming down the block. "What part of town is least likely to be hit by riots?"

Stellan and Elodie tossed out suggestions, but Luc stood. I just now noticed that he'd been doing things on his phone, too, ignoring his glass of wine. "We stay here," he said.

We all raised a collective eyebrow. The *Louvre*, when the town was descending into chaos?

"I've been watching what's going on all day. We're safe here. No one will question a strong security force around the Louvre during a threat to the city," he said. "And if you all don't want to stay, I have to anyway. This is my city now. I have to prepare for the worst."

Luc looked older than he had yesterday, a little of his sweet, care-free nature replaced with something more serious. To my surprise, it fit him.

"I think I should stay with him," Rocco said, breaking the silence. He turned to Stellan and me. "I'd like your permission to do so."

I glanced up at Stellan, and he nodded. "We'll all stay," I said. "It seems like the best thing we could do at this point is stick together."

Slowly, everyone agreed.

We all went in various directions, to change out of their funeral attire, or to get food, to assess the situation outside, or, in the case of Stellan and Luc, to check on their little siblings. I was sitting on a couch flipping between news stations reporting rioting all over the world when Stellan came back into the room. He sat beside me.

"How's Anya?" I said.

"Overwhelmed. Tired. But fine."

"When I said I don't think we should leave," I said, "I didn't mean you. You're a different circumstance."

Stellan had taken off his suit coat, and his tie hung loosely around his neck. He worked it the rest of the way off and tossed it onto the back of the sofa. "Do you want me to leave?"

I watched the footage of protesters in masks, shouting angrily and holding up signs in a language I couldn't understand. People worried that their government wasn't doing more, it appeared from the English headline. The virus had only actually killed a few dozen people at this point. I couldn't imagine what would happen if it got spread more widely. "I want you to do whatever's best for you and Anya," I said.

Stellan rolled something small between his palms and waited so long to answer, I didn't think he was going to. "What do you want for you?"

I wondered, just for a second, whether I should rethink not telling him how I felt.

Obviously I want you to stay here, I'd say. *I wanted that even before I realized how I felt about you, and now I can't stop thinking about how there is something between us, and it's been growing fast. I wish there was time for more than a few illicit kisses and a lot of hard decisions. I don't want to do this alone.*

I'd decided to fight for the Circle. I wished I could convince myself it would be right to fight for him, too.

"If it was entirely up to me, I'd want you to stay, of course," I said evenly. "But there's a lot more to it than that. Whatever you choose, I understand."

He rested his elbows on his knees. I finally saw what was in his hand: a small red block. It must have been what Anya had been playing with upstairs. "Thank you," he said. "I don't think you know how much I appreciate you letting me make that choice."

"Yeah," I said as a girl whose choices had been made for her her whole life. "I do."

The expression on Stellan's face was one I could only call tortured. From my side, he was leaving *me*, but from his side, it was more than that. He was leaving nearly everyone he cared about to keep one person safe. I'd been comparing my own decision to stay or go to my mom's, but really, *his* was exactly like the one she'd made seventeen years ago. He sat up and shifted, and his knee touched mine.

"There are so many toys here," he said, holding out the block. "Every time I go upstairs, Anya has a new favorite thing. And I've known Dahlia, the nanny, for years. Anya trusts her already. Which is especially fortunate since I have no clue how to take care of a seven-year-old girl."

That was not something he should worry about. He'd learn fast. I shifted closer so my hip touched his. As we watched Japan declare a state of emergency on TV, and the United States close its borders, "just until things are cleared up," he settled his hand on my thigh.

Stellan's forearms, like the rest of him, were slim but hard, powerful and graceful. I put a hand over his and traced the map of veins and scars and scrapes there. His long fingers tightened on my leg.

I was just about to decide that there were worse ways to spend what could be my last evening on this planet when he said, "Why did you come to Russia? You didn't have to."

My fingers tightened over his. "I—"

The doors to the library burst open. Stellan smoothly moved his hand, and Luc, Colette, and Elodie burst inside, carrying a pyramid of multicolored macarons, topped off with sparklers.

"Bon anniversaire!" they shouted.

CHAPTER 23

"What is this?" I scrambled to my feet.

"I heard there's a very important birthday today." Elodie batted a spark away from Colette's hair. "I guess the birthday girl *forgot* to tell us."

"You guys, no," I protested as they brought the macaron cake to the coffee table in front of me and the sparklers sizzled and flashed. "We can't have a *party* with all this going on."

Elodie pointed a finger in my face. "Avery June West. Korolev. Whatever. If you're going to be part of the Circle, you have a very important lesson to learn, and that's that you sometimes have to take your happiness where you can find it. The world is literally falling apart. There is nothing we can do about it tonight besides what we've already done and planned."

"And—sorry, but it's true—you might die tomorrow," Luc added. Everyone frowned at him. "We all might! The Circle could turn on us at any moment. An asteroid could hit Paris. There could be a zombie apocalypse! Who knows?"

Elodie nodded. "Exactly. So we could sit around all night and worry, or we could have a party."

She and Luc high-fived solemnly.

"I—" I didn't know what to say. Colette and Luc took it as agreement and broke into the happy birthday song in French. I tried in vain to blow out the sparklers.

We ate macarons, and they gave me presents. I had no idea how they'd done all of this without me knowing.

Colette got me white slippers so pretty and fluffy, I could hardly imagine they were meant for feet. "Because stilettos are fun," she said, "but no one actually *likes* wearing them for more than a few minutes." I kicked off my shoes and put the slippers on.

Jack handed me a folded piece of paper. I opened it to find a stick figure drawing of what looked like two people fighting a dragon. "I drew this when I was ten," he said. "Fitz found it and gave it to me. The girl's you. Or, it's Allie Fitzpatrick, anyway. I thought you were pretty great back then. Not that I don't think you'd be able to fight a dragon these days, because you could," he said quickly.

We told the story of Fitz's setting us up when we were kids, of Allie Fitzpatrick and Charlie Emerson. "Thanks," I said quietly, and Jack just inclined his head, and I could feel a moment, just a moment, of what might have been. But this was how we should be, and I knew it. "Thank you," I said again.

Elodie got me a new knife. Its handle looked like pearl, with gold-and-silver inlay. Elodie showed me how to close it. "Easier to carry," she said. "But still plenty deadly. You can stick it in your bra when you don't want anyone to know it's there."

It was a testament to what we'd become together that it wasn't weird at all when I reached into my shirt right there in front of everybody and lodged the knife in my bra. "I love it," I said, and I genuinely meant it. I never thought I'd get so excited about a knife. "Thank you."

"I have to show you your present later," Luc said mysteriously.

Stellan, still sitting beside me, was quiet. The last thing he'd said before they'd burst into the room knocked around in my mind. *Why did I come to Russia?* He'd said it like it mattered.

I'd thought I was feeling calm about the experiment tomorrow, but suddenly, it was hitting me hard what it meant.

I could die tomorrow.

It might not matter to me whether Stellan left, because I could be gone. Just like I'd accepted that my life was going to have to go on without my mom, his life, and the lives of the people who I had come to care about so much, might go on without me. After all the times we'd been chased and shot at and stabbed and I'd survived, I might be handing my life over voluntarily.

I tried not to be too obvious about staring at everyone's faces, memorizing them. Tried not to hug the presents to my chest too hard, or press my foot into Stellan's too obviously. Tried not to linger too long on my last bites of macaron, wondering whether this might be the last birthday dessert I'd ever get to eat. Tried to tell myself I was being overly dramatic. Knew I really wasn't.

"Thanks, guys," I said. How do you soak up the last bits of what might be your last few hours in the world when you've only just realized how full your world really is? I'd spent plenty of birthdays wondering if this year would finally be different. Now, for the first time, I could guarantee it would be. "This was really nice of you."

"She's funny," Luc said. Sometime during the festivities he'd ended up with a glass of something harder than wine in his hand. I couldn't blame him. No matter how strong he acted, it had been a hard twenty-four hours. He pointed gleefully at me with his drink. "You're funny. You must not know us at all if you think that's the end of what we have planned. Everyone get dressed. Black tie required. You have fifteen minutes."

"Until what?" I said, but Elodie and Colette were already bundling me out the door.

Colette had half a dozen dresses hanging from the four-poster bed in one of the bedrooms. "What will be the best for tonight?" she mused. "Sparkly?" She pulled down a dress that was slinky and low cut, with thousands of sequins and beads leading down to a full train.

"She wouldn't be able to move," Elodie said.

"What are we doing?" I asked again.

"Maybe romantic?" Colette held up two more dresses, ignoring me, and I gave up.

One of the dresses was white lace with a high neck and a flowing skirt, and one was pale pink and intricately embroidered, flowers and birds and vines snaking across the bodice and down to the hem. I reached out to touch it, emotion threatening to overwhelm me again. This could be the last time I got to wear something that was a piece of art.

"Let me choose," I said. In the closet, I pulled aside hanger after hanger of charming dresses and slinky dresses and fancy dresses, and then I saw it. I peeked at the tag. My size.

Elodie was sprawled on the bed, sunken into the fluffy comforter, Colette sitting over her. They looked up, and Colette clapped her hands. "Sparkly *and* romantic *and* sophisticated. Perfect."

The dress was a gossamer gray-blue lace with a sheer back. It had lace cap sleeves and tiny pearls sewn everywhere, giving it a subtle simmer. It nipped in at the waist and flowed to past my knees when I held it against me.

Colette looked at her phone. "Seven minutes!"

"This is the one, then," Elodie said, and I put on the dress, carefully avoiding the bandages at my shoulder. Elodie did up the tiny buttons down my back while Colette emerged from the closet in a navy-blue low-cut dress with a full skirt.

"There," Elodie said. "Those will be fun to unbutton."

"Elodie," I scolded, but I felt my skin get hot at the implication.

She poked her head in front of me, raising her eyebrows. "That was not intended as innuendo. I was simply saying the buttons are difficult. But I think we can all tell where the birthday girl's mind is."

I felt myself flush even hotter. "I didn't mean—"

"I think you did," Colette singsonged, arranging the lace over my shoulder bandage.

"She did," Elodie said. "She seems to think no one knows they're all over each other all the time—"

"Not *all the time*," I cut her off, then realized I'd just dug myself in deeper. I would be blushing for the next ten years.

Colette giggled. "We're just teasing," she said, surveying me like I was a doll to dress. "We won't talk about it anymore unless you want to. And if you do want to talk about it, we will always be here. We just want you to have fun."

"Oh, she will—" Elodie said.

Colette kicked her.

"What are *you* wearing?" I said to Elodie, but they were completely, embarrassingly right. Ever since Stellan and I had talked on the couch downstairs, I'd been thinking about how tonight was very possibly all we had, in one way or another. And I was thinking about what I wanted that to mean.

Colette stole the vase of flowers off the dressing table. They looked like miniature roses, white with a hint of blush pink, and woven between them were a navy-blue thistle. She broke off stems one by one and hummed while she stuck them into my hair, then kissed me on the forehead. *"Très belle,"* she proclaimed, then swept her own hair up and ran out of the room to tell the boys we'd be just a minute more.

Elodie tried to give my hair a sarcastic eyebrow raise, but it turned into a smile. "Very Colette," she said, and thrust her makeup bag at me and hurried into the closet.

I put on mascara in the mirror. Colette had given me a subtle flower crown, tucking the tiny roses and the thistles and a few lush leaves into it so they stood out against my dark hair, and pulled a few strands of pink out around my face. During my time with the Circle, I'd worn lots of fancy clothes. I'd looked cute, or sophisticated, but I'd hardly ever worn anything that was as *pretty* as this whole look was. It felt a little unlike me, but in a way that I liked.

Elodie still hadn't come out, so I picked up her makeup bag and peeked into the closet.

She was standing in front of the full-length mirror. She wore a strapless, shimmering gunmetal gray top that hugged her torso to the waist, and a pair of slim-fitting trousers that stopped just above her ankles.

She was holding her platinum wig in her hands.

Elodie had always been gorgeous, but the blond hair pulled a lot of focus. Without it, her delicate features took center stage. I'd seen it when she'd had it off before, but it was even more obvious now.

"You look beautiful," I said.

Elodie jumped, and I remembered that I was trespassing on a moment that wasn't mine. She scowled at me in the mirror. "Beautiful *and* badass," I said, backing away. "Definitely badass. I'll see you downstairs."

She studied herself in the mirror again, and I tried to slip away, but she called, "Makeup bag, please."

I handed it to her. She gestured for me to sit on a stool and swiped eye shadow across my lids, then turned to herself. I couldn't help but look at her back, now that I was closer. It was not as scarred as Stellan's, but now that she was wearing something more revealing than usual, I could see obvious scars there. And in the center of her back, vertically down from the Dauphin tattoo on her neck, was a small rendition of the Order tattoo I remembered seeing on the men at Prada so long ago. "How has no one ever noticed the scars or the tattoo?" I said, and then, nodding downstairs, because if I wasn't mistaken, both Jack and Stellan would have seen her with no shirt on, "How did *they* not notice?"

She shrugged. "I kept it covered. Always. Literally always." She finished putting on lipstick so dark it was almost black, smacked her lips together, and smiled at herself in the mirror.

She picked her wig up from the dresser where she'd set it, stared at it for a moment—then put it back down. "Ready?"

When we got downstairs, almost everyone did a double take at Elodie's hair. Stellan's gaze, however, skipped straight to me. He was dressed in a classic tux, leaning against a wall with his hands in his pockets, one foot propped over the other, like he had been the very first time I'd met him, at the prom in Minnesota. Just like that time, he met my eyes and smiled. Unlike that time, the smile was so warm I couldn't help but smile back.

I didn't notice Nisha until we got to the bottom of the stairs. That warmth cooled to ice.

"Nisha's going to hang out with us," Colette said. I breathed again. "She needs a break, and the others are taking over for a few hours."

Nisha had her arms crossed uncomfortably, looking around the Dauphins' formal living room. "Are you sure?"

Jack, of all people, said, "Of course. Stay."

Nisha was about to answer when the lights fuzzed, then blinked out entirely.

There were a few curses, and some scrambling, and then phone screens were turning on.

"Electricity out. That can't be good," Elodie muttered.

"Merde," Luc whined. "My birthday present."

"It'll still be fun," Colette assured him. "Maybe more fun. Do you have candles?"

While we all went in search of light, Elodie took Nisha upstairs to find a dress. Then Luc led us through his family's apartments, into a passageway that looked like it should be for mail deliveries, and onto an elevator. And when we got out—

"Bon anniversaire!" Luc said, and it echoed through a hall the size of a football field. Moonlight filtered in through frosted glass, but other than that and the candles we all held, throwing erratic shadows over our faces, everything was completely dark and silent. I could still tell exactly where we were, and a smile crept onto my face as Luc said, "I got you the Louvre!"

CHAPTER 24

This is Julien," said Luc. "It might appear that he's trying to kill that goose, but they're best friends. They are having dancing lessons."

We were standing in front of a gleaming marble statue nearly as tall as me, of a little boy and a bird. Luc had stories he'd made up as a child about every piece of art in here, and he was giving us a personal tour.

We'd come through a side entrance to the museum and made it halfway up this hall, ducking into galleries along the way.

The Louvre was all ours for the night. No guards. No alarms. For as much time as we'd spent in Paris, and even in this complex, the only time I'd actually been inside the museum was when Jack and I were looking for Napoleon's diary. And then we were being chased, dodging tour groups and blending into crowds. I tried not to think about the fact that *this* time here could be my last.

"This one"—Luc spun, his dress shoes clicking across the checker-board floor to a statue of a cherub reaching to the heavens—"this is Felipe. Doomed from an early age to go into politics because of his family name, but his real love is opera."

He cut off when the wail of a siren started up nearby, and then another, and another, a mechanical chorus. We all glanced at each other.

"Felipe sings in the shower," Luc continued defiantly, his candle spotlighting the cherub's cheeks, "and one day, he was discovered by a famous singer walking by his window, and now he's onstage every night in Vienna."

My arm brushed Stellan's. We were standing close enough that I could feel the warmth coming off his body.

Luc ran across the room, his candle flickering dangerously. "Here!" he said. Elodie grabbed Colette's hand and twirled her in the moonlight. Colette's hair clip fell out, letting her strawberry-blond curls loose. They'd both already ditched their shoes, and were barefoot in their formalwear.

"One of my favorites!" Luc's voice echoed off the stone arches. "Sven, the butcher."

Stellan took my arm lightly in his hand. As Luc rushed ahead, he whispered, "Can I show you something?"

I glanced after the rest of the group and followed him into a dark gallery. "My favorite in this wing," he whispered.

The statue was of a man, larger than life, his torso twisted, emerging from a block of stone.

"*The Rebellious Slave,*" Stellan said, setting his candle at its feet. "No one knows why it's not complete. Some people say it's on purpose, the juxtaposition of beauty and roughness. Some say Michelangelo abandoned it when he couldn't achieve the perfection he wanted."

From the next room, music started up, something jazzy and old and scratchy. Stellan reached out and touched the rough chisel marks at the statue's side, thrown into greater relief by the small, flickering light at its base. I couldn't help touching it, too, the marble cold under my fingers.

"I like it *because* it's unfinished," Stellan said. "I like that you can see the chisel marks. See where it came from. It makes it so much more."

The music had been getting farther away, and now there was a shriek. We jumped, and Stellan picked up his candle. But the shriek was followed by a burst of laughter.

Stellan's face relaxed, and he held up his candle. It bathed me in soft light, his eyes tracing over my dress, the little buttons, the lace. The flowers in my hair, fragrant enough that I could smell them every time I moved my head. Especially by candlelight, I must have looked like a Jane Austen heroine. The sultrier version—the one where lace and buttons weren't quite so prim and proper. If I had been trying to wear something he'd like, I could tell I'd gotten it right.

"You clean up okay," he said huskily. "Not that *covered in blood* isn't a good look for you . . ."

I smiled down at my flickering candle, then brushed a tiny piece of lint from his jacket. "You don't look terrible, either. I guess."

I tried not to think about how, whether I died tomorrow or he left the next day, this might be the last time he looked at me like this. It might be the last time I teased him. It was so unfair, and it was the way it had to be.

"I almost forgot," I said. My voice was surprisingly level. "I got you something."

"*You* got *me* something? It's your birthday."

I felt around in the tiny bag over my shoulder and handed it to him.

He set down the candle and twisted the top off the little pot. A tangy, medicinal smell wafted out. "Lotion?" he said.

"I asked Nisha to try this while they were doing their other experiments. It's for your scars. To make them not hurt anymore. And if you don't want it, for Anya."

Stellan raised his brows.

"I only told Nisha. I know she won't tell anyone."

He stared at the little pot of cream. Then he put one finger in it and spread it over the scars on his opposite hand. After a second, a surprised smile came over his face. "It feels—" He shivered. "Strange. Tingly." He pushed experimentally on the scars and looked even more surprised. "Different. I think it might be working."

He put the cap back on the cream and stuck it in his pocket, then looked up at me with the same tormented look he'd had on his face a few times over the last day.

"Birthday girl! Where are you?" Luc called.

Stellan smiled ruefully down at his candle. "Shall we?"

We followed the tinny music and the laughter into a new gallery. Stellan's hand brushed mine. I looked down at it. So did he. Our fingers slid together.

I let out a low breath. This was not just secret kissing. This was a declaration that, at least for tonight, it was more. And that neither of us was making a secret of wanting that.

Still, I glanced self-consciously at our hands, then in the direction of our friends. One, specifically.

"Jack knows," Stellan said.

I wasn't even surprised that he'd understood. "Are you sure?"

He shrugged. "I told him. It would have been bad manners not to."

I couldn't help a small, desperate laugh at that. "You told him what?"

"Well, I didn't go into *detail* . . ."

I elbowed him, and he grinned. "I told him that . . . I like you."

I wasn't sure how I could be thinking so much about dying and still have this kind of giddy smile keep creeping onto my face. "Oh," I said. "Okay, then." I linked my fingers more tightly through his as we walked under the portraits of stern-looking men and women gazing down at us from the walls.

It turned out our friends paid no attention to us at all. Everyone's candles were on the floor. Luc and Rocco and Jack all had their tuxedo jackets off, and the three girls were sitting on them like sleds.

"À vos marques," Luc said, crouching like he was at the starting line of a race and gripping the arms of his jacket, *"prêts, partez!"* They took off, the boys pulling the girls, dress shoes echoing on hardwood floors. Colette fell off Rocco's jacket immediately, collapsing in a laughing heap on the hardwood. Elodie's and Luc's feet got tangled up, and Luc yelled as they fell.

"We win!" Nisha exclaimed. She leapt up before Jack had even stopped, and tackled him in a hug. He picked her up and twirled her around with a grin that made me think of all the time Jack had spent getting briefings from the scientists the past couple days, and wonder, just for a second, whether there was something going on there I hadn't seen. I squinted behind them. "Is that the *Mona Lisa*?"

"It is," Stellan said. I let go of his hand and ran across the room, sliding in my slippers on the hardwood. *Don't think about the fact that this might be the only time you'll see it,* I told myself.

"It's so small!" I said.

Elodie stood beside me, crossing her arms and squinting at Mona's enigmatic smile. "At least you get to see it up close, without six thousand people taking selfies in front of it."

"Ugh." Luc came up behind me. "It's so boring, and so *terribly* overhyped. That's the valuable one." He gestured over his shoulder at a painting on the opposite wall that must have been twenty feet tall. "It's a portrait of the Circle from centuries ago. We made up that the *Mona Lisa* mattered so no one would ever make a move against the one we care about."

This was something almost no one in the world knew. Almost no one in the world had run around the Louvre at night, or flown in a private jet all over the world. Whatever else the Circle had done to my life, I'd also gotten to do some amazing things.

From outside, there was a boom so loud, we all went quiet.

"Firecracker," Stellan said after a second of silence. "It was just close."

Jack nodded. I still couldn't help but watch the walls like I could see through them to what was going on outside.

Luc grabbed both my hands. "It was only a firework, *chérie*. They set them off every New Year's, and it sounds like the world is ending. Do you like your present?"

"This is the best birthday I've ever had," I said truthfully.

Luc pulled me down the corridor and everyone else followed, Rocco ducking into gallery after gallery and shouting out what we had to see. Nisha gave us a lesson on one of her favorite paintings, and Colette and Luc contorted their bodies into the poses of statues while Elodie took pictures. With the domed skylights overhead letting in silvery moonlight, we crowded down a short flight of stairs, and then suddenly, we were in the Louvre lobby.

The outside of the Louvre was one of the most iconic images in the world, but inside was just as beautiful. The pyramid overhead formed a giant skylight, putting the Paris night sky on stunning display. Through the lattice of metal and glass, I could see part of the Louvre façade and beyond it, fireworks from the rioting all over the city. It was the most beautiful and most terrible thing I'd ever seen.

I was still staring when a new song started up on a tiny radio Nisha was carrying.

"Oh!" Luc said, and started to sing along.

Stellan set down our candles, then swept me into his arms and sang something off-key, but enthusiastically. "What song is this?" I asked, but they ignored me.

Luc and Rocco started dancing, too, and Elodie did a ballet leap across the open expanse of floor. When I looked up at the glass above, I could see the reflections of all our candles flickering.

Stellan twirled me, and I caught a glimpse of Jack, leaning against a pillar with his arms crossed over his chest, but smiling. I smiled, too, at this thing that looked suspiciously like joy, pushing defiantly through the terror and sadness.

The song broke into the chorus, and Jack joined in, a deep baritone that rose above the rest of the voices. One by one the rest of them dropped out, and we all turned to stare at him. When he realized everyone else had stopped, he cut off in the middle of a word. "What?" he said.

Elodie giggled and ran up the spiral stairs in the lobby's center to look out of the pyramid into the Louvre courtyard. The rest of them followed. Jack was the last to leave, and I could tell he was waiting to bring up the rear of the procession, always vigilant. When he realized Stellan and I were still dancing, he gave a quick nod and jogged off to catch up to the rest of them.

My heart squeezed and I rested my forehead on Stellan's chest, feeling the *thump-thump* of his heart. I pulled away just enough to look up at him, to run a finger down his jaw, down his neck, to the glowing white of his tuxedo shirt. Then I reached up and kissed him along the same line.

He shivered. "What was that for?"

"Because why not?" I whispered. I might be keeping some of my feelings in check tonight, but in this, I saw no reason to hold back.

"Well, in that case—" He leaned over and pulled at my earlobe with his teeth, and I got goose bumps.

"Come on," I said. I dragged him across the open expanse of floor, awash with moonlight and the distant flickering of our candles, and held his arm up to twirl myself again and again so my dress fluttered around me. I giggled, felt dizzy, went crashing back into his arms. "Ow!" I squeaked, cradling my injured shoulder. I couldn't stop laughing. My eyes were filling with tears. I pulled away from Stellan and sank to the floor, still holding my arm, my lacy dress pooling around me. There were more green and red pops through the triangles of glass, blurred now as my eyes swam. I wiped away one tear, two, but didn't let it go further than that.

Stellan stood above me, his hands in his pockets, looking at me in a way that made me feel unsteady. *"Kuklachka,"* he said roughly.

I held out my hand. "Come here."

He unbuttoned his tuxedo jacket and settled beside me, propping himself up on one elbow. That look was still on his face, the soft, quizzical one with a hint of apprehension behind it. He seemed to make a decision.

"I need to tell you something," he said, lying back to stare up into the sky. Through the delicate web of metal filaments holding the pyramid up, I could pick out three bright stars.

A ball of nervous light sparked in my chest. Was this it? Was he going to tell me he was leaving—or he was staying? I thought he'd wait to see what happened tomorrow, but now I steeled myself. "What?"

I turned my head to see his throat bob with a hard swallow. "I need to tell you that I've been lying to you all night."

My hand, on its way to grasp his, froze.

Stellan kept his eyes trained on the sky. "I think I didn't know how to handle this, especially with what's coming up. And so, I lied. I've lied to you over and over and over. For a long time."

The floor hadn't seemed cold before, but now it did, seeping through the lace of my dress. What was he saying?

Stellan propped himself on an elbow over me and I was paralyzed as he tucked a strand of hair behind my ear. "I lied to you earlier when I said you looked *okay*," he said. "The truth is, when I saw you coming down those stairs, I forgot how to breathe."

That . . . was not what I'd expected. "What?" I choked.

"And it's not just the fancy dress," he went on. "That happens every single day."

My head reeled, like I'd held my breath for too long.

"And I *definitely* lied when I said that I like you." He looped his fingers through mine. The light in my chest trembled. "It's just that I spent so many years persuading myself not to—persuading myself I wouldn't be *able* to—feel anything real for anyone that I don't think I quite believed it when I fell hopelessly, desperately, *absurdly* in love with my fake wife."

The light exploded into a million stars.

He cupped my face in his hand. "*Kuklachka*. I know everything's uncertain right now, and this is just about the worst time to be doing this. But it's also the only time. So, I love you. I've been falling in love with you for a long time, and I still don't know what's going to happen in the next few days, but whatever it is won't change that fact. I love you."

My heart was thumping as violently as it had when we were being shot at. "No one's watching in here," I teased shakily, regretting the words before they were out of my mouth. As much as I was trying to learn, I didn't know how to do this. I knew how to push people away. I knew how to convince myself something was less than it was. I didn't know how to believe in it.

"I hope not," he said. It was guarded. *Answer him*, I told myself, but the words weren't working. It was like in the hallucination—all I could do was stare at him, silhouetted above me against the panorama of the night sky.

His hand fell from my face. "I'm not expecting you to feel the same way. And that's okay. I just had to tell you, in case this is the only chance I have—"

I stopped him with a hand in the center of his chest. His heart was racing.

Footsteps thundering down stairs made me startle. "Hel*lo*!" Elodie called.

"Hi." I had forgotten they were there.

"We're going to eat snack bar chips," Colette declared, gesturing across the lobby. "And drink snack bar wine."

Stellan just waved, like it was the most normal thing in the world to be lying on the floor of the Louvre. My fingers tightened on his chest.

As soon as they disappeared around the corner, I pushed myself onto an elbow. "I—" The words still wouldn't come, so instead, I pressed my lips to his.

Of all the times we'd kissed—the ones that were desperate and wild, and the ones that were halfhearted and artificial—I'd never felt one like this. This kiss was careful, slow—but fierce. Final. This was a kiss that left no doubt about what it meant. And when we broke apart, I saw it reflected in the softness and sparkle between us as clearly as if we were saying it out loud: *I love you I love you I love you.*

It felt dangerous. It felt amazing. It felt like of course the lights were out, because all the electricity in the city was in my veins.

I felt whatever was restraining us snap, and I was kissing him more deeply, my leg hooked over his, the floor hard under my shoulder. The only thing I wanted was to be as close to him as possible, saying everything I couldn't seem to say out loud yet.

He pulled away, breathing heavily. And then he got to his feet, hauling me up with him, grabbed our candles, and headed without a word toward the sound of voices.

"What—" I said, but we rounded a corner.

There was a temporary baroque furniture exhibit off the Louvre lobby by the little cafe. Luc and Rocco were curled in an oversized gilded throne together. Elodie lounged on a rug, and Colette sat next to her, running her fingers absently over Elodie's short, spiky hair. Jack and Nisha sat at a small table. "Want some M&M's?" Colette held the candy out. "Or we have Snickers."

I remembered Cannes, unbuttoning Stellan's shirt, how he'd drawn that line I'd tried to cross. Wondering if he was drawing it again, considering the circumstances.

But he gave an exaggerated yawn. "I'm getting tired. Big day tomorrow. I think I'll be going to bed."

Oh.

"Me too," I said quickly. "Tired." Stellan ran his thumb across the inside of my wrist, and I felt goose bumps rise on my arms. "Good night. Thank you, guys. For everything."

Stellan pulled on my hand, and we headed back to the lobby, toward the elevators. "Was that ridiculously obvious?" I whispered.

"Yes," he whispered back. He held the candle far enough away that it wouldn't catch my hair on fire, and kissed me until the elevator doors opened and dumped us out.

The hallway was pitch-black. We came to a stop in front of a window with a view out over the Louvre. It was odd to see the pyramid dark and have none of the lights on the outside of the museum, or the street, lit up. In the moonlight, I could see dozens of police officers in the square. Stellan kissed me again.

My bullet wound ached and the cuts from Russia stung and the cool air on the skin he'd just kissed tingled and his mouth on mine felt so good it was like my whole body was alive. This *did* feel like jumping off a cliff, and I'd never wanted anything more.

"I love you," I whispered.

His grin in the half-light was so surprised and sweet that I took his face in my hands and brought his forehead to mine. "I love you," I repeated. Now that I'd said it out loud, I couldn't stop. "I *love* you."

"You don't have to sound quite so surprised. It's slightly offensive," he teased, because he couldn't do it, either. We were two people who didn't know how to feel this for each other, much less how to admit it, feeling it out in the dark.

"I've been thinking it . . . a lot," I admitted. "Since before you said it. It's different to say it out loud."

He swept me up in his arms so fast, I squealed. We kissed on a grand sofa in a sitting room, on a windowsill in the hallway.

How had it taken me this long to realize I loved him? I'd thought for so long he was just a detour on my path, but that was ridiculous. This felt like the only possible end to the collision course we'd been on for so long.

Maybe it was because I'd always thought being in love would feel . . . fluffy. Cute. *Kitten-bliss kiss* type of sweet. But that was not how this felt at all. It wasn't just that saying those words—*I love you*—made me grin so big I could barely kiss him. It was that this could be forever, or it could be just tonight, and it didn't make me feel any differently. It was the pinprick of sorrow that my mom wouldn't get to see me happy. It was the knowledge that we could never just be two normal people in love, no matter what happened. And the fact that every time I thought I was drowning, he helped me breathe again. Love wasn't perfect, but that didn't make it less. Like all of tonight, there was sadness and fear, but beauty and joy, too, brighter because of the contrast.

"I think I've been falling in love with you for . . . way longer than makes sense," I whispered. "I wasn't going to tell you. That's why I was so surprised when you said it. I was afraid it'd make everything harder. But—"

He set me on a windowsill so my face was level with his. "It's so much better."

"*So* much better," I whispered, and wrapped myself around him again.

We left his jacket over the back of a sofa in the Napoleon apartments, a section of the Louvre usually full of tourists. We left his shirt— I wasn't sure where. Someone would find it eventually.

We ducked into a room with a gilded ceiling that glowed and glittered in the light of our candles, but I barely saw it. Everything was him. After so long pretending I didn't want to, I couldn't take my eyes off him. The way his lips parted a little when I stroked the back of his neck, barely ghosting over his scars. His arms, straining in a way that told me he was barely holding back, but so gentle tucked around me. How he watched me openly, letting me look, letting me touch him as much as I wanted, his eyes tracing my every movement like he was as amazed by me as I was by him.

"What's this scar from?" I whispered. I touched a mark under his arm, hard and translucent against his smooth skin.

"Training fight. I was thirteen."

I traced the sharply cut lines down his abdomen, the slide of muscle at his hip bones that vanished into the waistband of his trousers. I made my way back up over his arms, arms that had held me after I'd almost drowned, arms that had carried me out of danger in Russia while the stars had spun in my head. Farther up, where the ends of the translucent scars curled over his shoulders.

"This one?" I stroked a thin mark at his collarbone.

"An operation in the Ukraine that was almost a disaster."

I wanted to ask about it. I wanted to touch every one of his scars and know the story of his whole life. Maybe we'd have time for that later. Maybe we wouldn't.

I really had changed. I'd been taught over and over that everything good was also temporary, and it was worse to lose something than to never know how it felt at all. Tonight was the opposite of that.

No matter what, though, I didn't want to think about the future right now. The past was easier. I touched another scar. "What's the story of this one?" I said, but he could tell something was wrong. He stroked the back of his hand over my cheek with a questioning eyebrow raise.

I circled my finger around the scar on his shoulder and whispered, "I'm just trying not to think that this could be the only—"

He plucked a sweet-smelling white flower from my hair. "I know."

"We need mint tea to concentrate on," I whispered.

He took another flower from my hair, and I knew we were both thinking about how he'd taken out my bobby pins that first day on the plane, when we had just met and the intimacy of it was completely inappropriate. "I'm relatively certain," he said, "that I'll be able to find other ways to distract you."

This time, I was the one who took his hand and pulled him out of the room, and for the rest of the night, I didn't think about the future *or* the past. The present was enough.

He guided us past the wing that had been closed off after the Dauphin family had been infected. Past the hall where Luc's bedroom was. He plucked another flower from my hair, and another, tossing them on the floor like a trail of bread crumbs up narrow stairs, to a hallway that was never meant to be for the public. To a bedroom. Small, all white.

"Your room," I asked around the edge of a kiss.

"Is this okay?" he said.

"Yes." It was warm and still and soft inside, homey and cozy like the Dauphins hadn't touched it since he'd left. Stellan pulled the small round window open a crack. Outside, a firework exploded in the distance with a pop and a sizzle.

"*Kuklachka.* My little doll." The single candle on a tall bureau threw a pool of light against the wall, enough to illuminate the small room softly. I could tell he wanted to say more, but he wasn't sure how. I understood anyway, and instead I kissed him again. And again. And again.

I was so afraid that we'd been playing at being kings and queens, and under it all, I was nothing but a girl, after all. Terrified that nothing I did mattered. Terrified that it did. But I wasn't scared of this. Is this what being in love was? I wasn't worried about doing or saying too much, or the wrong thing. I wasn't worried about *feeling* too much or the wrong thing.

My head swam with heat and the scent of the candle and the taste of his skin. Being so close to him was overwhelming, and all I wanted was to be closer. We made our way across the room slowly, until the backs of my legs hit the end of the bed.

The flutter and snap of the curtains, candlelight golden and glowing on his skin and on mine, flickers of life painting a canvas. The world was exploding around us, and we were a glow at its soft, warm center.

My skin took every careful touch and multiplied it by the electricity in my blood, and my heart beat in time with my thoughts, with every kiss, with every time I whispered *I love you, I love you, I love you.*

He checked in with me every step of the way, and I knew that if I wanted to stop, we would. But I didn't. So we didn't. And I was his and he was mine, and for tonight, that was all that mattered.

CHAPTER 25

As was often the case, Stellan and I were awake hours before anyone else the next morning.

Last night, we'd managed to let ourselves forget about what was going to happen today. Though we didn't so much as mention the scientists or the mice or the virus this morning, I could tell he was trying very hard to distract me enough that neither of us would think about it. It didn't work, of course, but it managed to keep the knot of nerves in my throat at bay until we couldn't deny reality any longer.

We'd told Nisha I'd be ready by nine. When we made our way downstairs, I was tousling my freshly showered hair with one hand, holding Stellan's hand with the other. Luc looked up from his crois-sant. "Good morning," he said, and grinned at me and Stellan, then cut his eyes pointedly at the next chair over, where Stellan's jacket and shirt were folded neatly. "How did everyone sleep? You two cer-tainly look . . ."

Colette, sitting next to him, smacked the back of his head.

"Ow," Luc pouted. "I was just going to say well rested. And . . ."

clean." She tried to smack him again, and he ducked with a grin. And then his face dropped.

We all turned to see Nisha standing in the doorway. "All the mice are still alive." Her voice was bright and confident, but she was twisting her hands nervously.

I wasn't a mouse. None of us said it. Stellan's hand clenched in mine.

For a brief moment, I wanted to take it all back. I couldn't do this after all. This wasn't how I wanted everything to end. Maybe there was another way.

There wasn't.

I took a single, shuddering breath. "Okay," I said. "Let's go."

All the way to the lab, Jack and Stellan and Elodie grilled Nisha about specifics, even though they knew nothing would change my mind now.

I sat in a chair. Nisha rolled over a jangling cart of medical supplies and wrapped a piece of elastic tight around my arm. She felt for a vein on the inside of my elbow.

A tear slipped down my cheek, then another and another.

Colette tried to wipe them away until she realized it was futile. Luc kissed me on both cheeks. Elodie pressed her lips together and squeezed my knee hard. Jack hugged me so tightly, my ribs almost cracked. Stellan sat beside me, holding my hand and stroking my hair.

I don't want to die, said the voice in my head. *I don't want to die. I don't want to die.* The tears flowed more freely.

As I held out my arm and Nisha swabbed the inside of my elbow, Stellan leaned close to my ear and whispered about random distracting things like dogs in strollers in Japan. I was shaking now, hard enough that he had to steady my arm for Nisha, but he just kept talking, smoothly, about how once he'd seen someone walking three cats on leashes in a Tokyo park, and I laughed through the tears.

Nisha pressed the needle into my arm and pushed down. There was a second when I felt only the cool of the liquid going into my veins. Then, the cool turned to fire, and I screamed.

CHAPTER 26

I woke up to Nisha on the computer, her back to me. I silently assessed my body. Everything felt like it was where it should be. "What happened?" I croaked, and Nisha startled.

A chair scraped and Stellan was standing over me, the relief in his posture palpable. "How are you feeling?"

I hauled myself to sitting, and found everyone else crowded around the couch I'd been lying on. "Fine, actually. Just dizzy. Did it work?"

"The good news is that you're alive," Elodie said.

At that word—*alive*—my brain woke up. It was like I'd stopped breathing for too long and suddenly air rushed through me.

"Being *alive* is too much cause for celebration lately. We've really lowered the bar." Elodie glared from me to Luc, but I could hear the relief in her voice.

I felt giddy, euphoric, dizzy with it. Hot tears pricked at my eyes. I realized then just how *sure* I'd been that I'd never hear one of Elodie's sarcastic comments again.

Stellan sat down next to me. "How does it feel being a lab rat?"

he murmured, his voice husky with suppressed emotion. He hadn't thought I was going to make it, either.

I clung to his hand, marveling at the feeling of it, at the air going into my lungs with each shaky breath, at the sunlight through the window. I'd never known quite how amazing being alive was until I thought I'd given it up.

"The bad news," Nisha said slowly, "is that it didn't work. We have no vaccine."

"Wait, what?" I was still light-headed. I hadn't heard right.

She got out of her chair. "We've looked at your blood already. If the modification was going to take, it would happen quickly, and it hasn't. It appears the Great modification does nothing to you. Maybe Olympias designed a safeguard that you two wouldn't kill each other. We may never understand how, just like we don't understand how she created the virus in the first place. But it also means we can't make the vaccine replicate like we wished to."

"Then why did I pass out?"

"The pain? The fear? Perhaps some of the other agents we put in the serum? You should be fine."

Another wave of dizziness hit me, and I curled back into the couch cushions. "So what do we do? We have no vaccine and no plan, and the meeting is set to happen sometime in the next twelve hours."

"That is the million-dollar question," Rocco said, his hands on the back of Luc's chair.

Stellan got a text and went upstairs to retrieve Anya, and soon she was sitting on the floor at our feet coloring while everyone tossed out ideas. If we could get ahold of the Saxons' virus supply, we could destroy it. But without someone on the inside, that seemed unlikely.

Maybe we could somehow force the Circle to take the cure. And Colette could post a video warning people in the cities not to drink tap water in case the Saxons released it anyway.

"That would cause a whole new level of mass panic," Jack said. "And if the virus were released in aerosol form, it'd be no use at all."

He startled when Anya tapped on his knee and handed him a crayon and a page out of her coloring book, saying something bossy-sounding in Russian. Jack looked taken aback but obeyed, sitting cross-legged on the floor and shading in a bright orange sun.

"What if . . . " Luc started hesitantly. "What is the word in English? When you are playing cards and you lie about what you have."

"Bluff?" I said, sitting up.

"Yes. We bluff. If we thought distributing this vaccine could work, the Circle will think so, too. For all they know, we could have sent out the vaccine the second Lydia made the threat."

For once, no one shot down the idea immediately.

I held a velvet cushion in my lap. "So we'd go to the meeting. We tell the Circle we've mass-released the vaccine and their territories are safe from the virus. We tell them the Saxons' plan to kill them, and we give *them* the vaccine in small doses, just in case. Then we get them to . . . physically overpower the Saxons, all before Lydia can pull the trigger?" I said doubtfully.

"Or hope enough of them side against the Saxons that it's no longer in her best interests to pull the trigger at all." Elodie had moved to lie on one of the couches, her feet in Colette's lap. She chewed her thumbnail thoughtfully. "Even if the Saxons themselves don't take our bluff, actually releasing the virus on a grand scale has got to be their last resort, right? Dealing with the fallout from that would be messy and difficult and not what they want at all."

I looked outside. It was late morning. We had a few hours until we'd know where the meeting was. A few hours more until it was all over. "Let's say we decide to do this. What are the problems?"

"It'll be incredibly dangerous," Jack said. "Fitz tried to make me promise that we wouldn't do anything like this."

"Yeah."

"That doesn't mean I don't think we should do it," Jack said quietly, tapping a crayon on his hand. "I think it might be our only hope."

"Okay, next," I said. "How would we convince them we're telling the truth? You heard what Luc said yesterday. The Circle doesn't know what to believe, but I bet anything *we* say comes in last on that list."

Anya handed Stellan a finished picture of a purple-and-green castle, and he grinned at her. "Everything is our word against theirs besides the actual science of the virus and the vaccine," he said. "How can we use that?"

"Yes," I said excitedly. "We show them. We bring a mouse, vaccinate it, then expose it to the virus."

"A mouse won't prove anything," Nisha said, "and they'll know it." She was sitting on the arm of the sofa nearest me. Anya thrust a new coloring page at Jack, with a picture of a princess on it, and Jack looked up helplessly. Nisha rolled her eyes and joined them on the floor, taking the page out of his hands and attacking it with a red crayon. He pulled out yellow and pink and handed them to her, too. I did a double take at the familiarity that had sprung up between them, thinking suddenly of the times I'd seen them together last night. Jack caught me watching, frowned at what he read on my face, and gave me a warning look.

"Maybe it shouldn't be a mouse." Colette hadn't said anything the whole time we'd been plotting, but now she sat up straight, her hand wrapped around Elodie's ankle. "I've taken the vaccine. Infect me."

We all looked at her, her strawberry-blond curls forming a halo around her heart-shaped face in the midday light. "Colette, you don't have to—" Stellan started.

"Just because I'm not good with a gun like the rest of you doesn't mean I'm useless. All I've wanted since Liam died was to make sure it didn't happen again. And then I'm the one who took you all to that show where Cole—" Her big green eyes flicked to me, and away. "We know the vaccine works. I'll be okay. Let me do this."

Elodie pressed her lips together, but nodded. "Okay. And if we can prove we're telling the truth about the vaccine, they'll be more likely to believe the rest. Just one *tiny* problem: despite the fact that they heard Lydia saying those things on tape, some of them still don't believe it. And the ones who do are afraid of us anyway. They might not even let us into the room."

Luc was pacing to and fro, coffee cup in hand. "They might be afraid of you, but you're still part of the Circle. We initiated you. You have a right to be at any Circle activity as much as I do."

The back of my neck prickled. All this time, I hadn't been thinking of it that way. We didn't have to hope they'd let us be one of them. We already were.

But Elodie waved a dismissive hand. "They'll say the initiation wasn't finished. We don't even have the tattoos."

There were murmurs of agreement around the room.

I glanced at Stellan. He smoothed the edges of Anya's picture over his knees. "So we get them," I said. All the murmurs stopped. "We finish the initiation, and we get the tattoos. Then we're official."

Next to me, Stellan opened his mouth, closed it again. His silence made me pause. I should have asked him first. I might have survived this experiment, but my future with him was still uncertain. And if he was leaving tomorrow, committing to the Circle might not be what he'd want.

But I *did* want it. This wasn't a marriage ceremony I'd just committed us to. We'd figure out *us* whenever he was ready. This was me, pledging myself.

"I guess I should say *I'll* get the tattoo," I said. "Nobody else has to."

"Yesterday *was* her seventeenth birthday," Elodie said. "That's when Circle members usually get their tattoos. And technically, only one witness from another family has to be present."

Luc raised his hand.

I glanced at Stellan, and his eyes were boring into me. I gave him as good a smile as I could muster, and he gave a small one back. *I love you*, I thought. *You love me. It sucks that that's not automatically enough.*

"It's settled, then," Colette said. I tore my eyes from my fake husband's. "Let's make you official."

We'd designated the Dauphins' grand library as our ritual space. We'd pulled the shutters closed, and it was dark enough inside that it might as well have been night.

We stood around a table in the center of the cleared room. The only illumination was the pool of light from a single lamp.

"Each family has a book," Elodie explained. "It's their history, their motto, everything that matters to them, and you swear your loyalty on it, to the Circle and to your family. Your family doesn't have one, so you'll need to swear on something else."

I looked around the room. "You all. You're what I want to swear on. I know it's cheesy," I said when Elodie cocked an eyebrow, "but there's nothing else that makes more sense."

Jack cleared his throat, then put his hand on the table and looked up at me. I smiled. Elodie shrugged and placed her hand over his, then Colette, then Luc. I motioned to Rocco, and he came from where he'd been standing a few paces back and put his hand on the pile, too, and finally, Stellan put his on top. I placed my hand over all of theirs.

Elodie read some passages from a book in Greek, her face lit from below by the lamplight. I pressed my palm down, feeling the slight movements of all these people I loved holding me up. "Do you pledge your loyalty as long as you remain a member of the"—she looked up—"the Korolev family?"

I met Stellan's eyes. "I do pledge my loyalty," I said, then repeating the Circle motto, "By blood. And—"

Before the Circle ceremony where we were to become the official thirteenth family, we hadn't only discussed what name our family would take, and what symbol. We'd talked about the family motto. These had been Alexander the Great's words first, declaring how much of the earth would be his. But they meant more now.

Stellan nodded, and I finished the pledge. "I pledge my loyalty. By blood," I said, "and to the ends of the world."

CHAPTER 27

An hour later, I was sitting in an armchair, wincing as a tattoo artist Elodie had paid to come here during a citywide lockdown and paid more to keep quiet about it inked the symbol from my necklace onto the inside of my left wrist.

I hissed through clenched teeth, loud enough that Elodie laughed. "That hurts," I said.

"You were shot in that arm," Elodie reminded me. I made a face at her.

As the needle buzzed, Stellan stepped up beside me. He'd been quiet since I sat down. Now he stared at my wrist and chewed his lip. "It looks good."

It did. It was almost finished: the thirteen-loop symbol from the necklace I'd worn practically my whole life, now inked into my skin, part of me forever.

"I suppose we won't be quite official if I don't get one, too," Stellan said after a pause. I'd been trying to not think about it, trying to let him bring it up when he was ready. I glanced back at everyone else. Nisha had just come in to give an update on the new experiments they were doing on the vaccine, and Jack and Elodie were asking questions.

"You don't have to," I said.

"I know I don't."

The knots in my stomach drew tighter. I'd just declared my intention to take my place as part of the most powerful group in the world, but I was afraid to ask what exactly he meant. It didn't have to mean he was staying. He'd told me he loved me yesterday—but he'd also said it might be his only chance to say it. This could be the last thing he did with us before he left for good.

I should just ask. Get it out of the way. I was scared to.

The tattoo artist wiped a rag over my wrist one more time. There it was: our family's symbol.

I couldn't stop staring at it. Stellan took my wrist, ran a thumb around the edge of the tattoo. "I'm getting it," he said. "If that's okay with you."

"Yes," I said, to whatever it meant. Just like I'd still be in love with him if he had to leave the Circle, I'd always feel like he was part of the thirteenth family. Same for Jack and Elodie.

We repeated the ceremony, and Stellan pledged his fealty, too, to the Circle and to us, *to the ends of the world.*

"To the ends of the world," the rest of the group murmured.

A few minutes later, Stellan and I were left alone in the room. He shrugged off his shirt and tossed it across the tattoo chair, then turned to me, spreading his arms in the low light. "Where do you want it?"

I blinked. "You want *me* to choose?"

He looked down at himself, holding his blond hair out of his face with one hand, gesturing across his body with the other. His skin glowed golden in the lamplight. "Back's taken up already, but anywhere else is fair game. Unless you don't want to decide."

"I want to decide."

My gaze flitted over him. Maybe I could put the tattoo on his arm. The bicep was classic. Jack's tattoo was on his forearm—that was always a possibility, too. I looked over the chest I'd woken up on this morning, broad shoulders tapering to a narrow waist, hints of his ribs along his sides when he breathed in. On his rib cage, maybe. I felt a surge of possessiveness at his scars, since I now knew the story behind all of them. I was fairly certain that, as recently as we'd come into each other's lives, I knew plenty of things about Stellan Kololev that no one else in the world did.

And yet, we were still in this no-man's-land between forever and just today. I touched my fingers lightly to his chest. I had to know. He could still get our tattoo if he was leaving—but I couldn't stand it any longer. I started to open my mouth, but he cut me off.

"Tokyo," he said.

Oh. I felt my shoulders droop.

I tried to gear up my happy face. The one that said his going to the other side of the world was probably for the best. The one that said of course I was sad he was leaving, but I understood.

He reached out for my hand. "I want to get you Tokyo. For your birthday."

A draft blew through the room and the candles flickered. "What?" I said.

"I didn't get you a birthday present last night, and I realized today it's because I want to get you the whole world. Tokyo is the strangest, most amazing city. They have things called cat cafes—you literally pay a fee to pet cats. And I don't think you'll like sake—it's rice liquor—but I want you to taste it."

I shook my head to stop him. "Wait. You're not saying you're leaving?"

"Tokyo's a long flight. If I left the Circle, I'd have to fly commercial, and who wants that?" he said, with feigned flippancy. When I just stared at him blankly, his face softened. "Avery, I'm saying I'm sorry it's taken me so long to realize it, but it looks like we're the official thirteenth family. If you'll have me."

I realized then that as much as I'd hoped for this, I hadn't expected it. I'd truly thought he'd leave. "But what about *your* family? Anya?"

He ran his fingers over my knuckles. They'd healed. I hadn't been getting up in the middle of the night to punch things lately. "I suppose you're my family now, too. I never wanted to leave *you*."

"I know that, but—"

"I don't think I really even wanted to abandon the Circle. Well," he continued with a smirk, "that's not true. When I was a Keeper, I wanted out every day. But now, seeing how things could be . . ."

"You want it," I said, surprised. "The Circle. The power. The . . . world."

The golden ring around his pupils glowed in the low light. "It used to be that the only thing I wanted was to leave the Circle behind so Anya would be safe. Somewhere along the way, though, I realized I could have left—but instead, I'd been following *some girl* to the ends of the world. To save people I thought I hated, nonetheless."

I grinned up at him, but his face was still serious.

"I really did almost leave after Jerusalem. But I couldn't. I finally understood that you weren't just some girl. And that Jack was right. This is who I am. And it turns out that matters to me." He took my wrist, ran a finger around the edge of my tattoo. "*Kuklachka*, yes. I do want this. I want us to be part of the Circle. I want to make things better, and I want—the world, I suppose, yes. We're being handed this life that could be more than I've ever dreamed of. I want to take it. With you."

There were voices outside the door, but I ignored them, the reality of what he was saying crashing over me, fizzing and popping in my veins. He wasn't just agreeing to stay for me. He *wanted* it. Just like I did.

"But Anya—"

He nodded. "Yesterday, when you were talking about your mother, I started to think that if I left, I'd be doing the same thing. Living half a life, and forcing Anya to live half a life, all for the illusion of safety that could shatter at any time. This way, she'll be with me. She'll be as safe as she can be. She'll grow up surrounded by people who care about her, in a way neither of us got to do. And . . ." He twisted his fingers around mine nervously. "She could use a big-sister type. If you're okay with that. I know asking you to raise a child with me is not the normal topic of conversation on what's essentially a second date—"

I laughed past an unexpected tightness in my throat. "I am very much okay with it." I was almost embarrassed at how quickly I'd said it, and at the catch in my voice that made it mean so much more. I cleared my throat. "You and I will never have the kind of relationship we would have had if we'd met in calculus class and had to make out in your car after school like normal people."

A smile ghosted across his face, but more than a smile. Relief. "And I know the Circle does not love that I'm one half of this couple," he said. "It'll make it harder, and I'm sure there are many people who would be a better partner for you in this than I will. But I'll learn, and we'll have Luc to teach us, and Jack and Elodie to help—"

I threaded my fingers with his. "Stop," I said. Had he really been worrying that *I* would reject *him* for any of these reasons? "You know how to lead so people want to follow you, and you know the Circle from the inside. You care about people more than you care about politics. You're *exactly* what the Circle needs."

His eyes went soft, surprised in a way I'd never seen them. Was it possible that no one had ever told him that? People told him how good-looking he was. They told him he was talented at being a Keeper—but his ruthless, trained-killer side was his least favorite part of himself. I remembered him talking about how Jack was such a good person. Could it really be that he didn't believe the same things about himself? I promised myself right then that I'd appreciate all those other parts of him, and I'd let him know it.

"The Circle would be so lucky to have you," I said again. "They don't deserve you, really. But I hope I—I hope *we* do. Us. Me and Jack and Elodie and . . . our family."

The warmth of the candles around the room flickered over his face, and he gazed down at me like he had on the plane after we'd rescued Anya, like he couldn't quite believe I was real. "I've been waiting for something for so long," he said. "I didn't know what it was, but it . . ."

"Hurts," I whispered.

He nodded. "I kept noticing that I felt different, but it took me a long time to realize what it was. When I'm with you, I don't ache like something is missing anymore. I think maybe that's what it feels like to love someone. When being with them makes that ache go away."

He was right. For the first time I could remember, I didn't feel empty. I'd always felt so much more *alive* around him. That was exactly what this feeling was. "I love you," I said. We'd said it last night, and last night had been amazing. But something in me had been holding back, still guarding my heart. Now that I didn't have to, it was like a hundred doors inside me had blown open at once, and I couldn't hold back if I tried. "I should have realized it so much earlier than I did. I think I've been accidentally falling in love with you since . . ."

"The train," he said.

"Train?"

"For me it was earlier than that—in the water in Greece, I think. It made me feel like when you were attacked at Prada. When even though I barely knew you, I lost it at the thought of something happening to you." He shivered. "But the first time I thought you might feel something, too, was that morning on the train to Cannes. Do you remember that? I woke up with my arms around you. It only happened because I let my guard down, and I was ready to write it off, but the way you looked at me—like it was a mistake, but not like you were upset. Like—"

"Like it was a mistake because I liked it," I whispered.

His free hand came to my hip, pulling me against him. "I want to sleep with you on lots of trains in the future."

I raised my eyebrows, and his grin turned sheepish. "I did not mean it like that. Although . . ."

I giggled, my other hand cupping his neck, gently over his scars. *I love you*, I thought. *I love that you make inappropriate jokes without even meaning to, and I love that it always makes me laugh even if it shouldn't.*

"Little doll, I want to see the whole world with you. I want us to jump off a cliff into the ocean in Thailand. I want to know whether you'll scream or laugh."

"Scream," I whispered, and the smile on his face grew.

"And Sweden. We used to visit where my mother grew up, and in the summer, it stays light there until after midnight. I want to show you. I want to do all of that and so much more while we're *not* running for our lives."

I stroked one fingertip over his chest, watched goose bumps rise there.

He was beautiful. He was a cocky pain in the ass and the most broken person I'd ever met, and also one of the strongest.

I love you, I thought again. But now, the words felt so much fuller, thrumming through me like a heartbeat. I love you.

I flattened my palm in the center of his chest. "I love you," I whispered again.

He exhaled softly. *"Kuklachka,"* he said, and my own heart sped up to the rhythm of his, fluttering under my hand.

I'd been wrong before. I did want him to need me. I wanted us to need each other.

My eyes were drawn back down to my hand on his chest.

"Here," I said. "Get the tattoo here."

The door cracked open and the tattoo artist stuck her head inside. She stopped short just inside the door, and said in French something I was sure had to be "Am I interrupting?"

Stellan ducked his head to plant one firm kiss on my lips, then turned to the tattoo chair, plucking his shirt off it and sitting in its place, balling the shirt in his lap. "Ready," he said.

I sat in another chair a few feet away, and we didn't say another word, but I watched the whole time.

When his tattoo was done, he shrugged his shirt back on but left it open so the tattoo peeked out, dark and slightly irritated on his skin. Beautiful. Right in the place where part of it would peek through a shirt with a deep V neckline, but otherwise, it'd be secret. Earlier, I couldn't stop staring at my tattoo. Now I couldn't stop staring at his.

"We match," I whispered, holding my tattoo up next to his. Stellan took my wrist and stared at my tattoo in the candlelight, the black of the symbol and the tiny blue veins underneath. He brought my wrist to his lips. And when he pulled me into his lap in the tattoo chair, it was really, really hard to remember that there were people right outside this room waiting on us.

Finally I stood up and straightened my clothes. "We have responsibilities," I said, with as harsh a frown as I could muster. "Stop distracting me."

Jack and Elodie's voices murmured in the hallway outside, and it sobered me. "What about Jack?" I said. "Will that be weird if we're actually together and he's our Keeper?"

Even if Jack was fine with us being together, the three of us would always be something—something that wasn't Stellan and me, or Jack and me, or Jack and Stellan. Another thing, together, the three of us, that ached a little when I prodded it, but not in a bad way. In a way that somehow made each of the individual relationships stranger, and richer. Like the unfinished *Rebellious Slave*. The messiness of it made it not less, but more. At least that was how I felt. I didn't know how Jack felt, and that was the problem. "I don't want to hurt him," I said.

"I don't either. Trust me, I've thought about it a lot. But I think he'd be offended if we gave him a full bank account and a mansion and told him to go have fun. Being a Keeper is his life. So I'd say it's his choice. What do you think? And what about Elodie, for that matter?"

Shadows passed the sliver of light under the door. "I think it feels really strange to be discussing the lives of our friends like they're chess pieces."

"Welcome to the Circle."

He was right. We were a Circle family now. This was only the first of many situations that weren't likely to come naturally to me.

"I say we tell both of them we'd like them to get our tattoo and be part of our family if they want. And if they ever change their mind and no longer want to work for us, that's fine, too," I said.

"I completely agree."

In the end, we needn't have worried. We did the ceremony twice more, and while the two of them were getting their tattoos done—Elodie's on her wrist, matching mine, and Jack's on the forearm opposite his compass—Luc, Rocco on his heels, came in with news.

The meeting was to be held in Rome. At the Vatican. And, because everyone had known it would be somewhere in Europe and so all twelve families were close by, it would be in just a few hours.

Stellan and I followed Luc and Rocco down the hall to a room with one whole wall covered by TV monitors to talk strategy. Rocco was falling easily into a Keeper role here in the Dauphin household. I had a feeling a lot of lines the Circle didn't like blurred would be blurring for all of us.

The news on the TV showed a car on fire in one of Paris's ritzy shopping districts, and footage cut to a police officer tackling a guy into a closed storefront, shattering glass all over a display of high-fashion boots.

Luc was studying the screens. He turned to Stellan. "I'm sure you thought I was just ignoring all that. My father would not have allowed it to happen. He would have sent troops out to crush any rioting immediately."

"Iron fist," Stellan agreed.

Luc nodded. He looked only slightly self-conscious when he looked at Rocco, and then at Stellan, both as head of another family and as past Keeper of his, who probably knew strategy better than he did. "I didn't do that, but it was on purpose. I understand why they're rioting. It's not unreasonable. The world is a frightening place right now. Feeling like their leadership is unsympathetic toward them might not help matters. I had our troops contain and protect, and do what they could to minimize damage. We'll address the rest once it's over."

Stellan looked surprised. I had a feeling peace and compassion were not generally recognized Circle tactics. "Rome looks like this, too. What's the strategy for getting to the Vatican safely?" he said.

As we talked, it hit me how terrifying it was for us to be entirely in charge of our own fates like this. We'd been playing at it for so long, but this was real. I used to think all I'd be to the Circle was a symbol. A pawn. But we were a lot more than that. This was quieter and less glamorous and a million times more important than the tabloids and the parties. When we'd first met up with Fitz again, part of me had wanted to let him tell us what to do. But we didn't need that. Throughout history people our age had done this, learning as they went. And we could, too.

Maybe this was how the world worked. You weren't ready for something, but you did it anyway, because you had to.

When Jack and Elodie appeared, their tattoos freshly finished, and Colette followed, the conversation shifted to refining the plan for once we got into the room where the Circle would be signing the treaty.

I sat back in my chair and looked around at them. Luc and Rocco, a newly crowned young king and the person he trusted before the rest of us did. Colette, our fierce mother hen, who embodied everything we were trying to *save* in the Circle. Jack and Elodie, our two warriors, each so loyal in their own ways. And me and Stellan.

I thought it was weakness how we kept needing each other more and more. But no matter how many times we put each other back together, we weren't broken, neither of us. *Any* of us.

That was strength.

I'd been so soft and afraid when I'd come here. I'd melted and reformed into glass, hard and brittle. But now? I felt like steel. I sat down, and all seven of us decided together how best to save ourselves, and the Circle, and the world.

CHAPTER 28

Jack, Stellan, Elodie, and I were in a car in Rome a few hours later. We'd flown with Luc and Colette on the Dauphins' plane, but we'd parted ways on the tarmac as they took a helicopter the rest of the way. We wanted to keep our presence here a secret until the whole Circle was assembled. If any of the families was prepared to shoot us on sight, or lock us up, they weren't going to have the opportunity to do it until the rest of the Circle was watching and could remind them of their code.

Luc had left Rocco in charge of his security forces in Paris, and Nisha and the science team were still working on replicating the vaccine. Fitz, for his part, had made it very clear he didn't think we should be doing this. When he realized we couldn't be dissuaded, he'd reminded us to take the vaccine ourselves, just in case, and wished us well. Once this was over, maybe I'd actually have time to get to know my grandfather.

We'd meant to be at the Vatican half an hour ago, waiting to go into the meeting the second it started. But traffic was at a standstill, and every shortcut the driver tried was met with police in riot gear or crowds congregating in the streets, most of them in surgical masks or with bandanas tied over their faces.

I tapped my fingers nervously on the cab's cracked leather seat as I strained to see out the back windows. We didn't have time for this. Luc could stall for a few minutes, but if the treaty was signed before we arrived, it was all over.

"We have to get out," I said.

"And do what, run? We're still miles away." Elodie craned her neck over a crowd burning something in the street.

A memory came to me. Istanbul, holding on to Jack like my life depended on it, the stolen motorcycle we were on flying through the city streets while people we thought were the Order chased us.

There was no shortage of motorbikes in Rome. I looked around and spotted a few parked in front of a gelato shop half a block away. "Can you guys hot-wire those?"

We jumped out of the cab. No one gave us a second look while Jack fiddled with some wires in one bike's ignition and Stellan did the other. Both bikes roared to life, and I climbed on behind Stellan while Elodie held on to Jack. "See you there," I yelled, and I clung to Stellan as we sped off down the street.

We maneuvered around crowds of people who paid no attention to us, and police officers who yelled in vain for us to slow down. When our lane slowed, Stellan swerved into oncoming traffic, nearly missing a wall of cars coming the other way. I dug my fingers into his chest and we flew up onto a sidewalk to a chorus of angry honking, and then made an abrupt turn onto a bridge flanked by stone lions. He hit the gas and we flew over the Tiber River, the gold dome of St. Peter's Basilica approaching fast.

And then I looked around him at the road ahead.

"Stop!" I shrieked, but Stellan was already slamming on the brakes. I lurched forward, and Stellan braced us hard. Jack and Elodie ground to a halt next to us. The bridge was blocked by hundreds—no, *thousands*—of people.

"It's St. Peter's Square," Stellan said. "It's so crowded, it's spilled all the way out to here."

"Is the pope speaking?" Jack asked.

"Maybe. Or maybe this is just where people feel safe," Stellan said.

I looked at my phone. "Twelve minutes until the meeting starts."

We left the bikes on the sidewalk. Stellan took my hand, I took Jack's, and he took Elodie's, and we started weaving through the densely packed crowd.

The sun wasn't down yet, but the pilgrims were holding candles already, a vigil for those who had died, and a prayer for those who still might. Some chanted, some cried. A group of stoic old men held signs in English proclaiming the end of the world, and every few feet someone silently lifted a cross to the sky, eyes closed, lips moving in prayer. Some eyes shifted to us as we pushed by, and there were a few shouts in languages I didn't know, but most of the crowd ignored us, their eyes straight ahead to a glowing balcony, where the pope stood to give blessings.

I wondered for just a second whether we should try to evacuate all these people. If the Saxons were to release the virus on the Circle and it got down here . . . But we had no way to do it, and no time.

As we got closer, the crowds grew thick enough that we were getting nowhere. A wild-eyed man jumped in front of us and screamed something, waving a hand-painted sign, and I recoiled while Stellan waved him off. Jack let go of my hand and climbed up on the base of a light pole to look over the crowd, then jumped back down and led us in a different direction. "Excuse us!" Elodie shouted, and repeated it in Italian and French before we resorted to using our elbows. We skirted a group of nuns, not one of them taller than me.

And then, we were at the front of St. Peter's Basilica. To get Alexander's bone, we'd traipsed into their most sacred archives and taken anything we wanted—Circle privileges. Now we hopped the low fence only to be stopped immediately by a group of the Swiss Guard. Stellan said a few words to one of them, and he went to get a superior while the rest held weapons on us. When a priest appeared, Stellan murmured something to him, and he looked over the four of us, surprised—and opened the doors, gesturing for the guards to step aside.

The priest—the Circle's main contact here at the Vatican, Stellan whispered to me—showed us inside St. Peter's Basilica.

The same panic that had driven some people to riot outside had driven others in here, to seek comfort another way. The pews were packed with worshippers. Chanting, sonorous and trancelike, floated up like the wisps of smoke from the braziers. Saints and angels rendered in gold looked on from their perches high above the congregation, and the last rays of the evening light slanted in, blinding off the cathedral's gilded accents, like the heavens had opened right above us. Our footsteps echoed hollowly.

We followed the priest up some stairs and into a room filled with Circle members. The second the door opened, every head swung our way. Everyone but Luc and Colette looked like they'd seen a ghost. Quite a few of them gestured to their Keepers, and in moments, half a dozen guns were trained on us. We'd known this would happen.

We'd considered blurting out everything the second we walked in the door. We'd decided against it. Without any preamble, no one would believe us. They might just kill us.

So we just put our hands up and walked calmly inside, like we were meant to be here.

The whole Circle was sitting around a long table, like they did at council meetings. In front of each of them was what looked like a contract and a pen. I immediately found Lydia, at the far end of the table, by my father. I let out a soft breath.

I hadn't actually seen Lydia since Cole had died. In Russia, we'd just heard her voice. Her long dark hair was gone, in its place a severe, choppy pixie cut, messy enough that she'd probably done it herself, and not carefully. She was wearing an oversized coat, and she had no makeup on. This was the first time I'd ever seen her less than perfectly put together.

Next to her was my father. Alistair Saxon was at the head of the table, pretending, as he did, to be in charge. He half stood when we came into the room. And then he sat back down and sighed, and my last, small hope that he would stand up for what was right died.

I didn't think my father was evil. My mom never would have fallen for him if he was, and Fitz's story had confirmed it. But he'd broken a long time ago, and had never put himself back together. Maybe it should have made me feel sorry for him, but it just made me angry. He might not be evil, but he was allowing evil things to happen because of his weaknesses, and that was just as bad.

"Avery." Lydia smiled, but there was no emotion behind it at all. It hit me who she reminded me of. She looked as vacant as I'd felt in the weeks after my mom died. I remembered exactly how little I cared about anything then, and how dangerous that was. "If we had known all it took was a council meeting to make you turn yourselves in, we would have done it long ago."

"Take their weapons," my father said.

We'd expected that, too. We let two men I recognized as a Saxon

Keeper and one of Rocco's old cronies search us and set our weapons at the far end of the room. The guns on us slowly lowered, but the atmosphere didn't grow any more welcoming.

"We're not here to turn ourselves in," I said. Stellan and I ignored the murmurs of disapproval and made our way confidently around the room to the head of the table, where the Saxons sat. Jack and Elodie followed us at a distance. This was part of the plan, too. Tonight, we'd be what the Circle had wanted us to be all along.

Ryo Mikado stood. "You have no right."

Most of the table nodded, angrily or warily. Even kind Arjun Rajesh looked disappointed in us—if *disappointed* was the right word when someone thought we'd been trying to bring down the whole world.

"You initiated us," I said. We'd decided I'd do most of the talking. The Circle were intrigued by Stellan, but I was more familiar to them. I held up my wrist. "And we completed the tattoo ceremony with the Dauphin family as witnesses. We're official. What's more, when you initiated us, you did so knowing we'd technically be the Circle's leaders. So yes, we do have the right to be here. But we're not here to exercise our rule. We've come here tonight to tell you the truth."

"The only thing you've done by coming here is allow us to punish you as we see fit," Lydia interrupted. "The only question will be who to terminate first. The two of you, or the Keeper who murdered my brother." Her eyes flashed at Jack.

My father held up his hands. "Once all the treaties are signed and witnessed, we can discuss the fate of the thirteenth family. Until then, please stay on task."

No one else protested. Instead, they picked up their pens reluctantly. They were too afraid of the Saxons. I'd been wrong to believe they didn't care about their people—they cared so much, they were going to ruin their own lives to save them. And they didn't want to speak up and take any chances.

Instead, we were taking the chance for them. This was the moment we could be sentencing the world to die. Or maybe the Circle. Or maybe ourselves.

"Don't sign the treaties," I said.

A few people with pens in their hands paused, but most just frowned up at me warily.

"Releasing the virus won't work." I was impressed with how confident I sounded about the lie. "That's what we've come here to tell you. We have a vaccine for the virus and we've distributed it in your territories. Your people won't die. You don't have to sign the treaty to save them."

CHAPTER 29

There were murmurs around the table. My father turned in his chair to face me. A set of massive doors with curtains pulled partway across them opened to a balcony behind us. It looked out on St. Peter's Square below, full of people as far as I could see. We must be in the room connected to the balcony where the pope always addressed the square.

"She's lying." Lydia got her phone out of her pocket. She must have had the trigger to release the virus programmed.

"We're not." Every head at the table swung from Lydia to me as though they were watching a tennis match. "We tried to tell you about the vaccine, but no one would listen. You should listen now, and not just because of the treaty—but because if you sign it, the Saxons plan to release the virus in *this room.*"

It took a second for that to sink in, and then the table erupted with protests.

"What do you mean by that?" Mr. Wang demanded.

"They're having you sign over everything you have," I said over the din. "And then they'll kill *you* so your families will be too destroyed to fight back. But we have the vaccine, and you should all take it." I nodded at Colette. She pulled a bag full of small vials out of her purse, and began to hand them out.

"Don't be stupid." Lydia's bored indifference cracked just a tiny bit. "They're obviously infecting you."

My father squinted at the vial in front of him quizzically.

"Why should we believe any of this?" Ryo Mikado said, but I noticed he'd pushed his paper away.

Arjun Rajesh opened the vial and sniffed it.

Outside, the wailing and chanting was growing louder as the sun went down.

"Because I vouch that it's true." Luc stood up at the center of the table.

Lydia laughed. "They killed Hugo and Celine Dauphin and left Lucien alive because he's in on their schemes. That means nothing."

Colette set her bag down. She stepped up to the table. "Lucien is right." Every head turned to her. "I've seen it all. There's no way I'd be siding with people who killed Liam, or who killed my aunt and uncle. Those of you who have also lost someone, ask yourselves whether you think I'm telling the truth. And if you don't believe that, believe this. I've taken the vaccine already." She walked around the table to Stellan and me. She opened a small pocketknife. I held out my arm, and Stellan did, too. She cut me and wiped a bead of my blood on her hand, then cut Stellan and mixed our blood together.

"Colette!" Mr. Frederick cried out, slamming both hands on the table. Colette must have been like family to him. She'd dated his nephew Liam Blackstone for years.

"I'm doing this for Liam's memory," she said. "He would never have wanted to see you die over this. Any of you. Now you'll have to believe us." She put her hand to her mouth.

Mr. Frederick looked at her with wide eyes. Mr. Emir's mouth fell open. Zara Koning, whom I'd talked to at the party in Jerusalem, gasped from her place behind her father.

As the entire Circle stared in shocked silence, Colette wiped a tiny bit of blood daintily off her lip.

"More lies, more manipulation," Lydia said, but no one was listening to her. All eyes were on Colette, watching for any sign of the virus taking hold as she made her way back around the table to the seat behind Luc.

Elodie was right. "Alive" was a pretty low bar, but in this case, it was all we needed.

"Take the vaccine," I said again.

"It's a trick," my father said, but even he sounded uncertain.

Stellan's hand came over mine. "Mr. Saxon," he said, cutting through the murmurs building in the room. "You brought Avery into this against her will. You tried to marry her off. You used her own blood to kill her mother and made her watch, and then you ruined the world with it and blamed that on her, too. And somehow she's managed to stay good and kind and care that the Circle would fall." He turned to the table. "She is the one who convinced us you were worth saving. Let her do it."

I was still watching Lydia's finger poised over her phone. While Stellan was speaking, she turned it off and put it back in her pocket, and I loosened my grip on the edge of the table. Maybe she believed us about the vaccine getting out. Or maybe she could see the tides turning against her.

And then she gestured to one of her minions. The guy trained a gun on Stellan. "Who votes to terminate the ex-Keeper now?" Lydia said.

"What? No," I said. Arms came roughly around me from behind, dragging me back from the table. On my other side, two more men seized Jack and Elodie. Stellan backed slowly away from the table, his hands spread warily.

"He's a Circle member," I protested, clamping down the panic in my voice. "It's forbidden to terminate a Circle member without a trial."

Lydia ignored me. "He's responsible for killing members of over half the Circle families. All in favor of termination?"

Around the table, David Melech's hand went up, Mr. Hersch's, and, of course, my father's.

"You heard the recording," I protested. "Lydia admitted *they* did all those things. Not us."

The hands remained in the air. I remembered what Stellan said earlier—some of the Circle didn't like him. They weren't going to let an ex-Keeper be one of them no matter what. I struggled harder.

"You can't do this." Luc stalked toward Lydia until another of her guards pointed a gun at him. He stopped and turned to the table. "He's technically your *leader*. It has to be a three-fourths majority for termination even of a distant family member."

"I have to agree with Lucien," said a worried-sounding Arjun Rajesh. "What if they're telling the truth? Even if they're not, this is against code."

"He's right," George Frederick spoke up. "I'm not against a trial, but—"

"We're not voting on Avery now," Lydia coaxed, ignoring them. "This one was a Keeper who turned on us. It was a mutiny. Even if he does have the mystical powers it seems like he does, it's in his entire bloodline. There are plenty more in the world who can fill that place."

Two more hands went up hesitantly. Slowly, Mr. Koning put his hand in the air. Zara met Luc's eyes across the table. "Father, no," she said, low, but he ignored her.

"That's a majority," Lydia said.

"No!" I screamed.

I didn't even stop to think. My elbow connected with the Keeper's stomach and I wrenched out of his arms, throwing myself between Stellan and the gun. "*Kuklachka*, get out of the way," he growled.

"Stop!" my father yelled, pushing back from the table. The guard with the gun paused. "Don't shoot her! We don't want her dead."

Behind us, the chants and prayers of the crowd outside had turned into a frenzied wall of sound. A warm breeze swirled in from the balcony.

"Just let them both die," Daniel Melech said. "Most of this is her fault, anyway, and we'll take all the blood we can from her as she bleeds out. All in favor?"

"Now hold on one minute," my father said, leaping from his chair, but some of the same hands went up as had voted to kill Stellan. Even with the incentive of the virus and the vaccine, the rest of the Circle had none of the vague attachment to me my own family seemed to have.

Daniel didn't even stop to count. "Do it," he snapped to his Keeper.

The Keeper raised his gun, aiming right at my head.

I hardly had time to suck in a quick breath and start to duck before the gun went off.

Then I was being tackled to the ground. Screams echoed in my ears.

I was on the floor, half on the balcony. My father was lying across me, a pool of blood spreading under him.

Lydia screamed.

She dropped to the ground by Alistair's head. Stellan was there immediately, pulling me from under my father's body. I stared at Alistair's blank face. He'd saved me. After everything, my father had given his life for mine.

Lydia was sobbing, huddled over him, digging through his pockets. She came out with his phone, her bloody fingers sliding clumsily across the screen. It could be a city she was about to infect, but I was willing to bet her focus had narrowed. Stellan and I started toward her, but with the hand not holding the phone, she pulled a gun out of her coat. "Stay back!"

We froze. She turned back to the screen.

"Take the vaccine!" I shouted. "Drink the vial! Now! Everybody— Keepers, too. You're going to die if you don't."

Arjun Rajesh took his, then handed a second one to his Keeper. So did the Mikados and the Vasilyevs, and surprisingly, the Emirs. A few more families held their vials nervously, watching those who had taken the vaccine for any sign of imminent death.

"Take it!" I yelled again. I looked to Stellan, desperate. His shirt fell open at the collar, and I saw our tattoo, dark and strong and sure on his chest.

Our tattoo. The thirteenth family's.

I touched Stellan's chest and took a breath. "I *order* you to take the vaccine."

"Yes," Stellan murmured, but only a few people heard me above the commotion. Stellan squeezed my hand and nodded to Lydia.

I let go of him and turned to my sister. Stellan's voice boomed across the room behind me, "We are the thirteenth family of the Circle of Twelve. We're your leaders. And we order you to take the vaccine we've given you. We order you by blood."

Without looking to see whether they were responding, I inched toward Lydia.

She was huddled against the balcony railing, gulping back sobs, wiping the phone's screen on her shirt. Behind her, the worshippers in the square had heard the gunshots and seen the activity, and the square had gone quiet. A sea of faces turned up to us, tens of thousands—*hundreds* of thousands—of people expecting their pope to give his blessing, but instead getting this.

"Don't, Lydia. You don't have to infect the Circle."

She looked up at me, shaking and wild eyed, and pointed the gun at me again. "I do. I have to. I promised. It's the only way. He was right."

"What?" I held my hands up. "Who was right?"

"He said we'd never have to worry about our family being hurt again." She dragged her sleeve across her tearstained face. "He helped me before, but then he was gone. I had to do it alone. Until yesterday. He said this would be the only way to make sure everything I set in motion could happen. That if all the family heads were gone, things would be easier. And he was right. They're turning on us. I should have done it earlier."

"Who are you talking about?" I was right—someone had been behind Lydia's schemes all along, and it wasn't Alistair. I had a sudden disturbing thought. Had something sent her a lot further over the edge than I'd realized? Was this all in her head?

"I didn't want Oliver to die, Avery." I startled at the sudden change in topic, but she went on, "How could I possibly want that? He was my *brother*. But he did die. I was part of it, and I didn't even realize it. It wasn't Cole's fault, either. It was—it was all this. It's taken everything from us. And *he* said—"

I fell to the ground beside my sister. Beside our dead father. "Who are you talking about?" I said again.

"I don't know!" she shrieked. "I never met him. He was Oliver's friend. He said he'd help make sure it never happened again. That our family was safe. That the Circle would be better off in the long run. He was the only one who would help me."

"It's okay—" I tried to make my voice soothing, and inched closer to her, but she pulled the gun again. I put my hands back up. "All of your family is gone, Lydia. Whoever was telling you to do this was wrong. Stop before more people die. It's over."

She shook her head again, frantically, glancing at the phone's screen. "He said no one would understand. He said I was the only one strong enough to do it. It would have worked if it hadn't been for you."

I surreptitiously tried to reach for the phone, but she held it out of my reach, her thumb over the screen.

"If you release the virus in here, you'll die, too," I said softly, changing tactics. "You think you have a cure, but you don't. Don't do it."

Lydia looked down at Alistair again—at our father, who looked so much like both of us—and burst into tears. She lowered her hand and I took the phone out of it.

I rubbed my face. "Now tell your side to put the guns down, and we'll talk like civilized—"

The doors opened. It seemed like everyone with guns couldn't decide whether to point them at the door or at each other. Someone walked in. A priest.

The priest was holding an ornate metal ball on a chain, the kind they swung during Mass to spread incense. Smoke came from inside the ball, wafting up toward the ceiling.

The priest pushed back his hood, and my heart stuttered.

It was Fitz.

No. He couldn't be here. He was going to try to do something heroic to save us, but I couldn't watch him get killed. Again.

"Jack!" I screamed.

He was already pushing past people to the door. "Get out of here," he yelled to Fitz. "It's not safe—"

Fitz held up a hand and looked around the room. Everyone was paralyzed. Those who knew him had thought he was dead. Those who didn't had no idea who this "priest" was. Smoke still poured from the holes in the contraption.

The vaccine. It had to be. Nisha hadn't thought they could aerosolize it and get the concentration high enough to work, but they must have.

Fitz's gaze finally landed on me, and he made a beeline for the balcony.

"I'm okay," I called.

"You're stronger than that," he said.

I jumped up.

But Fitz looked *past* me. "You're stronger than that, Lydia," he said.

Now *I* froze. "What?"

"What?" Lydia echoed, and behind Fitz, I saw the same sentiment on Jack's face, and Elodie's.

Fitz walked right past me and swung the smoke near Lydia and the guards on the balcony.

"What are you doing?" I asked him.

"You were doing the right thing for your family all along," Fitz said to Lydia. "I wish you'd been able to finish it. I wanted that for you. At least you can know your family is at peace."

Across the room, someone coughed. Fitz pushed past me back

into the room and tossed the ball in the middle of the conference table. The smoke was coming out more quickly now.

I took a step back, staring warily at him. "What's going on?" Stellan said at my elbow.

"I don't know—"

"Oh God," Lydia said. She was staring at Fitz, wide-eyed. And then a drop of blood fell from her left eye.

I heard a cough and wheeled around. At the far end of the room, David Melech was leaned over, hands on his knees, racked with coughing. So was Daniel next to him.

That smoke. It was not the vaccine. It was killing them. That meant—

I turned back to Lydia just as she downed the contents of a small vial from her pocket—not the one we'd brought, but one she already had. The "cure," I was certain. She looked up at Fitz accusingly. "It was *you*?" she choked.

The understanding that had been trying to break through finally hit me like a punch.

Fitz had come in here spreading the virus. Fitz had talked to Lydia like he knew her. Like he'd given her orders she hadn't followed through on. Lydia had been under the command of some mystery person, directing her in her efforts to take down the whole Circle for the "good" of her family.

It was Fitz. All this time, it was Fitz.

He'd conned the Saxons into doing all of this, throwing the Circle into the kind of chaos it hadn't seen for two thousand years.

Now he stood, calmly, right in the middle of the chaos. "Take the vaccine," I said, and I could barely hear myself, like I was underwater. "Take the vaccine!" I yelled to the room. "The smoke is the virus! Take it now!"

But it was too late. Mr. Koning opened the vial and tossed the contents down his throat, but it came right back up in a cough and a spout of blood.

I turned back to Fitz. "How?" I sputtered. "Why?"

"So for the first time since the Circle came into existence, the world could go back to *peace*." He took me by the arm, trying to steer me out of the room, but Elodie smacked his hand away.

"What the *hell*?" she said.

Jack was still standing next to us, speechless.

"You've been guiding Lydia since the very first assassinations to stir the Circle into turning on each other?" I said. "Did you get kidnapped on purpose to get closer to her?"

"That was not originally part of the plan, no. I'll tell you everything, Avery. And you too, Charlie, Elodie. But we have to leave *now*. All of us do. It also wasn't part of the plan for some of them to survive this."

There was more coughing around the room, more screams. At the end of the table closest to us, Jakob Hersch collapsed, blood streaming down his face. Colette ran from person to person, trying to help, but it was no use.

"We were your pawns all along?" I said. "*I* was your pawn?"

"This was *for* you," Fitz pleaded. "For the future. For the world, but mostly for *you*, Avery. The Circle has taken so much from us. My research was always about giving you back what you should have had. So was this."

"The cure's not working!" the Melech Keeper yelled. Daniel Melech was holding a vial like Lydia had, laboring for breath, and his father, David, was choking, spraying blood across the table.

I heard a whimper, and turned to find Lydia trying to stand, blood running down her face.

Fitz tried to pull me toward the door again, but Jack grabbed him. I dropped beside my sister. Even though there was enough blood in Lydia's eyes that I couldn't see the expression in them, I could tell by the way her head darted around that she was terrified.

"Lydia," I said. "It's okay. It's going to be okay. Sit. Come here."

Her head whipped around, her blind eyes trying to find me. "Avery," she choked. I was the only family she had left. She grabbed for my hand. "Avery. It was a lie. It's only in a few cities. Paris. Tokyo. Moscow. Mumbai. We didn't have enough of your blood. I didn't want to do it." Her voice dropped to a whisper. "I knew some people would have to die. I didn't want to kill kids, whole families. I didn't want—"

She coughed. Blood painted her teeth red. "He said everything would be better if we— I believed him—"

She started coughing and she couldn't stop. I knew what would come next. She'd keep bleeding. Her lungs would collapse, and she'd die choking on her own blood. I saw my mom, her blond hair matted with red, her eyes going from frantic to dull and dead, but not before a lot of blood and pain.

I should let the same happen to Lydia. There couldn't be a more fitting revenge.

I reached into my top and found the new knife Elodie had given me.

Lydia whimpered and tried to pull herself to standing, not giving up even now. Behind her, over the top of the stone balcony, I could see the crowd losing its composure. There were screams, pointing up at us, some parts of the crowd moving, running, making it look like one huge living thing. At the back of the square, something was on fire.

"Lydia, try to relax. You'll be fine," I lied as soothingly as I could. I gathered her to me, her blood soaking my shirt.

"I'm sorry," she whispered. "I lost Oliver. I lost you. Then I lost Cole. I thought if I did this—"

I felt unexpected tears fill my own eyes. I opened the knife.

Lydia coughed again, choking, her whole body tensed with panic.

"Shh," I said. "You didn't lose me. I'm here."

She rested her head on my shoulder. I wasn't sure whether it was on purpose or she couldn't hold it up anymore. I wiped my wet face with the back of my hand and positioned the tip of my knife between her ribs, where I was pretty sure Stellan had taught me the heart was. Could I really bring myself to do it? What if I didn't hit the right place—

Stellan knelt in front of me. He readjusted my hand. Inside the room, someone wailed.

"I'm sorry," Lydia whispered again, and I nodded at Stellan.

I had been waiting for so long to get revenge on my siblings. Now Stellan and I together slipped my knife between my sister's ribs.

Lydia shuddered, and I held her tight, and then she sagged.

Stellan ran his hand over his face. I laid Lydia gently on the concrete balcony, and then let him help me up. He swiped his thumbs across my cheeks and we pushed through the curtain to a bloodbath. Too many people to count were on the floor, their bodies racked with coughs, or already dead. Some were just starting to show symptoms, panicking anew.

Jack and Elodie had Fitz restrained.

I glanced over my shoulder. The riot was getting worse. "Where's the pope?" I said. "The actual pope. Someone go find him."

A couple of people darted out of the room.

"The Order did this!" someone I didn't know shouted. He must have been a Keeper.

Stellan stepped forward. "The Saxons orchestrated it, on the command of one rogue Order member. We'll have justice—"

The man raised a gun at Fitz. "We're not waiting for justice anymore."

Jack stepped in front of him, still the noble knight, after all this time. "Jack—" I said.

But he didn't move. "The way to solve violence is not with more violence."

From behind him, Fitz met my eyes. We were all doing the same thing, I realized. Us. Lydia. Even him, behind it all. Each of us trying to do the best we could for the people we cared about.

Maybe everything depended on how you framed it. Family. Power. Love.

"Put down the gun," Stellan yelled, but it was too late.

The Keeper was pulling the trigger.

I lunged for Jack, but as I did, I saw Fitz shove him out of the way. Then I was on the floor, Elodie on top of me. Jack and Stellan were in a heap next to us. All four of us had jumped in to keep one another from being hit.

Jack sat, dazed, and looked up at Fitz.

Fitz dropped to his knees, his eyes wide behind his round glasses. And then he fell, a pool of blood beneath him.

Elodie clapped her hand to her mouth. A sob escaped from mine. The only sounds in the room were the hacking coughs and wet, rattling breaths of the dying.

The doors to the room opened, and a man in all-white robes came inside.

The pope surveyed the carnage. He murmured under his breath

and crossed himself, then calmly stepped over the bloodied bodies littering the floor. Two priests in red followed, and they flipped some switches and adjusted what must have been a microphone at the pope's collar. He stood at the doors to the balcony composing himself for just a moment before he stepped outside, over Lydia's body. His voice boomed out of the speakers surrounding St. Peter's Square.

The crowds outside fell immediately silent. The pope started to pray, and his assistants pulled heavy velvet curtains shut behind him, closing us off from outside.

Luc stepped to the head of the table, breaking the eerie silence that had finally fallen over the room. "Everyone, guns down," he said quietly. "Put your weapons on the table. All of you." People looked at each other, then guns and knives were tossed down next to the unsigned treaties and the no-longer-smoking weapon of destruction Fitz had brought.

Luc turned to me, Jack, Stellan, and Elodie. "You too," he said. "Thirteenth family."

Jack and Elodie reluctantly relinquished their guns. My knife was still in Lydia's chest.

"Now," Luc said. "Back away from the table. There will be a lot to discuss. This atrocity. The Order and what to do going forward. But there will be no more death today." He looked at us. "It's over. It's all over."

EPILOGUE

All in favor?"

Hand after hand went up. Stellan and I looked at each other, and I raised my hand, too. Ten to three. Passed. It wasn't a major issue—we'd voted not to touch any of those for a while—but any kind of agreement was a positive.

"Korolev family?" Zara Koning said. "Your floor."

"For the third item on the agenda, I outlined the pros and cons yesterday," I said, "and now we'd like to put it up for a vote." The Mikados asked a question, and I explained.

Stellan was watching me, little frown lines between his brows that said he was taking something seriously. I wasn't sure why. We knew exactly where we stood on this issue.

"Excuse us for one moment while we discuss." He closed the laptop.

"What's wrong?" I said.

He framed my face with his hands and kissed me hard. "You really have to stop looking like that while discussing trade agreements. I can't concentrate. I'm going to accidentally put in a motion for Luxembourg to invade Belgium, and it'll be entirely your fault."

I hid my grin as he opened the computer back up. "Thanks for your patience," he said seriously, turning the floor back over to me.

"If there are no more questions, we'll take a vote," Zara said. She and her brother were both at the meeting. Zara was older, but in the past, her brother would have been next in line, as the male heir. That was one of the items on the docket for future vote, but for now, families were allowed to have anyone they wanted present at council meetings, and all thirteen families took turns leading them. When we'd voted and the issue passed, Zara said, "And with that, the meeting is adjourned. Reconvene tomorrow, at the same time."

We all nodded, Luc gave a little wave of his fingers I knew was meant for us, and I gave one back. Stellan closed the laptop again. "Another day as a Circle family down," he said.

After the Vatican, we'd brought the remaining Circle together and made a plan for the near future. We had to rebuild, within the Circle and in the world. We'd be meeting every day, but for the sake of both peace of mind—lots of the families still didn't trust each other—and each family's efforts in their own territories, we'd do it remotely for now.

The world had quieted some in the weeks since that night. Once the pope had calmed the crowds, any world leaders left alive in the room assembled, showing not only the half million people in the square, but news cameras streaming around the world that we were a united front. The story, according to the press, was that the politically motivated terrorists responsible for the carnage all over the world had attempted to attack again that night, but had been killed. With all the chaos that had been captured by the news cameras, people believed it. There had been no more attacks since then.

The Circle was trying to recover. Our first order of business had been to make sure the places hardest hit by the Saxons—Jerusalem, and Paris, and Rome, and Beijing—had help putting their cities back together and trying to heal.

The heads of six families had died. Every family had at least one direct heir to take over—except for the Saxons.

The closest Saxon heir still alive was me.

For now, Alistair's cousin—the father of Sunday Six drummer Noah Day—was second closest, and he was acting head of the family. I wasn't worried about him trying to overthrow me. Like Noah, he had no love for the Saxons. Plus, he was an influential politician in his own right.

We, the thirteenth family, the Korolev family, had no territory of our own. That would be put to a vote sometime soon, but for now, we were in an "undisclosed location." Someplace far away from Paris or Rome or Russia, where we could be certain we were safe while everything settled.

Stellan stood up and unbuttoned his crisp, collared shirt. It had looked a bit ridiculous with his orange swim trunks. I took a second to admire our tattoo in the center of his chest. I'd chosen the placement well. It made me want to touch his chest even more than I already did. The cuts across his back from Lydia's attack in Russia had healed to nothing already. The salve Nisha had made was helping with the pain. She'd given us more, and now we were putting it on Anya every day, too. It didn't offer much relief to the thicker burn scars on Stellan's back—but it was something.

And as they worked to learn more about the Great modification, Nisha and the science team were beginning to discover that it might have more uses. It was especially promising in cancer research. And they were still, secretly, working on a way to better distribute the vaccine for the virus, just in case.

I pulled my dress over my head to expose my own neon-yellow

bikini. Stellan raised his eyebrows appreciatively. "Have I mentioned that I have the most beautiful girlfriend in the world?"

"About a hundred times a day."

He scooped me into his arms. "A hundred times is not enough."

"Cheesy," I admonished, looping my arms around his neck. "I'm going to get tired of you if you turn into a big cheeseball all the time." This was a lie. I'd seen him smile more in the past week than I had the whole time I'd known him. I would never get tired of that.

"But cheese tastes good, yes?" He leaned down and kissed the bullet wound on my shoulder. "Healing nicely," he said, carrying me outside.

"Going to have some weird tan lines," I mused, picking at the small bandage.

It was an act, the smiles and the flirting and the fun. I didn't know how long it would be until we felt whole again. But we were safe. The world was okay. We were trying.

Stellan set me down on the porch of our bungalow, and we looked through the row of palm trees out to a wide white sand beach. This little island could only be reached by boat, and even on the mainland, we hadn't seen a single person in all of Thailand who gave us a second glance. No Circle, no paparazzi.

"Speaking of tan lines," I said, "when was the last time we put more sunscreen on her?" Anya was crouched in the sand, playing with the nanny she'd grown up with, whom Stellan had tracked down in Russia and brought to live with us. "She's going to be a lobster."

Stellan grimaced and shrugged. We might have more to learn about the *being responsible for a kid* thing than the *being part of the Circle* thing.

I grabbed the bottle of sunscreen and started down the beach. Anya jumped up when she saw me coming. "Avie!" she screeched, and ran up the beach, kicking up sand and grabbing my hand to drag me back to the water's edge. She'd started warming to me, finally.

The sun and the sand and the steady diet of mango shakes and green curry had relaxed us all a little. I'd even been sleeping better, and Stellan had, too—though I'd realized now that we were together every night that he had more nightmares than I did. When one of us woke, the other would wrap them up and whisper nonsense until we both fell back to sleep, and if we were up with the sunrise, which we still often were, we had a beautiful beach just outside our door waiting for a morning swim.

Anya dropped beside the pile of wet sand she was sculpting into some kind of creature, and chattered away to me. I still didn't understand a word, but I smiled at the nanny over her head. Farther away, down the beach, a sheer cliff rose out of the water, craggy and dramatic against the turquoise water. At its base, Elodie was panting and sweaty, just back from a run.

Jack stood on the hard-packed sand nearby, with a boy named Maxim. He was the son of Sofia, the nanny, and Stellan had known him for years—their family had been friends with the Korolevs when Stellan was a kid. Max was my age, and had been in Russian military training for the past year. When we asked Sofia to come on full-time with us, we'd brought Max, too, since the two of them were the only family either had. We hadn't said it yet, but we were hoping he could take over as Keeper at some point. So Max had been training with Jack every day, and Jack was impressed so far. We were not at the point to trust anyone we didn't know with our secrets, but for now he knew he was training to be bodyguard to a family who paid very well while treating him like an actual human being, and that was good enough.

We needed a new Keeper because once Jack and Elodie felt comfortable with his progress, they wouldn't be staying with us full-time anymore.

Something had happened in the days after the Vatican. Jack wasn't the same. None of us were, but he had taken it especially hard. Then one day, he and Elodie had asked to talk to us.

They had decided to join the Order. Both of them.

After what had happened, Elodie felt like she'd be more useful with the Order than she would with us. Jack wanted to go with her. He confessed that he'd been secretly considering working with Fitz already, and after what Fitz had done, it only strengthened his resolve. Both of them saw potential to reinvent the Order as a complement to the Circle rather than an adversary. They'd do it aboveboard, and in full collaboration with us.

It took me a few days to wrap my mind around the most faithful Circle member I'd ever met joining the *Order*, but Jack looked happy with his decision. It might have to do with the fact that he'd been talking to Nisha every day, but I really did think his new path was good for him, too.

The rest of the Order claimed not to have any knowledge of Fitz's campaign to make the Saxons destroy the Circle, and we believed them. There just weren't enough of them for it to be a big conspiracy. The Order was going to pull their spies out of Circle households, and there was no more need to prevent purple-eyed girls from being born. In return, the Circle would stop hunting them, and the two sides would communicate regularly, through Jack and Elodie and Nisha.

I heard a laugh and squinted behind where Jack had just knocked Max onto his back in the sand. In the shade of the cliff, watching, was Mariam, the driver we'd met in Egypt. She was wearing a sunny yellow hijab and eating a mango.

The idea of offering her a permanent position with us had been Elodie's. We could have gotten anyone—movie stunt drivers or military or trained bodyguards—but we'd gotten used to being *us*. We liked the idea of building our family's crew in a way we could all grow into together. It turned out while we were in Egypt, Mariam had told Elodie how jealous she was of our travel—she had always dreamed of seeing the world, but she couldn't since her family relied on her earnings from her taxi to pay the bills.

Now her family never had to worry again. Mariam had accepted our offer just as she'd done every strange thing we asked her to on those days in Alexandria, with enthusiasm and without so much as a moment of pause.

Not all of us were here in Thailand. Luc was in Paris, rebuilding the city and his life—though he sent whiny texts at least twice a day about how unfair it was that we were on the beach. Luc hadn't introduced Rocco to the Circle yet as anything official. Their relationship would be one thing, but Rocco's past with the Circle would be a bigger deal. They were going to wait until things had settled to address it.

Colette was just starting to film a movie with a director she'd been wanting to work with for years. It was an artsy, awards-bait movie, and Colette couldn't be happier. Elodie had just gotten back from a few days in Paris helping Luc, and then visiting Colette on set, and we fully expected her to tell us all the gossip over dinner tonight.

Anya put a shovel in my hand. I made some sand into a row of spikes down her creature's back, and she grinned, pleased. When Stellan came down the beach, she jumped up again and he swung her around until she screamed.

I wasn't naive. Our personal demons might be locked away for the moment, but they weren't gone. The temporary tranquility in Circle and Order relations would erupt sooner than we wanted. Eventually we'd have to be grown-ups. But at least the world had something that looked like a fragile peace, and we had something far less fragile than that.

Stellan set Anya down. "Sand castle," he said in English, pointing to it.

"I think it's a dragon," I whispered. He consulted with Anya in Russian.

"Ah, of course," he said. "Unicorn-dragon."

"Unco-dagon?" Anya repeated, and I high-fived her.

Stellan reached for my hand and I let him pull me up. He pointed at the cliff. "What do you think?"

That day at the Louvre, he'd said he wanted to jump off a cliff in Thailand with me. I'd been hoping he'd forget. Despite everything, I still wasn't the world's biggest fan of heights. But I took a deep breath. I could do this. I wanted to do this. "Yes," I said. "Okay."

We had to hike off the beach and around the other side of the cliff to get to the top. When we got there, the salt air blowing our hair, the sun on our cheeks, the smell of lemongrass and garlic cooking in tonight's dinner wafting from the direction of our bungalows, I looked down at all our friends.

We hadn't talked much about the worst parts of what had happened. That didn't mean I didn't think about it. I sat down on the cliff and looked out over the ocean, picking at the vines growing out of the rocks.

"Do you think Fitz was actually doing it because he cared about us? That's not—" I shook my head. I was done with the days when people did what they thought was good for me without consulting me about it. "I do believe he loved me, and all of us. But that wasn't enough. I can't believe it wasn't partially about power, and politics, and I know that's the world we're in now, but . . ."

Stellan came to sit behind me, cocooning me against his bare chest. He smelled like sunscreen and salt water, and I nestled back into his arms. "I will promise you something right now," he said. "I will always love you more than I care about the Circle."

I leaned my head back on his shoulder. "We've been together for about five minutes," I said, because one of the first things we'd promised each other was to try to talk our worries out, even if it was awkward. "How can you be so sure?"

"It has been only a short time since I've been able to do this whenever I wanted," he said, kissing my neck in a way that brought goose bumps up on my arms despite the scorching sun, "but we've been a lot more than that for a lot longer than that. Jack and Elodie and Anya have been my family for a long time, but I can't remember anymore what it was like not to have you as part of it, too. And I will always put our family, and the people we love, first. I guess nobody can be sure about anything, but I'd say I'm as sure as I can be that I'll feel this way for the foreseeable future. Is that rational and boring and uncheesy enough for you?"

I craned my neck around and pulled his lips to mine. He tasted like the sea, too.

"It was earlier than the train," I murmured.

"What?"

"When I started falling in love with you. Maybe in the water in Greece, like you? No, earlier than that. When we were standing on that balcony in Venice. Or maybe when you let me *stab* you at Notre-Dame so we could escape."

He grinned and touched his shoulder, where the wound had hardly left a scar. "I find it hard to believe you were in love with me then. You enjoyed stabbing me a little too much."

"Okay, I didn't realize how I felt at the time," I said, giggling. "I thought you were obnoxious."

He laughed, low and rough. "To be fair, I was. So what we're saying is we've both been falling in love with each other for a very, very long time."

"Yeah, I think that's right," I whispered, and I kissed him again. Mint tea and honey weren't going to be the only things I'd associate with kissing him from now on. It was the Louvre, and looking up through the pyramid. It was candlelight on a white wall. It was a sea breeze and the hammock on the porch of our bungalow and cool, crisp water and a whole lifetime of things we had yet to experience. It was all that and more, to the ends of the world.

"Come on," I said, standing up.

We held hands, and stood back from the edge, and on the count of three, we ran forward and jumped. For a few seconds, we were flying, the whole world stretching in front of us. And as we plummeted toward the aqua water, I laughed—and I screamed.

ACKNOWLEDGMENTS

Finishing a trilogy (!) is a task that requires a whole team, and I have the best team around.

Katherine Perkins—you are Superwoman. How much you did for this book in how short a time is mind-boggling. Thank you so much for getting Avery (and me!) to the end of this story—I will be forever grateful for your intelligent, patient edits. Arianne Lewin—your astute guidance has been instrumental in making this series what it is. It's been such a privilege to work with you! Thank you a million times over for believing in Avery and the crew and helping me tell their story. To the Penguin team: Theresa Evangelista for the gorgeous covers of the first two books, Dana Li for the third, and Marikka Tamura for the lovely interiors. Marisa Novello and the Speak team for all you've done for the paperbacks. Lauren Donovan, Katie Quinn, Anna Jarzab, Rachel Lodi, Madison Killen, Tara Shanahan, and the rest of the marketing and publicity team for your hard work and clever ideas. Amalia Frick for all your help. The crew who produces the Conspiracy series audiobooks, and especially to the inimitable Julia Whelan, who narrates them.

To the WME folks: My agent Claudia Ballard—thank you so

much for championing these books from the beginning. Caitlin Landuyt for being so on top of things this year. Laura Bonner for sending the trilogy abroad. To my foreign publishers for letting the books travel as much as Avery does, and especially to everyone at my French publisher, Collection R, for being so lovely and welcoming. So glad I got to meet you all this year!

To all the indie booksellers out there who have championed the Conspiracy series—*thank you*. And especially to Bookworks, my wonderful local indie. To bloggers and reviewers—thanks for doing so much for the bookish community!

To the friends who are always available to talk me through story problems or writing freak-outs—and for this book, especially Dahlia Adler, Sofia Embid, and Kim Liggett, who have dealt with my whiny emails over and over. To a whole lot of other bookish friends—the ones I've met during events and travel this year, and the ones I talk to online—you make this whole publishing thing fun. I want to list all of you, but if I did, these acknowledgments would be as long as the book. To my family—my parents, my brothers, my in-laws, my cousins-in-law . . . Thank you for being endlessly excited about the books! To Andrew—as always, thank you for putting up with my book stress and especially for always being willing to brainstorm and help me with story problems.

And last, to the Conspiracy fandom—your emails and tweets and Instagram posts and fan art and general excitement about the series are truly the best thing about this job. I am such a lucky author to have you guys, and I'm so glad to have shared this story with you all. These books are yours as much as they're mine.

MAGGIE HALL indulges her obsession with distant lands and far-flung adventures as often as she can. She has played with baby tigers in Thailand, learned to make homemade pasta in Italy, and taken thousands of miles of trains through the vibrant countryside of India.

She graduated from the University of Southern California and worked as a bookstore events and marketing manager before making the switch to writing. When she's not on the other side of the world, she lives with her husband and their cats in Albuquerque, New Mexico.

For bonus *Conspiracy of Us* content
and all the latest news,
join Maggie's newsletter at:
maggiehall.com/newsletter